"The ghosts of hard-boiled legends such as John D. MacDonald ...and—yes—Dan J. Marlowe himself haunt these pages. Pure pulp pleasure."

—Wallace Stroby
Author of *Shoot the Woman First*
and *Kings of Midnight*

"Author Jed Power has the...touch...it doesn't get much better..."

—Charlie Stella
Author of *Rough Riders*
and *Shakedown*

"...Jed Power channels the tough-as-nails prose of Gold Medal greats Peter Rabe and Dan Marlowe."

—Shamus & Derringer
award-winning author
Dave Zeltserman

Praise for *The Boss of Hampton Beach*

"Fans of Dennis Lehane will revel in the settings and atmosphere ...an absorbing read...a hard-charging plot...Boston nitty-gritty."

—Charles Kelly
Author of *Gunshots In Another Room*
a biography of crime writer Dan Marlowe

D0104603

Other Books in the Dan Marlowe Series by Jed Power

The Boss of Hampton Beach

Hampton Beach Homicide

Jed Power

Blood On
Hampton Beach

a Dan Marlowe Novel

Dark Jetty Publishing

Published by
Dark Jetty Publishing
4 Essex Center Drive #3906
Peabody, MA 01961

Cover Artist:
Brandon Swann

ISBN 978-0-9858617-5-9

10 9 8 7 6 5 4 3 2 1

Acknowledgements

Again I would like to thank my editor, Louisa Swann, for her continued excellent work on the Dan Marlowe series.

Also thank you to my wife and first reader, Candy.

This book is dedicated to my best friend,
Dr. Stephen Dulong

Chapter 1

I COULD SEE two bullet holes in her head. The seagulls I had just chased away had worked on the wounds, making them large and jagged around the edges. As I stood there on the beach looking down at her, my stomach rolled in time with the waves of the ocean. I didn't attempt to touch her; a simpleton could see the woman was dead.

I had left my cottage for a morning run twenty minutes earlier. I usually head out for my daily run around eight o'clock. This morning I woke up early and had been unable to get back to sleep, so I was almost two hours ahead of schedule. It was the middle of June, a week before the tourist flood began. When I came out through the dunes, the only person I could see on the beach was a lone figure—I couldn't even be sure if it was a man or a woman—hurrying south along the beach. They had already passed my spot. Whoever it was saw me too, because the person looked toward me, then quickly looked away. They were about fifty yards from me, moving diagonally across the sand, hurrying toward the dunes. I stopped to watch. All I could make out were a baseball cap and a long coat. Strange for the season. I watched until they'd disappeared up and over the dunes in the direction of the state park and then forgot about them.

I focused back on why I was here on the beach. The temperature was moderate now, good running weather. It would warm up later. Except for a few gray early morning clouds the sky was clear. I could see the Isle of Shoals and make out a few buildings on the island. I was wearing black, lightweight jogging pants and a black T-shirt. I had my Walkman in my hand; Jimmy Buffet came through the earphones. I didn't have a hangover. It was a good start to the day.

I did a few minutes of warm-up exercises, then walked down to the hard sand near the waterline and began to jog south toward the jetty that marked that end of the beach. When I reached the jetty, I did a slow turn and headed north.

I'd just gone by the path through the dunes where I'd first entered the beach when I saw birds circling far up ahead, maybe a half mile or so. They were down near the water and it looked as if they were almost across from the playground on Ocean Boulevard. At first I thought it was just one of the Bird People. There were a couple of them—local characters who fed the birds daily and usually had a large flock swirling around them. When I finally got a bit closer, I saw that I was wrong. Some of the birds were hovering in the air but others were on the sand surrounding what looked like a log or large piece of driftwood. There was no sign of Bird People or any people for that matter. I guessed that maybe a lobster trap or two had broken free and the birds were enjoying a gourmet feast. When I got closer still, I saw that I was wrong again.

I came up on the birds quickly. They didn't scatter like they usually do at the sight of a fast-approaching human. I had to wave my arms and shout. That's when I first saw that it was a woman on the sand. She was at the waterline, stretched out flat on her stomach. Her face was sideways on the sand; what I could see of it looked like a horror mask. Her hair was knotted and twisted around one of her thin arms. The hair looked blonde but the red splattered throughout the strands were an ugly contrast. The tide had reached her body, and she was wet, so I couldn't tell if she'd been dumped from a boat or shot there. She had on light blue shorts and what looked like a white top, stained with blood in several places. She wore sneakers and I couldn't see any jewelry.

I stood there for a minute, staring down at her. I was successful in keeping the contents of my stomach where they belonged. Wasn't so good with my heart and breathing rates—they were off the charts. When I snapped out of my shock, I quickly looked along the beach in both directions. The only people I could see were up at the other end of the beach, near the Ashworth Hotel. There wasn't a soul in my vicinity.

I broke into a run and headed across the sand toward Ocean Boulevard. The soft sand was a tough run and I was out of breath by the time I reached the steps that led to the concrete boardwalk. I didn't slow down; I ran north past the playground in the direction of the Seashell Stage and the Chamber of Commerce building. My feet slammed against the concrete. I did see some people now but I didn't stop.

When I reached a white cinderblock building that held the women's restroom, I ran around the corner to a bank of about half-a-dozen pay phones attached to the wall. I pulled change from my pocket—I generally grab a coffee after my run—dropped some coins into the closest pay phone, and punched numbers.

When I heard the Hampton police operator answer, I gulped for air and tried to sound coherent. "My name's...Dan Marlowe. There's a...dead woman...on the beach."

I don't remember what else I said; it's just a blur.

Chapter 2

I WAS UP by the boardwalk—cement walk really—which separated the sand from the municipal parking lot. Beyond that was Ocean Boulevard, Hampton Beach's main drag and commercial area. The strip was lined with the usual T-shirt joints, jewelry stores, and nautically themed bars and restaurants, all facing the ocean. In the center of the district stood the Casino, a two-story, two-block long building that housed arcades, fast food joints, and a variety of businesses designed to appeal to tourists. The predominant odor was a toss-up between fried dough and pizza. That changed at night during the summer season, when car fumes from kids continually circling the Ocean Boulevard/Ashworth Avenue loop took first place in the smell category.

I'd given a statement to the responding police officers and shown them where the woman's body was located. It hadn't taken long for a crowd to gather on the boardwalk to watch the police activity down on the sand. I stuck around for a while but I didn't feel that well. I was sure that some local would start asking me questions any minute and I didn't want to deal with that right now. I asked one of the cops if I could go. He said yes; they all knew me pretty well. He also said that the detectives would probably be asking me to come down to the station for a talk.

When I got back to my cottage on the Island section of the beach, the first thing I did was dig out my prescription bottle of Xanax. I took one of the pink pills with tap water. I had been doing pretty good with them lately. I rarely needed one of the tranquilizers and had thought my anxiety might be finally under control. Today was an exception though, if there ever was one.

Less than an hour later, after taking a shower and trying but failing to eat breakfast, the pill finally kicked in. Somewhat at least. Not as good as the Xanax usually worked but that was understandable considering what I had just been through.

I didn't have to be at the High Tide for my bartender duties until ten thirty. I couldn't just sit around the cottage until it was time to leave for work. I had to do something to keep my mind from rehashing what had just happened. TV was as good as anything. I plunked down in my easy chair and flicked it on, hoping to catch the news.

The president again! And on all channels. Clinton had just been elected to his first term in November and already it seemed he'd held more press conferences than old man Bush in his entire four-year presidency. I didn't wait to hear what it was about. I turned the TV off in disgust.

Just then I heard a car crunching onto my gravel driveway. I set the clicker down on a side table. Two car doors slammed. Footsteps clomped up the stairs to my porch and there was a firm knock at the door. I glanced at the clock, shook my head, and got up to answer it. At the beach, it could be anybody.

When I opened the door, it wasn't just anybody standing there—it was two Hampton police detectives. The first one was Lieutenant Richard Gant. His iron gray hair was slicked back and he was wearing a sport coat and pants with creases so sharp they could have cut your throat. Behind him was Steve Moore. Steve was younger and sported a brown buzz cut, short-sleeve shirt, and chinos. His pistol was prominent on his hip. Gant was his superior.

"Marlowe, we want to talk to you," Gant said. He didn't sound too friendly but that was to be expected. We'd had a run in or two in the past and there was no love lost between us.

I felt my anxiety level go up a notch despite the pill I'd taken. I stepped aside and waved them in. When they'd both stepped inside, I said, "Have a seat."

Neither of them moved. I could see Gant giving my small bachelor cottage the once over. It didn't look like the Merry Maids had just been through, but I didn't think it was too bad for a guy living alone. By the sneer on Gant's face, he didn't agree. I suddenly had an urge to defend every seashell and beach-themed knickknack in the room.

Finally Gant spoke. "Before we sit," he said, "I want to know why you left that scene up there? You were told to stay."

"I wasn't told anything about staying. I asked one of your men if it was all right to leave. He said it was and you'd be in touch later and here you are."

"I don't know who said that. But he shouldn't have and you should've known better."

They both sat on the couch that faced my easy chair which I quickly reoccupied.

"Can I get you anything?" I asked. "Soda? Water?"

"Nothing," Gant said quickly. "Feel free to have a beer if you want."

I didn't miss the dig. "It's too early even for me," I said.

Gant smirked at that. He leaned forward, put his arms on his legs. "That's good. Because we want to ask you some questions and I don't want any fuzzy answers."

I looked at Steve. He was a good friend of mine. A friend who looked awfully uncomfortable. He didn't look at me as he took out a small notebook and pen from his shirt pocket.

"All right," I said. I didn't have anything to hide, so I wasn't too worried.

Gant stared at me intently. "Tell me exactly what you were doing—before you found the body?"

"I jog," I answered. "Every other morning."

"This morning?" Gant spit out.

"Yes, that's when I found her."

"What time?" Gant said.

"A little after six o'clock."

"Six, huh?" Gant said. "Could it have been earlier?"

"No. It was after six." I looked at Steve. He looked at his notebook, didn't look up.

Gant leaned back on the couch, put his hands on his thighs. "You always go at that time?"

"Once in a while. I woke up early today. Couldn't get back to sleep." I noticed the Xanax didn't seem to be working quite as well any longer.

"When do you usually go?"

"Around eight."

"I thought so," Gant said, smiling and nodding his head. "Something different about today of all days?"

"Only that I woke up early."

"Maybe. We'll see about that." He had a satisfied look on his thin hard face. "You see anything? Anyone else?"

I thought for a moment. "No." I remembered then, hesitated, and added, "I did see one person."

"Oh?" Gant raised an eyebrow.

I told Gant and Steve about the lone figure who had disappeared over the dunes in the direction of the state park.

"And you couldn't tell if it was a man or a woman?" Gant said, making a face I didn't like.

"Too far away. Besides, whoever it was had a long coat on."

"Sure they did," Gant said. "It's odd though. There's a dead body on the beach the one morning you do your little trot two hours early. You find it...no one else around. Except, of course, the phantom in the long coat. On a summer day."

"People have worn stranger clothes," I said. I heard Steve clear his throat.

"And you didn't see anyone else?" Gant said quickly.

"Just when I found the body. There were some people up near the Ashworth."

"So there were other people all over the beach and they didn't see anything?" Gant said.

"I didn't say 'all over the beach.' I said they were near the Ashworth. They probably never got to where I did." I had a sick feeling in my stomach. I had an idea where Gant was headed. I didn't like it.

When he spoke, it was like he hadn't heard me. "But yet they saw nothing? And you find a dead body at a time you never jog?"

I shrugged. "I didn't say I never jogged then, just not often. And I said they probably didn't see anything because they never got to where I did on the beach."

"So you just happened to go for a run two hours early today?" Gant said. "And you just happened to stumble across a body that no one else on busy Hampton Beach saw? Coincidence? And is it coincidence that the body just happened to be across the beach from the bar where you work?" Then he threw in, "You know, Marlowe...the place you used to own." He smirked again.

The man was making me angry; I wished I could have smacked him. But in reality I couldn't even give him a good dose of shit—he'd make my life a living hell if I did.

"It was awful early," I said. "Of course not many people were around. And coincidences happen."

"Not on my beach they don't," Gant said. "You tell me everything you goddamn know about this, Marlowe. Otherwise, you'll wish you had."

Now it was my turn to get hot. Enough was enough. I had no reason to lie. Even if I had, I knew Gant would have chewed me up like a medium rare steak. "I told you all I know. Now if you haven't got some type of warrant, there's the door." I gestured toward it.

"I don't need any warrant to question an ex-junkie like you, especially during a murder investigation."

I jumped up. "Get the hell out of my house."

Gant flew out of his seat followed by Steve who finally spoke up. "All right, all right," he said. "Dan says he's told us all he knows. Let's go, Lieutenant. No sense letting this get out of hand."

Gant shot Steve a hard look. "Dan, is it?" Then he looked back at me. "We're done with you for today, Marlowe. But we'll have more questions and we'll be watching you, too." Then his look hardened. "So you better hide your stash."

I had to fight to hold myself back. Gant turned, went to the door, and walked out. I followed Steve to the door. "Thanks for the support," I said as he started to leave.

He turned to look at me. "Believe me it could have been a lot worse. He wanted to get a search warrant for this place. I talked him out of it."

"Thanks," I said grudgingly.

When they were both gone and I heard the car tires crunch over my driveway and fade away, I returned to my easy chair. I thought over what had just happened and tried to calm myself down.

I had a very sick feeling. And who wouldn't after the police had just talked to you and almost accused you of being involved in a murder? I had no involvement, so why was I so anxious? I remembered what Steve had said about the search warrant. What did I have in the cottage that could be used against me? This was New Hampshire, so Betsy, my double-barreled shot-gun, and my .38 pistol were both legal. And as far as Gant's wisecrack about dope, those days had been over a long time ago. So I had nothing to fear.

That knowledge didn't help me to relax, though. Earlier this morning I had been out for a pleasant run. Now, just a few hours later, I was being questioned as a witness in a murder investigation. I hoped that was all it turned out to be.

Chapter 3

I WAS LATE when I got to the High Tide Restaurant & Saloon. I entered through the rear door, as usual, and into the kitchen. The smell of baked haddock filled the air. I said hello to both Dianne, the owner, and Guillermo, the head cook. I didn't stop to chat as I sometimes did. Instead I walked the length of the kitchen, pushing through the swinging doors into the restaurant section of the business. A couple of the waitresses puttered around getting the tables and booths ready for lunch. I headed around a chest-high wooden partition that separated the dining room from the bar. The partition had a well-stocked aquarium on top of it that ran almost the entire length of the room. When I turned the corner, I was in my domain—the bar area.

The first thing I saw when I rounded that corner was Shamrock Kelly, the dishwasher and all-around handyman at the Tide. He was seated on a stool down near the far end of the L-shaped mahogany bar. He had a copy of the *Boston Herald* spread out in front of him. He was wearing his restaurant whites as he almost always did, and had his elbows on the bar. He was holding his face in his hands.

"Hello, Shamrock."

He turned, looked at me with a sad look on his Irish face. "Danny, I never win at this thing," he said, his brogue even thicker than usual. He batted the back of his hand at the newspaper. He watched as I walked past him and came around behind the bar.

"I told you before—you're just paying them an extra tax when you play the lottery." I moved as I talked, getting ready to set up the bar. I was behind schedule.

"Yes, you have, Danny. And one of these days I hope I listen to you." He folded the newspaper up and pushed it disgustedly away from him.

Suddenly he became animated. "What do you think of that?" He pointed through the large picture window that looked out on Ocean Boulevard, the municipal parking lot, and the ocean beyond. Of course I knew what he was talking about but he didn't give me a chance to answer. And that was good. I had work to do and I was late. He began to recite everything he knew about the incident on the beach and then some.

As he talked, I grabbed a green five-gallon bucket and left to get ice for the bar. When I returned Shamrock was still chattering away like I'd never left. I made a few more trips, filling two sinks, one at each end of the bar. I then attacked the fruit—limes, lemons, oranges—slicing them and filling two fruit trays. Again, one for each end of the bar. When I finished, I got the money banks ready for the waitresses, filling three coffee cups with nickels, dimes, quarters, one- and five-dollar bills. All the time I was listening to Shamrock going on and on and trying to politely respond to him here and there.

Finally, I caught up with my work. I glanced up at the Budweiser Clydesdale clock and saw that it was 10:55. Five minutes until opening. I slid clean ashtrays along the length of the bar. When I reached Shamrock, I swapped the ashtray he'd been using for a clean one. He was still looking out the window, speculating on what had happened. I stopped, looked in the same direction.

Across Ocean Boulevard, I could see several media trucks—a couple from Boston television stations and one from New Hampshire's Channel 9. There was yellow police tape curled around the railing that separated the boardwalk from the sand, the tape stretching as far as I could see in each direction. There was also a large throng of people scattered along the railing. They all had their backs turned to the Tide.

"I found the body, Shamrock," I said.

Shamrock stopped talking, turned, and looked at me. "You're kidding me." He had a big smile on his rosy face.

I didn't say anything, just looked back at him.

"Sweet Mother of Jaysus, Danny, you're not kidding me." He wasn't smiling anymore.

"I found her on my run this morning around six."

"What happened? Who was it?" All of sudden he was acting as if he knew nothing about what he'd just been babbling on about.

"I don't know who it was, but it looked like she was shot in the head."

"Shot in the head? I thought it was a drowning. And was it someone we knew?"

"Like I said—I don't know, Shamrock. I didn't get a good look at the face."

Shamrock turned back toward the window, quickly blessed himself. "This is an awful thing."

I looked out the window with him. "It gets worse. Steve Moore and Lieutenant Gant came down to the cottage. Gant thinks I had something to do with it. And he doesn't mean just finding the body either."

Shamrock snapped around to face me. "No? He couldn't really think that, could he?" He stared at me for a long moment, then answered himself. "I guess he could. It is Gant after all."

I came around the bar and headed for the front door. "Keep the part about Gant thinking I'm involved between us."

"Of course. Christ, you know me."

Yes, I did. That's why I had said it.

I unlocked the heavy wooden door and used the eye hook to hold the big door in the open position. It was June, warm enough for open doors but not hot enough for the air conditioners. I could smell the salt air and hear the commotion of the investigators and the curious onlookers across Ocean Boulevard.

The first person through the door wasn't a surprise; he was a regular. It was Eli, a sixty-something-year-old housepainter. His head only came up to my chest and he had on the same white paint-stained pants he wore every day. Ditto for the matching hat. He made a beeline for his usual stool near the beer spigots.

He was barely seated when number two came barreling in right on time. Paulie, another regular, was a mail sorter on the graveyard shift. He looked anything but your average mailman with his shoulder-length brown hair. He was tall and rail thin. He grabbed his customary stool down by Shamrock at the L-shaped end of the bar near the big picture window.

I had just stepped back behind the bar when Eli blurted out, "Ya hear who got killed?" He looked down the bar at Shamrock and then at me.

Before either of us could respond, Paulie shouted, "Evelyn Kruel."

Eli spun toward Paulie. "What are you—an asshole? I was about to tell 'em."

Paulie smiled, brushed the hair out of his eyes, and fired up a cigarette. He blew a couple of smoke rings toward the ceiling.

"Ahh," Eli said, flicking his hand in Paulie's direction and shaking his head. "Where's my damn beer?"

I poured a draft Bud into an iced pilsner glass, topping it with a perfect white foamy head. I placed the glass in front of Eli on top of a cocktail napkin. I grabbed a bottle of Miller Lite for Paulie from the beer chest—he didn't use a glass. When I delivered the beer to him, he gave me a sly wink and tilted his head in Eli's direction. I frowned. I knew the two liked to aggravate each other but bartenders can't take sides. I didn't.

"Evelyn Kruel?" Shamrock asked. "You sure about that?"

I'd been surprised to hear that name, too. I knew her casually. Everybody on the beach did. She was a widow who had inherited a good-size chunk of beach commercial property when her husband passed away. She was known to be a tough, take-no-prisoners landlord, less accommodating with tenants when they had problems than her husband had been. If I had moved her head, gotten a better look, I would have recognized her. I hadn't though—moved her head or recognized her. I was glad I hadn't. The visual I already had was enough, thank you.

Paulie started to answer; Eli cut him off cold. "Let me tell something, will ya? Of course I'm sure. I was right over there." He pointed out the window in the direction of the beach and yellow police tape. "I know a lot of people and I was told it was her. And shot in the head, too." He raised himself proudly on his stool. Then he looked back and forth between Shamrock and me, apparently waiting for a shocked reaction.

We already knew the gruesome part and he was disappointed when he didn't get any response. He lifted his beer, took a long drink. When he placed the glass back on the bar he had a white mustache to go along with the white hair protruding from under his cap.

Shamrock pushed himself away from the bar. "I'll see you later, Danny."

"Okay."

Paulie and Eli were nursing their beers, smoking their cigarettes, their eyes glued to the overhead television at the window end of the bar. There was a twin of that TV at the other end. Both were on the same station. There was a game show on that my regulars enjoyed every day. The three of us watched it. During commercial breaks the talk about Evelyn Kruel and what had happened to her would start up again. I didn't tell them about finding the body. I knew it wouldn't be a secret for long and that I'd have to tell them soon before they heard it elsewhere. But within a half hour the lunch crowd would troop in and I didn't feel like having to explain how I'd discovered the body to each and every customer after they'd heard the news from Paulie and Eli.

With my elbow on the bar, looking up at the TV near the window, I found my eyes drawn to the scene across Ocean Boulevard. As I watched, my mouth dried up, my palms became moist, and my heart beat faster. To top all that, I was filled with a sense of dread. I wasn't sure if all of this distress was because of what I had found that morning or because of what Gant had said. Or was it my old abnormal anxiety paying me a visit? Or maybe it was all of it. There was nothing I could do about stumbling across Evelyn Kruel's body; that was done. The pills and beer would help with the anxiety. As far as Gant went, I could only hope he would come to his senses, realize I had nothing to do with the woman's death, and start accusing someone else. Preferably the guilty party.

Then I remembered what Shamrock had said about whether Gant could really think that I was involved. *I guess he could. It is Gant after all.*

My hope turned a little less hopeful.

Chapter 4

I WAS JUST about to turn over the bar to my relief when in through the front door walked Steve Moore. He stood there, gave me a look that told me he wanted to talk. I nodded toward a small empty table at the back of the room. He went to the table I'd indicated and sat.

I finished the last of my bar duties and grabbed my tips; they weren't anything to write home about. The day shift was a lot less stressful and the hours were better than nights, especially as a guy got older, but the money was a lot less, too.

I caught Steve's attention and he mouthed the word, "Coke." I got him one from the tonic gun and a tonic water with lime for myself. A few eyes at the bar followed me as I made my way to Steve's table. Almost everyone in the room knew who he was. Those few who didn't could easily figure it out by the gun he had on his hip. I set the drinks down, took a seat across from him.

"I enjoyed your visit this morning," I said.

He let out a little laugh, but I could tell it was forced. He cleared his throat. "Look, Dan, I'm sorry about that. With Gant and all. He dragged me along. I told him it was a waste of time. That if you'd seen anything else, you would have told the guys at the scene."

"Of course I would've."

He swirled the coke with his straw. "I know that. But I don't think Gant does. He's got a bug or something up his ass about you. I think he believes you actually had something to do with her death or that you at least know something about it."

"That's crazy! Why in God's name would he think I'd have anything to do with Evelyn Kruel's murder?"

Steve's eyes widened. "How did you know it was her?"

I waved in the direction of the bar. "Everyone knows."

Steve scowled. "That didn't take long to get out."

"On the beach nothing does."

"I guess." Steve flushed a bit. "Now look, Dan. Gant doesn't like you. He hasn't for a long time. We both know that." He looked at me as if expecting a reaction; I just shrugged. "He knows your history. I know you went through some rough times, and it was never anything *too* out there, but Gant? For some reason, he thinks you were Mr. Big on the beach at one time and that maybe you still are and that you're getting away with it to boot. He's even got some cockamamie idea that you really still own this place, not Dianne." He waved his hand over his head. "Like I said, the man's got a bug up his ass when it comes to you."

He looked down at his drink, hesitated, then said, "And there's something else."

I knew what was coming; how could I not?

He looked up at me. "Dianne and Morris Kruel."

I had known the subject might come up, and here it was. Morris Kruel was Evelyn's younger brother. About six months ago, Morris, newly divorced, had started dropping into the Tide. He always showed up at night, late. Being the day bartender, I never was there when he'd come in. I'd hear about his visits the next day from Shamrock, the night bartender, a waitress, or one of my regulars. Morris was the sibling of one of the largest landlords on the beach, so he could have been king of the bar if he'd behaved himself. Instead, he'd get drunk—and with an ego so big he needed a wheelbarrow to haul it around in—act like an obnoxious slob.

If it had been anyone but Evelyn Kruel's brother, I'm sure the night bartender would have shut him off. Apparently, my night counterpart was intimidated by Morris and the awe some of the other customers seemed to hold him in. When I'd heard about Morris's escapades at the bar, I wasn't pleased. But I was just the day bartender, not the owner anymore. So I wasn't responsible. Then I heard he'd been bothering Dianne.

I guess he'd been at it for a while. Making lewd remarks, ogling her every time she was in the bar area, even calling her at the bar on nights he wasn't there, drunk again, asking her for a date. No one wanted to mention any of this to me. Finally, Shamrock did. I wasn't happy. I spoke to Dianne about it; she brushed it off. I got the feeling she, too, was afraid to toss the man out because of his sister and the possible blowback. I wasn't though.

I made arrangements for the night bartender to call me the next time Morris showed up at the bar. He did. I'd already had a few beers myself but made the walk to the Tide quickly. I took a seat down the bar from Morris, ordered a beer, and watched the show. Shamrock said the guy'd been obnoxious. He wasn't—he was *very* obnoxious. What did he look like? Your average preppy nerd.

I watched him holding court, some of the other patrons egging him on, buying him drinks. When Dianne came out to help as she often did nights, she was surprised to see me. She quickly looked at Morris and I could see the smile leave her face. She was probably praying he'd be on his best behavior. He wasn't.

"Hey, honey," Morris called. "I needs another drink." He held up the glass, wiggled it, and leered at Dianne who pretended not to notice.

Rick, the bartender, bounded over and tried to take Morris's empty. Morris pulled it away, slammed it down on the bar. "I want her to get it," he said with a cockeyed grin. "I like to watch her walk." He laughed, held up his hands, and made like he was driving a car with them. A few of the customers laughed along with him. Many didn't, including all the women. Dianne was flustered. She headed toward her office.

When she passed Morris's stool, the man actually reached out and grabbed her arm. She pulled it free. "Howshh about I show you my place after work. It's on the ocean. You can make my drinks and I can watch you walk around." He let out a vile little laugh. Again, some at the bar laughed with him. Most didn't. I was one of them.

I was off my stool and by Dianne's side faster than I can pour a draft. I was pissed and I got right in the man's face. "Why don't you take your drinking somewhere else, Kruel?"

Dianne touched my arm lightly. "Dan, please."

Morris made a face like I was dirt. "Who the fuck are you?"

Except for us and the TV, there wasn't another sound in the bar area. All eyes were on us, many watching in the bar mirror.

"I'm the man who's asking you to leave." I could feel my heart pounding.

Morris looked at Dianne; she looked at me.

"I'm not going anywhere," Morris said. "Don't you know who I am?" He turned and reached for his empty glass but he never made it.

I grabbed his other arm and yanked him off his stool. He stumbled several steps. I came up behind him, latched onto his shirt at the shoulders with both hands, and propelled him in the direction of the front door. Someone saw where we were heading and opened it for us. Morris's arms flailed as we went and he started calling me the kind of names he would have been thrown out for using anyway.

When we were out the door and on the Ocean Boulevard sidewalk I gave Morris a good shove. He lost his balance but didn't fall. Instead, he jerked around and took an awkward right hand swing at me. I didn't hesitate. I fired a hard right that landed square on his nose. The feel of his nose collapsing under my fist felt damn good. He landed hard on his ass on the pavement.

I looked down at him. He looked shocked. Blood poured from his nose.

My heart was hammering a mile a minute. "You ever come back here again or if I hear you're bothering Dianne, I'll break your freakin' neck, Kruel."

A minute later the first Hampton police car pulled up to the curb. They must have been passing by and seen the commotion. Morris was still sitting there with his hands up to his face, blood flowing out between his fingers. There was some back and forth between the police and myself, with Dianne in the middle trying to cool things off. The Tide's patrons had spilled out onto the sidewalk to watch the action, mingling with pedestrians who'd been passing by.

Within minutes, a red Hampton rescue truck pulled up. They loaded Morris and his nose onboard and headed for Exeter Hospital, sirens screaming. The cops cuffed me and tossed me in the back of a cruiser for the short ride to the police station. The last thing I saw before we pulled away from the curb was Dianne standing next to Shamrock at the front of the throng watching me get hauled away. Dianne was mouthing, "I'll get you out." Shamrock was nodding vigorously.

She did too. They both showed up at the station and posted my bail on an assault and battery charge. I never went back to court. Morris didn't press charges. Apparently, he wanted the story to die. He wouldn't have looked good—drunk, hitting on women, and getting in street brawls. His big sister probably wouldn't have been happy with the publicity, either. So someone squashed it; I didn't care who. I was just happy that we'd never have to see Morris Kruel at the Tide again. I was right about that, too. He never made another appearance.

"So Gant's thinking that you had problems with the family," Steve said, pulling me back from the past. "There *were* rumors a while back that Evelyn was threatening to cause trouble for Dianne and the High Tide. I'm sure she wasn't happy after you gave her brother that thumping. So he's wondering if Dianne might have been involved in Evelyn's death, too. And Gant thinks Dianne's some kind of front for you here at the Tide anyhow."

"That's ridiculous," I said. "Dianne uses non-lethal mousetraps, for God's sake. You know her, Steve. And as far as threats from Evelyn Kruel, those were...rumors. I think all that talk was just people trying to stir up trouble during a dull beach winter. She probably didn't like her brother any better than me."

"Maybe," Steve said. "The jerk did deserve a pop in the nose after the way he treated Dianne. That's for sure. Still, Dan, if I didn't know you, I'd probably put you on the suspect list, too. So I can see where Gant's coming from. Plus, like I said, he's got it in for you."

"So what's it all mean, Steve?" I asked.

"It means at the best he's going to make life very uncomfortable for you. Maybe Dianne too. And Shamrock—Gant knows how close you two are—he called him your Mick partner in crime. And at worst? I hate to say it, Dan, but he might actually try to hang this on you. You're already halfway there. With the fight and the threats. And the man really believes you may have killed Evelyn."

My heart didn't speed up this time; it sank in my chest. Along with my stomach which hit the floor. Somehow I'd ended up involved in a murder case—as the main suspect! And from what Steve said, the best I could hope for was trouble and lots of it. For Dianne, too, maybe. And Shamrock.

"Great," was all I said.

Steve added one more thing. "He's also put a bug in the chief's ear and with the state cops, too. So watch yourself." He got up from his chair. Just before he turned to leave he lowered his voice. "I'll keep in touch. But we've got to keep it discreet."

I nodded. He gave a little salute and walked out.

I sat there, thinking about what I'd just learned. I felt almost as empty as if I'd just heard of a death in the family. I couldn't make any sense of it. In the space of twelve hours, I'd gone from being a relatively happy jogger and somewhat carefree bartender to a murder suspect. Unless the police caught someone, and soon, for the murder of Evelyn Kruel, I was in for an unpleasant summer on Hampton Beach.

Not just me either—there was Dianne and Shamrock to consider. Who had dragged them into this mess? Dan Marlowe, that's who. Of course, I hadn't really done anything. They were in jeopardy just because of our relationships. Still, whether intentional or not, I was to blame. So against my better judgment, I decided to look into Evelyn Kruel's murder. Just a little, I told myself. A few questions here and there and that would be it. After all, if I didn't look out for myself—and my friends—who would?

Chapter 5

THE NEXT MORNING I got up and headed for the only spot I could think of where maybe I'd have some luck turning up something—Plaice Cove. There wasn't much traffic so I breezed up Ocean Boulevard, past the Casino and Boar's Head, and pulled into a small dirt parking area.

I walked up a sandy path and past a bench I'd used to relax on many times through the years. Sea grass waved in the breeze on either side of me. The Atlantic Ocean stretched out from the beach as far as I could see. There were no boats, only the occasional gull diving for breakfast. I walked down the other side of the small dune and came out on the sand. I started walking north.

The homes were located up about ten to twenty feet from beach level. They all were protected from the surf by boulder or concrete walls. Most had wooden staircases that gave easy access from the house down to the beach. The homes ran the gamut from rustic, nautically-themed cottages that had been there for generations to newer, much more expensive, ultra-modern homes that had probably replaced previous tear downs. In another ten years or so, I figured all the older cottages would be gone and replaced by multi-million dollar

McMansions. The property was just too damn valuable and I couldn't blame the very rich for muscling in. Situated high up on the rocks, protected from nor'easters, with 180 degree ocean views interrupted only by the picturesque sight of the Isle of Shoals six miles off shore.

And the beach itself was about as private as a public beach could be, isolated as it was from the hustle and bustle of Hampton Beach. Even today, with the temperature already in the low 70s, and only a wisp of an occasional cloud to block the sun, I could see just one other person on the entire length of the beach. That person was at the other end walking in my direction.

I studied the homes as I strolled by. I had no idea which had belonged to Evelyn Kruel. I'd heard through the years that she had lived on this beach somewhere. I didn't see any police activity anywhere. In fact, except for that one lone figure farther down the beach, I didn't notice anyone at all. There was absolutely nothing to give me a hint of where she had lived. I realized I should have made a trip to the Hampton Town Hall and gotten that information before I'd come. I decided to do it later.

I continued my walk, checking out the homes as I moved, trying to guess which one had been Evelyn's. The woman had been loaded, so I was sure it was one of the pricier jobs. I looked for the most ostentatious—there were more than a few.

I'd just turned toward the ocean, when I caught a blur of movement out of the corner of my eye. I spun and lurched backward. A large Doberman pinscher raced toward me at full speed and came to a bounding halt only feet away. Sand flew as he slid to a stop. His teeth were bared and he was growling viciously. He lurched at me, snapping teeth that looked sharper than a fisherman's knife.

I held my left arm up protectively in front of me. "Easy, boy, easy." I doubted that would do any good but it was the best I could think of. I was scanning the sand for a rock or other weapon when the figure I'd seen down the beach came up behind me. I hadn't noticed before that he had a walking stick. It was thick and long, almost like a large police skull-cracker.

The man came around me with the stick held over his head. "Get the hell out of here, you dirty son of a bitch. Go! Go!" He came closer to the dog, swinging his stick as he did. I guess the dog didn't like the look of the stick, because he turned tail and ran toward the houses, disappearing behind some rocks.

"Those goddamn dogs are a pain in the ass," the man said, turning toward me.

I got a good look at my rescuer now. He was quite old but he was one of those people you would never call elderly no matter how old they were. He was dressed all in black. A black beret, black T-shirt, and matching black slacks. He wore sandals on his feet and a shock of pure white hair hung down below his hat. His face was heavily lined but healthy looking. His blue eyes looked me up and down.

"He would've bit you too," he said, spitting on the sand. "Lucky it was just the one."

"One?" I glanced quickly around the beach.

"From up there." He pointed in the direction of one of the old cottages; I noticed a ham radio antenna towered over it. "Two damn Dobermans. They get loose once in a while. I can barely hold them off with this thing." He raised his stick; shook it. "Owners don't give a shit. Winter renters, I think."

"Well, thanks anyhow," I said, feeling a bit embarrassed. "I'm glad you came along." I hesitated. "And had your walking stick."

He looked indignant. "It isn't a walking stick, son. I look like I need a walking stick to you?"

I shook my head.

"It's for them." He waved his stick at the same cottage again. "Can't walk around here without it since those dogs came."

"Well, thanks again." I stuck out my hand, he took it firmly and we shook. "My name's Dan Marlowe."

"Henry Fuller," he said. "What brings you here, Dan? I don't think I've seen you on the beach before."

It was an opening that I figured I should accept. It might save me a trip to town hall, if nothing else. "Evelyn Kruel. I figured I'd just take a walk by her house, see where she used to live. Problem is I have no idea which one it is. Thought maybe there'd be some kind of police activity or something to give me a hint."

Henry looked somber. "Christ, there'll probably be quite a few nosey people traipsing by in the next few days." He grimaced. "I didn't mean you, Dan."

"That's okay," I said. "I suppose it's just that murders don't happen in Hampton every day."

"I guess," Henry said. "Walk with me this way. I'll show you. It's before my place."

He started walking back the way I'd come. I fell in beside him. Not only did he look healthy, he was spry as hell, too. I had to walk faster just to keep up with him.

We hadn't gone far before he suddenly stopped and pointed his stick in the direction of one of the homes on the cliff. "There she is," he said. "Evelyn Kruel's monstrosity."

I hadn't been wrong earlier. He was pointing at one of the more elaborate homes I'd picked out. It was new, of a modern design that I didn't particularly like. Two-stories with more glass than a greenhouse. It had the customary wooden staircase leading down to the sand. On one side there was a similar home, another of the ones I had selected as possibly belonging to Evelyn. On the opposite side was what looked like one of the original beach cottages built many decades ago. I liked the older ones better than the new showplaces they were throwing up. The older ones looked like they belonged there, compared to the newer ones that could have been transplanted from some rich suburb. I stared at Evelyn's place for a bit but couldn't see any signs of activity.

"No police?" I asked.

"Oh sure, they're still there. Out front. Can't see them from here."

We stared at Evelyn Kruel's house for another minute, then Henry said, "Care to come in for a drink, Dan?"

Why not? Henry seemed like a nice gent, and besides, if I was going to find out what the hell was going on, I had to start somewhere.

"Yeah, sure, Mr. Fuller. I'd like that."

He frowned. "Dan, please. I feel old enough. It's Henry. My friends call me Hank though. You can call me Hank, too."

"Okay...Hank."

We kept walking in the same direction past a few more homes until Hank veered off and headed for the rocks.

When we reached a rickety staircase that led up to what I assumed was his home, he went up first. I fell in behind. I held the rail tightly with one hand and I could actually feel the stairs sway in the light wind. I wondered how they survived a nor'easter.

I wasn't surprised by Hank's home—it was one of the smallest and most rustic on the cliff. He led me through the door into a kitchen area that seemed to belong to another era. It was clean, but everything there was old. From the refrigerator that produced an odd noise to the furniture that probably had graduated years ago from second-hand status to antique, at least in the mind of any Yuppie who saw it.

Hank motioned to a chair at the cloth-covered table. I sat. The house had an old people's odor. Reminded me of my grandparent's home when I was a kid.

"What can I get you to drink—Beer? Coffee? Water? You like coke?"

I chuckled. It was too early for beer, so I asked for a water.

He came back with a glass he'd filled from a container in the noisy fridge. He brought a sixteen-ounce bottle of Knickerbocker beer along with a frosted mug for himself. I was impressed. It was a good beer, but not many people drank it anymore. If he'd pulled out an import, like I enjoyed, I would have been disappointed. The Knick fit both Hank Fuller and the scene perfectly.

Hank pulled out a chair, the legs scraping noisily against the floor. When he had himself seated he poured the Knick expertly into his glass, forming a perfect head.

I was impressed again. "Nice job," I said, nodding at the glass of beer.

He took a healthy swig of the beer, set the glass down. "I've had enough practice." He let out a little laugh. "Don't think I do this all day though. I only have one or two a day and I get up around four, so this is a lot later in the day than it is for a young man like you."

I liked that—me, a young man!

"You like beer?" he asked.

"Oh yeah, I like beer."

"What do you do for work?"

"Bartender. That's why I can appreciate that nice head you poured."

He smiled again and asked where I worked. I told him.

"The High Tide," he said. His eyes got a little dreamy. "I used to go there when it was The Anchor Bar. Closed the place many a night. That's back right after booze became legal on the beach."

I knew of the Anchor. It had been the original name of the Tide. There had been a couple of unsuccessful watering holes in between the Anchor's time and when I had purchased the business. "That's going back a few years," I said.

"Yes, it is." He let out a sigh, and his shoulders rose and fell. I could tell he was remembering some things from his past. They must have been pleasant because he was smiling. Finally the smile left his face. "You come up here much, Dan?"

"No. Maybe once a year or so. Plaice Cove is a beautiful area. I should come up more." He was sipping his beer; I took a sip of my water. I wasn't sure if I should take Hank into my confidence, tell him why I was really there. Then I realized that it most likely couldn't hurt and maybe I'd actually find out something of value. Anyway, I had no idea where else to go with any of this.

"I hate to disappoint you," Hank said before I could make a confession of any kind, "but this isn't Plaice Cove." I thought he was kidding; he wasn't. "No. Plaice Cove is a small area past those rocks." He pointed out the window in a southerly direction. "They say *Peyton Place* was written in a little house over there."

I stared in the direction he indicated, puzzled. "What's this called then?"

"There's been various names through the years, but it's North Beach."

"North Beach? Wait a second. North Beach is down there near Boar's Head."

Hank smiled. "That's right. And it comes right up to Plaice Cove over there." He pointed back toward the rock outcropping. "Then there's Plaice Cove...just a short little section. Then North Beach starts up again at those rocks and runs to the end of this beach near the North Hampton line."

I'd either lived on or been coming to Hampton Beach my entire life. I didn't think there was anything I didn't know about its geography. I'd walked this short strip of beach enough times to carve a path on it. And all this time I'd thought it was something it wasn't. I wondered how I could make a mistake like that.

Hank must have picked up on my feelings. "Don't let it bother you. You're not the first person who thought this was part of Plaice Cove. Christ, one of my neighbors said that before she bought her place here the real estate agent kept referring to it as Plaice Cove. She only found out a year after moving in that it wasn't." Hank let out a deep laugh. "Now a real estate agent *must* have known. But I guess it was a good selling point."

I could believe that. It was similar to what had happened in my own area. Not too long ago beach real estate agents had resurrected an old name that hadn't been in use for decades to refer to the area I lived on—*The Island*. I guess the name gave the area some class and was a good selling tool. The name eventually caught on.

"It is a beautiful area though," Hank said. "Whatever people call it. Especially in the off-season. There's not a lot of homes open year-round. Christ, I couldn't even afford to buy here now. I picked this damn place up over forty years ago. You'd hate me if I told you what I paid for it." He let out another little laugh, took a sip of beer. "You picked a nice day to check out Mrs. Kruel's house though."

I decided to tell him the real reason I was there. "To tell you the truth, Hank," I started uncomfortably, "I'm here to see if I can find out anything about her murder."

He looked at me quizzically. "You a private detective on the side or something?"

I shook my head and laughed. "No, although sometimes I feel like it. I'm just looking around because the police think a friend of mine was involved. He wasn't, and I was hoping I could come up with something to prove that."

"A friend, huh." He gave me a sly look. Apparently I hadn't fooled him. "Well, I don't know what you'll find here. The cops have already been all over the place. I'd be glad to help you if I can though."

I did have a few questions. "Did you see Evelyn around here much?"

"Sure, once in a while. She was a walker, too. I even saved her once from those damn dogs." He took a sip of beer, wiped his mouth with the back of his hand, and continued. "I even rescued Artie Neal one time."

"*Tiny Bastards?* He lives here?"

"That's him and he does. Way down near the North Hampton end. A second home, I guess."

Artie "Tiny Bastards" Neal. I knew the name well. Everyone did. The man was the host of one of Boston's most popular radio talk shows. A right wing talk show. Matter of fact, that's how he got the nickname of Tiny Bastards. Along with railing against almost every minority imaginable, Neal had a special vindictiveness toward what he called Welfare Queens. He went so far as referring to their children as "tiny bastards" on almost a daily basis. I couldn't stand the man and his views. Apparently some others couldn't either. The nickname had been used by a couple of alternative media outlets and had been picked up slowly by others. Eventually it stuck and was now commonly used by people who disagreed with Neal's bigoted philosophy.

"I think he came up on weekends during the cold weather," Hank continued. "I'd see him walking on the beach every so often. Once with Evelyn Kruel as a matter of fact. Not too friendly. I'd get a nod out of him in passing. That was about it. Until the day he had the same goddamn problem as you."

"Me?"

He took a slow sip of his beer, savored it. It made me want one. "Yeah, the dogs. I was out for my walk as usual, foggy goddamn day. Couldn't see twenty feet in front of you. I'd made the length of the beach, turned around, and was halfway home when I heard the commotion."

"Commotion?"

He scowled. "I knew right away it was those damn dogs. They was yapping up a storm. Worse, I could hear someone screaming his fool head off. I had my stick with me, of course, and I made a beeline for the noise. With the fog I couldn't see a damn thing till I got right on top of them."

"Them?" I interrupted.

Hank frowned. I apologized; he continued. "The dogs and Neal. And those mutts were snapping and biting at him like he was a juicy steak. I ran right up to them, swinging my stick. I just missed clobbering one of those dogs in the head, too. Wish I'd got him. Anyhow, they took off running back to their house. It was quite a sight."

"And it was Tiny Bastards?" I asked.

"It was and he was a mess. His pants were torn and he had a couple of small bite marks on his legs." Hank's face flushed just a bit. "Worse, the man was crying like a little baby."

"Crying?"

"Yup. Crying. It was damn embarrassing. I escorted him back to his place. He asked me to. Was shaking like a leaf he was so scared. I would've anyhow, of course. He gave me a half-hearted thanks when we reached his house. Didn't invite me in or anything. Just waved me off."

"Have you seen him since?"

He shook his head. "That was only a couple of weeks ago."

"So nothing out of the ordinary lately?"

"Nothing except for the murder. Not many people around here in the off season, Dan. Once in a while one of the other owners will come for a weekend, work on their place maybe. That's it."

And I guess that was it for me too—I couldn't think of anything else to ask. Apparently, I'd struck out. It wasn't a total loss though. I'd made a new friend.

Just then my new friend finished his beer and glanced at the clock on the wall. "I hate to be a bad host, but it's my nap time. Believe me...you get my age and miss that, it throws the rest of your day off."

I laughed, stood up, held out my hand. We shook.

"You don't have to go down the stairs," he said. "Your car at the little turnaround?"

I nodded.

"Take a right out the door and left on the street. You'll come right to it."

He escorted me the few feet to the door. "Thanks again for coming to my rescue with the dog," I said."

"No problem. One was easy." Just before I closed the door behind me, he added, "Don't be a stranger, Dan. Drop by any time you visit Plaice Cove." He smiled, a sparkle in his blue eyes. "I can use the company. I don't want to start talking to myself." Now we were both smiling.

On the way back to my car, I wondered if I'd gotten anything out of my little visit to Plaice Cove...North Beach. I couldn't come up with a thing. Except, of course, making the acquaintance of Hank Fuller. And that was a good thing, I was sure.

Chapter 6

I WAS LATE for work again. That was very rare for me. Made two days in a row. Christ, it was becoming a habit. I let myself in the back way as always and walked into the kitchen. Guillermo was playing with the fryolators. Dianne was prepping on the speed table. She saw me coming, turned, and walked right past me.

As she went by she said, "Dan, I want to talk to you," in a loud voice.

I fell in behind her and followed her back toward the rear door, around a corner, past one of the walk-ins, and into her office. She held the door and slammed it behind me.

I turned to face her. Her arms were across her chest, her lips tight, and her green eyes looked angry. She was a good actress; she had me fooled. She took a step toward me and wrapped her arms around my neck. We pulled together fast. The lips that had looked so thin a moment ago were full and lush and tasted wonderful now. We were flush against each other, fitting perfectly.

After a long minute she pulled her lips away; I didn't want them to go. She kept her arms around my neck, her body against mine. I caught the scent of perfume. I liked it. I liked everything about her.

Her black hair was pulled back, the way she wore it at work. It was slightly curly and long when she let it fall, and sometimes I'd catch sight of a lone gray strand. I'd kid her about that. Ninety-nine percent of the time she was the most beautiful woman in the restaurant. I don't know who the remaining one percent would have been but I had to cover my bases just in case a better-looking woman than her ever showed up.

I smiled. "I thought you were really mad."

She smiled too. "Scared you, huh?"

We both knew that most of the employees at the High Tide knew about us. Still, we kept it low-key at work. Dianne and I agreed that it wasn't a good idea to have the other workers see the boss rubbing noses with an employee. It might start talk of favoritism even though Dianne was as fair a boss as there could be. Just like I had tried to be when I owned the Tide. Besides, neither of us was really sure where it would end up. We weren't kids after all and had seen the fiery flames die out before. We couldn't be sure that wouldn't happen to us. Although we never admitted that to each other, I'm sure she felt the same way. So it was one of those things that everyone knew about, but said nothing.

"Yeah, you better calm me down." I tried to nibble on her neck.

She pursed those lips again. "Dan. We have to go back."

She was right, of course, but there was something I had to tell her and now might be the only time I would get. "Can we talk for a minute?"

She could tell whatever I had to say was serious. "Sure." She pulled away, walked over to her metal desk, and sat behind it. I plopped down on a love seat adjacent to the desk. There were two other metal chairs, a couple of filing cabinets, and boxes of paper products stacked in the corner. The room was windowless, and except for a few pictures that hung on the walls and the generally much cleaner and neater condition, it wasn't much different than when I'd sat on the number one side of the desk.

Her lightly clasped hands were on that desk. "This has got something to do with Evelyn Kruel, doesn't it?"

I nodded.

"I knew that would come back to haunt you some day, Dan." Her tone became angry.

"I found the body."

"What?"

I told her the whole story. Right through Gant and Steve Moore's visit to my cottage and the suspicion Gant had about my involvement in the murder. I also told her what Steve had relayed to me—about Gant thinking that Dianne could possibly be involved in the murder too and even his questioning her ownership of the Tide.

"That's ridiculous," she said.

"That's what I said. But I guess the jerk believes it. He's threatening to cause Shamrock trouble, too."

She let out a sigh. "What are you going to do?"

I leaned forward, my arms on my legs, stared at the floor. "I'm not sure." I raised my eyes slowly to look at her. "Maybe look around a little bit."

She leaned back in the swivel chair so hard it squeaked. "Oh, Dan. Not again."

I threw up my hands. "What else can I do?"

"I don't know." She jumped up from the chair. "We'll have to talk about it later." She headed for the door, stopped, and turned back toward me. I was up now and she took the few steps back to me, kissed me gently on the lips. "I'll help, you know that," she said. "But you better tell me everything that's going on. And for God's sake, be careful. Please."

Before I could say anything else she was out the door and I was following her. In the kitchen Guillermo glanced up, then quickly looked away. Dianne returned to prepping and I hurried to the bar.

I unlocked and opened the restaurant's front door. Paulie and Eli clomped in.

"Yer late," Eli said.

"Sorry."

The two of them headed to their stools like they were magnetized. Eli sat, as usual, near the center of the bar, adjacent to the draft beer spigots. Paulie ended up at his regular place at the L-shaped end of the bar with the plate glass window behind his back.

I got them both their beers and flew around trying to catch up on my work. Mixed in with the sound of the televisions I could hear Eli and Paulie going back and forth about the murder of Evelyn Kruel. I paid it no mind; I knew it would be the hot topic on the beach for a while. At least until something else came along to top it. A few other customers wandered in and I served them. A couple of families trooped through the door, heading for the dining area and an early lunch.

I noticed Eli and Paulie looking at me oddly every so often. I figured they knew about me finding the body, but for a change neither wanted to be the first to speak about it. I was just about caught up with my work and ready to come clean with the information when I heard Paulie say something that caught my ear—*Tiny Bastards*.

"Her place is just a bit down from Tiny Bastards' place," he said to Eli. "He owns the new one with the widow's walk and the giant American flag. And," he raised his voice just a bit, "one of my coworkers saw them going back and forth between their houses a few times."

"His name's Artie Neal," Eli said, "and I don't believe any of that shit. He's a good family man."

Paulie nodded his head sagely. "Sure he is." He took a puff on his cigarette, blew smoke rings toward the ceiling. He had a smile on his face.

I pretended to wipe the bar and maneuvered my way down close to Paulie.

"They had something going on?" I asked.

He shrugged. "I can't say for sure, but if the shoe fits…"

"Baloney," Eli bellowed down the bar. "He'd lose his radio job and his family for that."

I wanted to ask Paulie more but before I could, he said, "Couldn't happen to a nicer guy," loud enough so Eli could hear him.

Eli raised himself off his stool, grabbed the bar with both hands, and looked in our direction. "Whatcha mean by that? The man fights for the average Joe."

"Oh, sure he does," Paulie responded. I could see his face reddening. "He makes a million bucks a year and he fights for the average Joe. That's a laugh. He doesn't care about anybody but himself."

I could see Eli was pissed now, too, and he wasn't the type who cared who knew it. "He's against all them goddamn welfare queens, ain't he? He don't like them and their kids freeloadin' on our dough." He lifted his glass of draft, drained half of it, and banged it down on the bar.

Paulie wasn't backing off. "Why do you call them kids? Why don't you call them what your hero always calls them… the *tiny bastards*?"

"That's what they are, ain't they?"

I forgot about my questions for Paulie and put my hands up. I knew where this was headed. "Okay, okay, that's enough. There're women and kids here." I nodded at the restaurant section on the other side of the chest-high wooden partition. On top of the partition, a well-stocked aquarium ran almost its entire length. I knew they probably couldn't hear us over there, but I also knew if the conversation continued in this direction, that would change. And besides, a couple of other drinkers at the bar had started to toss in their two cents worth. And the rest of the gang looked uncomfortable. If I didn't step in, the disagreement could escalate into a shouting match. Easily. So I chopped the talk off. Both men quieted down, but they were still steaming. And you could feel the tension in the air.

It was just then that Shamrock Kelly came through the swinging kitchen doors.

"Hey, lads," he said with that Irish brogue of his. He was talking to the bar patrons at large. "I hear someone mention Tiny Bastards?"

I rolled my eyes. "It was nothing, Shamrock."

He leaned both his arms on the end of the bar and looked at my group of customers. "He's quite a piece of work, that man. Don't like immigrants. Once a week he reads the police blotter on his show. Every time he says the name of an Irishman arrested for anything, he plays a little of *Seven Drunken Nights*. Not only insults my countrymen but a great song to boot."

I quickly tried to change the subject. "Any action in the restaurant, Shamrock?" I raised my chin in that direction.

He wasn't having any of it. "I dunno, Danny Boy. I'm wondering though...does Tiny Bastards still own that summer place up the road?" Apparently, I was the only one on the beach who hadn't known about Neal's place.

Mel, one of my retired daily visitors piped up. "Sure he does. He's owned that place for at least ten years. Summer place. But what a joint. Right on the ocean."

"Must've cost him a bundle," someone else said.

"Christ, the man probably has more money than God," Shamrock said.

"And he deserves every penny of it," Eli said loudly, looking toward Paulie. "He's the best."

"He's a bigoted shithead," Paulie snapped back.

"That's it," I said. "Any more and you're both shut off." I didn't like saying that; rarely did a regular get shut off here. They knew that, too. They also knew how pissed off I must have been to say it. They both went silent and clutched their beers.

I glared at Shamrock. "Sorry, Danny," he said softly. He pushed away from the bar and slinked back into the kitchen.

Shamrock avoided me for the rest of the day. Finally, near the end of my shift, I grabbed him as he was trying to sneak a coke from the tonic gun, and told him what I had told Dianne. At least the part he didn't already know. He wasn't happy, but he promised to help in any way he could as I'd known he would.

There was one thing that had kept tickling at my brain for that shift—Tiny Bastards. Twice in one day his name had come up in regards to Evelyn Kruel. Whether or not it meant anything, I wasn't sure. But it was all I had, so I had to find out what their relationship had really been. *And* if it had anything to do with murder.

Chapter 7

WHEN I LEFT the High Tide, I returned to my cottage, took care of a few things, puttered around. Then close to seven o'clock I went out, got in my '86 green Chevy Chevette. The thing was an embarrassment and ran poorly to boot. I'd driven better cars back in the day. Anyway, I headed for Plaice Cove (I know—it's really North Beach, but I've grown accustomed to referring to it that way, so I will) for the second time in one day. When I got there, I cruised slowly along Ocean Boulevard past the turnaround I had parked at on my last visit. Just yards ahead began the only homes that sat on the beach side of Ocean Boulevard, except for less than a dozen others down at my own Island section and a similar number perched on Boar's Head. The rest of Hampton's ocean view properties, a much larger number, were all separated from the beach by the boulevard. I eyeballed the backs of the oceanfront homes as I drove. Like I said before, they ran the gamut from bare-bones beach cottages, to big buck, multi-story luxury homes that seemed barely contained by the narrow lots.

It wasn't hard to find Neal's. I couldn't miss it. The house had a huge American flag flying above it just like Paulie'd said. The damn thing was probably as large as any in D.C. I pulled into the driveway and parked behind a late model Cadillac. When I got out, I headed up a small walkway, unlatched a wooden gate, and went up to the back door. If there was any type of security, I didn't see it. Strange, considering the emotions the man played with on his radio show. Maybe he felt he was safe up here near the ocean in tax-free New Hampshire. I pushed the button. I heard the chimes play some tune I didn't recognize. I waited a minute. Nothing. I pushed it again.

When Artie Neal came to the door, I knew right away it was him. He was one of those few people who actually looked like their radio voice. He was a butterball of a man, with a very plain, pasty white complexion. His thin hair was dyed black with that odd red tint you see on some cheap dye jobs. He was a few inches shorter than me and was dressed in a maroon track suit.

"What can I do for you?" He said it like he didn't want to do anything for me, no matter what I said.

"Mr. Neal? I was wondering if I could talk to you for a minute?"

He held his pudgy hand up, shook it like he was waving goodbye. "I'm busy. Any questions you have, you can call the station. They'll answer them."

I stood firm. "This is important. And it has nothing to do with radio."

He reached for the screen door handle; jiggled it as if making sure the door was locked. "What's it about then?"

"I'd like to ask you a few questions about Evelyn Kruel."

"Evelyn Kruel?" He looked at me like I had two heads.

If that's the way he wanted it, I could play the game, too. "You know her. The woman who was killed. She lives a few doors down from you." I pointed off to my right.

"Oh, yeah," he said. "Heard about it. A real tragedy."

I lowered my head a bit, then looked up at him. "We can speak then?"

"No, we can't speak then. I don't know what you want, but if it has something to do with the show, like I said, get in touch with the station. Otherwise, get lost." He pulled the screen door tighter toward him.

I decided to find out right now if there was anything to the rumor Paulie had mentioned. "It's about you and your relationship with Mrs. Kruel."

The little fat deposits under his eyes quivered a bit. "Relationship? There was no damn relationship. Now get the fuck out of here."

I looked at him hard, tried another card. If this one didn't work, I knew I was done here. "All right. I'll come back in a week or two, see if you've changed your mind and want to talk." I turned, started to walk away.

I had taken about three steps when Neal called after me. "Wait a minute." I turned around to face him. "I don't know what you're talking about, but you can't be coming back here..." he hesitated, "my kids'll be here then." Bingo! He pointedly hadn't mentioned his wife. I was sure that was who he was really afraid I would bump into.

"I'll be back. I won't disturb them."

I heard the lock click. He slowly pushed open the screen door. "All right. I don't know what good it'll do. But I don't want you coming back to harass my children."

"*I* don't harass children," I said, squeezing past him into the house.

He directed me into a very large room. Matter of fact, I guess it would be called one of those *great rooms* you hear the homes of the well-off sometimes have. It was lavishly furnished with a chandelier, a huge fireplace, and a wet bar the

High Tide could have used. The thing that caught my eye right away though, and held my attention, was the floor-to-ceiling glass that looked out over the ocean. It was still light out and the view was dramatic. For a moment I envied the man, but then remembered who he was and how he had acquired the money for a place like this.

He pointed toward a chair that faced away from the ocean. It looked very old and expensive. I sat on it gingerly. He sat across from me on a couch that looked just as expensive.

"All right. What's this all about?"

"I told you, Mr. Neal. It's about Evelyn Kruel."

"I don't know anything about Evelyn Kruel."

I decided to go full out. "You were having an affair with her."

"You're crazy, ahh...What's your name, anyhow?"

"Dan Marlowe. And I have proof about you and her," I bluffed.

"Who told you such a thing, *Dan?*" He leaned heavily on the last word.

"That I can't tell you, *Artie.*" I leaned right back.

"Well, someone's kidding you. There's nothing to it. You might as well get out of here."

I wasn't going to let this guy intimidate me like I was a liberal caller on his radio show. "I'm not going anywhere until I get my questions answered. Unless, of course, you want me to talk to your wife."

His face flushed. "What is this? A shakedown, Marlowe?" The first name basis hadn't lasted long.

"I wouldn't lower myself, Neal. I just want to know about you and the Kruel woman. What do you know about her murder?"

"Murder?" His voice went up a notch and now it sounded just like the hysterical one I was used to hearing on the radio.

"I don't know anything about her murder. Okay, okay. Maybe I did speak to her a couple of times on the beach, but that was it. Why the hell would I want to hurt her?"

He was lucky that wasn't really a question because I could think of one very good reason—to keep his wife from finding out about the affair. I was an amateur at this and didn't know what else to say, so I said, "Did she tell you about any trouble she was having?"

He jumped up from his seat. "Would you like a drink, Dan?" Back to first names again. I shook my head; I had a flashing thought of a Mickey being dropped into a glass. He hurried over to the long bar against the far wall. He kept his back to me, but I could see him fill a large rocks glass with Jack Daniel's and toss in a lone cube from a silver ice holder. He took a drink before he returned. By the time he sat back down, the glass was half empty.

"Where were we?" he said.

"Was she having any trouble with anyone?"

"Not that I know of. She never mentioned anything like that." He swirled the drink, staring down at it as he talked.

I'm sure a professional would have had more questions. I wasn't a professional and I'd run through my short list of questions.

Neal must have picked up on my investigative inexperience. "Well, if that's it, Dan, I have a speaking engagement tonight." He looked at me dismissively, set his glass on the table.

I got up. He stood, too. He put his hand out. I almost didn't shake it but I wasn't sure I was through with this man yet. I might want to talk to him again. When I took his hand, it was clammy.

"Thanks for the time, Artie."

His eyebrow lifted just a bit. "A pleasure, Dan."

He walked me to the door, said goodbye, and closed it behind me.

Outside I didn't go directly to my car. Instead, I turned left and walked around the side of the house towards the front. I wanted to see what kind of a view the house really had. Stunning. One hundred eighty degrees, all ocean. The surf seemed louder and the air saltier here. I could see all the way to the Isle of Shoals. Bigotry paid off, I guess.

Just then I heard a sliding door open and Artie Neal stepped out onto his wide deck. I was a little behind him and he didn't see me. He walked up to the railing, stared out at the ocean. He had the glass in his hand. I watched as he raised it to his lips, drained the other half in one swallow. He set the glass down on the railing, placed both his hands on either side of it. I swear I could hear him sigh from here.

On my drive back to the cottage, I went over my talk with Artie Neal. I hadn't learned a lot but I had at least verified that he knew Evelyn Kruel. And that was something.

I'd also learned that he drank Jack Daniel's. And I wondered if he always drank it like he had in front of me. I hoped not; it was nice imagining I might have caused the man to up his alcohol intake even if it was for just one day.

Chapter 8

WHEN I RETURNED to the cottage, I had the best of intentions to just stay in, relax, and try to get a good night's sleep. It didn't work out that way though. After devouring a gourmet frozen dinner, I plopped myself down in my easy chair, turned on the tube. I couldn't find anything interesting. Or maybe I just couldn't get interested. I kept coming back to Gant's threat and what it could mean. Not only to me. I was worried about Shamrock and Dianne, too.

I couldn't push the thought of the trouble the three of us might be in out of my mind. After my talk with Artie Neal, I had no idea what to do next. My mind just kept going round and round, ending back at the same hopeless spot every time. Finally, before I drove myself crazy, I decided to get out of the cottage and go have a beer.

I didn't do that often anymore, but when I did, I stayed clear of the High Tide. I didn't believe in drinking where you worked. Instead, I usually went to a place called the White Cap Tavern. The Cap was on a lettered side street, a couple of blocks from the Tide. Convenient. One of the good things about living on the beach was that if you wanted to go out for a drink, there were plenty of watering holes within walking distance. You didn't have to worry about drinking and driving.

I made the short walk to the White Cap on automatic pilot. I still couldn't get my mind off of the Evelyn Kruel murder, even knowing that rehashing what I knew, and worse, what I didn't know, was getting me nowhere. Before I knew it, I was halfway to the Casino. I took a left when I came to the street I was looking for, went down a few buildings, and reached my destination.

The second I walked through the front door of the White Cap, I wished I hadn't. Too late. There was a shout from the middle of the bar. "Dan! Dan Marlowe! Get down here, boy."

The stools at the brightly lit bar were all taken but I could easily see who was calling me. He was standing on the leg supports of the stool he'd been sitting on, raising himself up and looking in my direction. Eddie Hoar. He waved me closer. I couldn't get out of it now; I was stuck. I walked through the crowd in his direction.

Seated beside him on the far side was a large, slow-looking man—his shadow and partner, Derwood Doller. Derwood looked up as I approached, a drunken grin on his goofy face. "Hey, Dan. How ya doin'?"

I nodded, forced myself to smile. "Eddie. Derwood." I felt stupid even saying it.

Eddie slapped me on the back. He was a short man with a thin pockmarked face. His greasy black hair was combed straight back. He had on a disco-era shirt and pants and wore a gold chain. I figured the chain to be either fake or hot.

He pulled me in close between him and Derwood and shouted to the bartender. "Give my friend here whatever he wants."

I knew Gene, the bartender, well. He gave me a sympathetic look. I just nodded.

I could smell Eddie's rancid breath as he loudly addressed the bar. "Here's the best bartender on Hampton Beach," he bellowed. Then looking at Gene he quickly added, "Well, tied for best, maybe." He forced a laugh.

He leaned in even closer to me. "I'm gonna pay you that bill we owe you in full tonight," he whispered in my face. I'd believe that when I saw it.

Eddie and Derwood were a couple of small time beach hustlers about my age. They weren't too successful at it either; the duo made so little that they usually had to move off the beach during the summer season when the rents went up. They came back in the fall when the rents dropped again and the tourists had departed. Eddie and Derwood had skipped out on one of our waitresses at the Tide without paying the bill a few months previously. Before they left they'd both devoured a huge fisherman's platter, drank imported beer, and swilled cognac. If I'd been there, I would have had my eye on them as if Charles Ponzi had been sitting with them, but it was at night and I'd been off. The night people were either a little naive or didn't know the pair's reputation.

Dianne had called the cops and they'd been picked up. Somehow they had convinced the judge it was just an error of judgment. They were ordered to pay. Of course, they never did. It goes without saying they were banned from the Tide.

Gene plunked a cold Heineken and frosted glass in front of me on the bar. I could barely squeeze one arm between the two men, so I just grabbed the bottle, took a large swig. I'd changed my mind about doing my drinking here; I wanted to finish this one and get the hell out of there.

"Thanks, Eddie," I said, trying to make it sound like I meant it.

"My pleasure, Dan," he answered. Then raising himself up again, he shouted down the bar toward Gene. "Set everybody up again, my friend."

I almost spit out the mouthful of beer I'd been about to swallow. I tried to catch Gene's eye but he was already dishing out various drinks and beers to the lineup at the bar. Some people had jumped up from the small tables a few feet away and approached the bar, hoping to get a piece of the free action. I'd seen a lot of things on Hampton Beach through the years, but this was a first—Eddie Hoar setting up the bar. And apparently this wasn't the first time he'd done it tonight. I heard shouts of "Thanks again, Eddie," from various patrons. I wondered if Eddie was running a tab; I hoped Gene knew what he was doing.

Gene delivered the last of the round to Eddie and Derwood. Derwood was drinking Coors Lite and Eddie had an imported beer along with a snifter of cognac. Gene looked at me. I quickly shook my head no. He went to the register, rang it crazy, and returned. He peered at the register receipt in his hand. "One hundred seventeen dollars even, Eddie," he said.

"No problem," Eddie said so everyone could hear. Then in a wide-open display, he pulled a fat roll of bills from his front pants pocket and with a dramatic flair peeled three fifty dollar bills off the top. He handed them to Gene. "Keep the change, my good man," he said, again so everyone at the bar could hear it. I *had* seen everything now. Almost.

Eddie turned to me, pulled off two more fifties, and stuffed them in my shirt pocket. "That oughta cover that check Derwood forgot to pay."

Derwood leaned his big head forward and looked at Eddie. "I didn't forget to pay, Eddie. You said..."

Eddie interrupted him. "You'd forget your head if it wasn't tied on, Dumwood."

The big goon looked like a hurt little kid. "I told you not to call me that, Eddie. You know I don't like it."

Eddie batted the air. "Ahh, drink your beer." Derwood did.

I took another large gulp of beer, anxious to get out of there. Of all the nights to come in here, I had to pick this one. At least I'd gotten Dianne's money for her. Eddie tried to talk to me, but fortunately for me, he was a rock star tonight. He had half the moochers on Hampton Beach hanging all over him, waiting for the next round. Most of these were people who wouldn't stop to spit on Eddie Hoar even if he was on fire.

While Eddie was being backslapped by the sponges, I noticed Derwood was occupied by another group to his right. I quickly drained my beer, dropped a couple of singles for a tip, and slid by Eddie, hoping to slip unseen out the door. I should have known better; my luck had been bad from the instant I'd stepped into the White Cap. It hadn't changed.

Just before I reached the door, I heard a shout behind me. "Yow, Dan. Hole up. I gotta talk to you." It was Eddie, of course. I couldn't ignore the request—the whole bar had heard it. I turned. He was coming off his stool, alternating sips of beer and cognac as he did. He dropped both glasses on the bar and grabbed Derwood's arm, gave him a pull. The lug almost fell backwards before he regained his balance. Eddie headed right for me, Derwood behind him, bottle to his lips. He slammed the empty on the end of the bar as he followed Eddie.

Eddie got right up in my face; I didn't like that. "I gotta talk to you, Dan. Important business." He raised up on the balls of his feet and still had to look up at me.

I faked a face like I was sorry. "I can't tonight, Eddie. Long shift. I'm exhausted. Got to get home."

I didn't expect his answer; like I said my luck was running cold.

"My car's out front. Me and Derwood'll give you a lift."

Great. Because the only cars these two had ever been known to have could be called cars only if you were very generous with the definition. I was trapped. Hopefully, the drunken fools wouldn't slam into a seawall before they dropped me off.

I stepped outside into the brisk beach air, the other two right behind me. I looked both ways. I couldn't see any obvious deathtrap.

"Which way?" I asked.

Eddie pointed toward the strip. We paraded up there. I hoped no one saw us.

When we reached the corner, we clomped across Ocean Boulevard. I stopped and said, "Where is it?"

Eddie scooted up beside me, a drunken smile on his pock-marked face. "Right in front of you, Dan. Can't you tell?" He pointed and pushed his chest out like a bantam rooster.

No, I couldn't, because he was pointing at a powder-blue convertible Caddy boat parked at the curb. Its top was down. I couldn't tell what year but the car was in cherry condition. It was the type Elvis might have bought for someone who had smiled at him back in the day. As I stood there looking at it, I realized that this was exactly what someone like Eddie would buy if...*if* they had suddenly come into money.

"Hop in back, Dan," Eddie said. He flipped the keys to Derwood who fumbled them for a minute then finally held on. "You drive. And don't you get a goddamn scratch on Baby either."

I crawled in the huge back seat, Derwood got behind the wheel, and Eddie slid in shotgun. Eddie put his arm up on the back of the seat and turned to look at me.

Derwood started the car up, moved north along Ocean Boulevard. The big man was fairly drunk but I hoped he could maneuver this thing all right, at least until I was able to get out at my cottage. I had a visual of him driving half blind up to Boar's Head, careening through the flower garden of one of the oceanfront homes, and plummeting down the cliff into the Atlantic. If the three of us were found dead like that, Dianne and Shamrock would spend the rest of their lives trying to figure out what had been going on. My kids not so much. My ex would let them know it was just par for the course.

As I nervously watched Derwood pilot the big car up Ocean Boulevard, I said, "I live down near the bridge, Derwood." I didn't feel any smarter using his name this time either.

Derwood nodded, kept driving north.

"Don't worry, Dan," Eddie said. He was looking over the seat at me with glassy eyes; he was a bit cockeyed, too. "We know that. We own this beach." He kept staring at me. I wasn't sure if he was studying me or just trying to focus on my face. Finally, he said, "I got a business proposition for you, Dan."

This ought to be great, I thought to myself.

Eddie flicked a finger at Derwood, then back at himself. "We got some merchandise we'd like to sell."

Merchandise? With these two *merchandise* could be anything from a hot baby carriage to ladies underwear. "Money's tight right now, Eddie," I said diplomatically. I was happy to see Derwood pull a U-turn right after Boar's Head and head south on Ocean.

Eddie waved his finger at my face. "Now wait'll you hear my proposition. You might come up with some dough fast or know someone that's got it."

"My asshociate here," he slurred, glancing at Derwood, "and I have access to some top-grade pot."

So that was it. That explained the generosity down at the White Cap and the new wheels. I was sure they'd probably just put a small down payment on the Caddy. A repo man would have a new assignment within a month or two if I knew Eddie and Derwood. I also was betting they'd ripped off some beach ounce dealer for a few pounds.

I shook my head. "Can't help you, Eddie. I wouldn't know what to do with it."

Eddie threw his head back and gave me a look like he thought I was joking. "You're kidding, right? Remember who this is, Dan." He thumbed his chest and then pointed his thumb toward Derwood. "We're businessmen, too. So we know the score."

Maybe they thought they knew the score, but they still had the numbers wrong. This wasn't the first time some indiscretions I'd been involved in years ago had come back to haunt me. Sure I'd done some things back in the day, when I'd been another person. But those days were long over. I was well aware, though, that some people would never believe that. People like Lieutenant Gant, for instance, and the two dimwits seated in front of me. They thought my story was just something a smart guy would say to keep people in the dark. It wasn't. But the more you told people it was the truth, the more some didn't believe it. They thought it was just a cover story. You could lug your baggage around with you for a long time, sometimes forever. I knew that for a fact.

"I can't help you, Eddie."

Eddie got testy; I don't like testy. "You gotta know somebody that can. You're not stupid. There's big dough to be made. You could get a piece."

"Sorry, Eddie."

"Shit," he said turning around in his seat. Then more sullenly, "I thought you'd want in on this for sure."

We were headed down Ashworth Avenue now. We stayed quiet for the rest of the trip until I directed Derwood to my cottage where he pulled up in front.

I hopped out. "Thanks for the ride. Sorry I couldn't help you, Eddie."

"Your loss," he said. "Come on, Dumwood, drive."

As they pulled away, I heard Derwood say, "I asked you not to call me that, Eddie."

I watched as they drove the Caddy all the way down the street and turned right onto Ocean Boulevard. I shook my head and wondered how long those two would keep it together—flashing money, buying drinks, and riding around in a powder blue Caddy on Hampton Beach. Not long, I figured.

I remembered the bills in my shirt pocket, fingered them. Maybe I'd had a little luck tonight after all. At least I'd gotten Dianne's money back before the two geniuses who had just departed were flat broke again. That wouldn't be long coming.

Chapter 9

MORNING CAME QUICK and the anchor-shaped clock on my wall said it was time to get ready for my shift at the Tide. After I had showered and dressed, I stepped out on my porch and locked the door behind me. Oh yeah, you have to lock your doors. Hampton Beach is a nice beach and most of the people are, too. But like everywhere nowadays, there are a few characters floating around who aren't top-shelf. And they like unlocked cottage doors.

The half-mile walk from my cottage to the restaurant was uneventful. It was a great June day so I walked on the beach side. Except for some puffy white clouds the sky was a bright blue. The sun sparkled off the ocean. A couple of sailboats decorated the scene and out farther the Isle of Shoals. You couldn't see those islands every day. Today they were as distinct as I had ever seen them.

Up ahead a large swarm of seagulls circled over the sand. It brought back memories of finding Evelyn Kruel. I pushed the thoughts from my mind. I was sure this time it was either the Bird Man or Seagull Sally engaged in their morning bird-feeding ritual. Most of the stores along Ocean Boulevard were open for the season now. Owners puttered around, getting ready for the start of the busy season in another week or so.

When I reached the Tide, I crossed the strip, made a bee-line for the rear door, and stepped inside. I walked through the kitchen, greeted Guillermo and Dianne, and went directly to the bar. Shamrock sat in his usual seat near the window. He saw me, closed the newspaper on the bar in front of him, and pushed it away.

"Thank God you're here, Danny. I've been waiting for you." He looked disdainfully at the newspaper he had just shoved aside. "I'm tired of looking at those damn numbers. Staring at the godforsaken things doesn't change them."

I chuckled. "What's up, Shamrock?" I asked, stopping beside him.

He pointed at me, waved his finger. "You. You. You didn't tell me that arsehole Gant said he'd get me, too."

I knew Dianne must have told him. I didn't mind—I hadn't told her not to. I was going to tell him myself, just hadn't gotten around to it yet. Now I'd have to bring Shamrock up to speed. Diane as well. I didn't need her mad at me. I had enough trouble.

"Hold on a second," I said. I went to the kitchen and asked Dianne if she had a minute. When I returned, I asked Shamrock to join me in a back booth in the dining room.

"What's wrong, Dan?" Dianne asked when she reached the booth and slid in beside Shamrock.

I told Shamrock everything I had already told Dianne, plus I told them both about Artie Neal and my encounter with him. I didn't leave out anything. They didn't interrupt me; even Shamrock held his tongue. I could almost see the black clouds forming over their heads.

"Well, that's about it," I said. "I thought you both should know."

Shamrock spoke first. "So you think Artie Neal was giving her the old shillelagh and maybe he killed her."

I shook my head. "I don't know. I do know he doesn't want his wife to know about it."

"Nobody would," Dianne said. "That doesn't mean he killed her."

"Somebody did," I said.

"But Gant thinks it was you," Dianne said. "Or all of us," she quickly added, twirling her finger in her hair. "How can he think any of that?"

"With me it's easy," I said. "He hates me. He's just dragging you two in because you're my friends."

"No," Dianne said. "It's because of that stupid fight with her brother and that was my fault." My hands were on the table. She put one of hers on mine. She squeezed gently. "I'm sorry, Dan."

"It wasn't your fault. I'd sock him again. He deserved it."

"He did, Dianne," Shamrock chimed in. "And what a shellacking you gave him too, Danny."

"That's nothing to smile about, Shamrock," Dianne said. "Look how it's ended up."

She stared at the table in front of her, her hand still on mine. I could feel her shaking just a bit. She didn't have on any makeup or lipstick; we were at work after all. She didn't need it anyway. She was a beautiful woman. I felt a sudden tinge of guilt that I had dragged her into this mess. If it wasn't for her connection to me, Gant would have no interest in her. Depression washed over me and I almost forgot why we were all sitting there.

"What can I do to help, Danny?" Shamrock asked, snapping me out of my fog.

"I hate to even ask you, Shamrock, but..."

Shamrock held his hand up. "No, no, no, Danny. I want to help. I'm involved now. And for the love of Jaysus, no one is going to besmirch the name of Michael Kelly on Hampton Beach. I've got a good name here to protect."

I smiled. The man did have a good name to protect. He had a heart of gold and he'd give you his last shirt—even if it was on his back—if you needed it.

"Well, do you think you could nose around?" I asked. "See if maybe Evelyn Kruel had any enemies?"

Shamrock beamed. "I certainly can. If there were any serpents slithering around the woman, I'll find them."

"She was a big landlord, Dan," Dianne said. "Lots of people probably didn't belong to her fan club."

"You're right, but I've got to start somewhere."

"What can I do?" Dianne asked.

"Nothing right now." Even though I wanted Dianne involved as little as possible, I was still speaking honestly. I had no idea what she could do at this time. I felt her hand pull away from mine. Shamrock saw it too. I added quickly, "I have a feeling there's going to be plenty to do before this is over. Just wait a bit. See what Shamrock can dig up first."

"I want to help, Dan." She sounded angry now. "And don't think it's just about you either. I've got a business to protect here, you know."

I noticed Shamrock was counting the light fixtures on the ceiling.

"I know, I know," I said soothingly. "We'll all work on this together."

"We'd better!" she said, sliding out of the booth. "I've got work to do now."

I looked at Shamrock. He rolled his eyes. I did too. But I think we both knew the real reason she was livid.

And it wasn't because I didn't send her on some wild goose chase. She was worried about me—and about Shamrock— and maybe a little about the High Tide. And probably even less about herself. That's the type of person Dianne was. That was one of the reasons I was in love with her.

Dianne went back to the kitchen. Shamrock got up, headed over to review his lottery losses one last time. And I sat there like a dunce. It wasn't just that I had nothing to ask Dianne to do in this predicament—I had no idea what to do *myself*. I was at a loss. I did know I couldn't just sit around and wait for other people, meaning Gant, to demolish my life and my friends' lives too. I'd have to come up with something to get us out of this situation. Before it was too late.

And that's what I thought about during my shift as I was going through the motions. I didn't come up with any ideas though. Not even a bad one. I had to fix that and fast.

Chapter 10

THE NEXT MORNING I still didn't have an answer. I did have four hours of troubled sleep to contend with though. Knowing that the police were trying to pin a murder on you wasn't conducive to a good night's rest. If I didn't want to end up with permanent bags under my eyes, I had to come up with something that would get the finger of suspicion pointed in the right direction. Only one problem—I had absolutely no idea what the right direction was.

I decided to go for my jog. It was my scheduled day and jogging often helped me think better. Maybe it would help me this time, too. I needed all the help I could get. I threw on my running stuff and headed out the door.

When I reached the street I noticed a maroon Ford parked on the other side, up closer to the dunes. I could make out two figures in it. I didn't recognize the car. Even though it wasn't summer season yet, strange cars weren't unusual at the beach. It looked like it might have been a cop car. A bit old and beat for that, though. I wondered for a moment if it was police surveillance...of me. Gant would pull something like that. The clouds were black and heavy, so I ruled out sun worshippers. Whoever it was, I had an uneasy feeling. I had to pass the car to get to the beach. I could have turned back and cut through the cottages, but dropped that idea as foolish. If it was the police, so what? More likely it was just a couple of day trippers.

I had just come abreast of the car when the passenger side door flew open and a large burly man stepped out. I could see the automatic in his hand as he came around the front of the car to cut me off. I stopped dead in my tracks.

He came right up to me, pushed me in the chest with his free hand. I stumbled backwards. He opened the car's back door.

He motioned with the gun. "Get in, asshole. Hurry up."

I looked quickly around, hoping to see a neighbor or someone who might at least call the police. This wasn't a plainclothes cop holding a gun on me; it was anything but. I didn't see another soul on the street. So I did what I was told and slid into the backseat. The big man came in beside me, using the gun to nudge me in farther as he settled himself behind the driver.

"What do you want?" I asked. The inside stank of cheap cigars.

"Shut the fuck up," the big man said, digging the gun roughly into my side. He looked like a bit player in a 1940s gangster movie. Sounded that way, too.

The driver backed the car up, turned it around, and headed up to Ocean Boulevard. It was early and the street was almost deserted. He puffed on a foul-smelling cigar as he drove. When we reached the municipal parking lot, the driver pulled in. He didn't go far. The south end of the lot had only a few cars scattered about. He parked there. He shut the car off, stubbed out the cigar in the ashtray, and turned to look at me. He hung his right arm over the seat. He wore an Irish Claddagh ring.

He had a long face with a sickly complexion. And he was tall. I could tell by the way the wispy brown hair on his head brushed the roof. "What's yer name, sport?" he asked. "Ya gotta name, ain't ya?" He talked with a Boston accent. Not one of those Harvard ones, but the poorer cousin kind. His voice was harsh, too, like the cigars had done some permanent damage. He was younger than his sparse hair made him appear—forty maybe.

I wasn't sure telling him was a good idea. I changed my mind when the big man sitting beside me jammed me hard in the ribs with the business end of his gun.

"Dan Marlowe."

"Good you didn't lie, Mr. Marlowe." He sucked at his teeth as he talked. "I want to ask you a few questions."

That didn't sound too bad. I glanced past him out the front windshield. All I saw was an old-timer with a coffee and newspaper sitting on a bench facing the ocean. A female jogger breezed by him. There was no help out there.

"Where's the merchandise?" he asked

"What merchandise?"

I knew it was the wrong answer the second I said it. The big man instantly let me know I was right. He was turned toward me, the gun in his left hand. The back of his large right paw flashed out and struck me hard on the side of the head. My head snapped back and my hands flew up to my face.

I lowered my hands, looked at the big man. He smirked. When I turned back to the driver, he said, "Let's try again. The merchandise. Where...is...the...merchandise?"

I almost spoke, hesitated, looked at the big man, then turned back to the driver again. I thought I chose my words much more carefully this time. I guess I didn't. "I honestly don't know anything about any merchandise. That's the..."

I didn't get a chance to finish. The back of the same hard hand caught me square in the forehead this time; my head rocked back. Those stars prize fighters talk about appeared for a few seconds. I shook my head to put them back in their place.

"You were with those two jerk-offs the other night," the driver said. I knew immediately who he meant before he added, "Hoar and Doller." I also knew immediately where Eddie and Derwood must have gotten the pot they tried to sell me.

"They just gave me a ride home." I flinched. The blow I expected didn't come.

The driver nodded slowly, a wicked grin on his face. "Sure they did, Marlowe. And there's no fish in the ocean either. We know all about you. We figure either you're the brains behind the rip-off or they're using you to get rid of it. Either way, for the last time, where the hell is the merchandise?"

I didn't say a word—I wasn't that dumb. Even so, the big man tried to gangster-slap me again; this time I was ready. When his hand shot toward my face, I grabbed it with my left, and yanked his body toward me. At the same time I fired my right at him and caught him flush on the nose. I was hoping he wouldn't dare use the gun in a public parking lot.

He looked shocked for a second. He held the gun on me and wiped his nose with the back of his other hand. He moved the hand in front of his face and stared stupidly at the blood smeared on it. After a few seconds he raised his eyes in my direction. They were red with rage. For a long moment, I thought he was going to shoot. He didn't. Instead, he hoisted the gun as if he was about to pistol-whip me.

"No, no, not here," the driver said. "We'll take him some-where quieter. Then you can have your fun with him. Maybe we'll get some answers that way. We aren't getting anywhere

here. And if that don't work, *Mister* Marlowe, we'll find out who you're close to and go after them. Even you must have friends. How do you like them apples, Marlowe?"

I didn't. Not one bit. He might as well have mentioned Dianne and Shamrock by name. Again, I may have gotten them involved in trouble, just because they knew me.

The driver started the car, backed out of the spot, and headed for the parking lot exit.

"You got anything for this bleeding, Rudy?" the big man asked.

"I said no names! *Santa!*" The man named Rudy glanced angrily in the rearview mirror. He continued driving for half a minute, then pulled out a used handkerchief and tossed it behind him. "Try not to get it all over the car. Blood's a bitch to get out."

With the cloth pressed tightly against his nose, Santa said to me, "You're gonna be one sorry bastard you did that, Marlowe. And I'm gonna love every second of it, too."

There's nothing like knowing you're being driven to your own pistol-whipping to make your mind latch onto any possible idea to avoid it, no matter how desperate the idea was. The idea my mind came up with wasn't anything new, but it was all I had. It was early, foot traffic was light and few businesses were open. I was also betting again on Santa's reluctance to shoot in the middle of Hampton Beach in broad daylight.

Rudy stopped the car at the parking lot exit. Santa had looked away from me in the direction of an attractive woman on the other side of the street. I waited until Rudy stepped on the gas and pulled out onto Ocean Boulevard. Santa was still glancing from me to the woman and back. I waited until we had traveled a half block before I made my move. I lunged over the front seat and slammed Rudy's head into the window beside him; the thud was sickening. It did what I hoped though—stunned, his foot floored the accelerator. At the same time, I grabbed the steering wheel and spun it to the left. We careened across the road and banged up and over the curb, blowing into an area of temporary plywood business stalls.

I had known it was too early for any of those businesses to be open. Good thing, too, because I wouldn't have tried it otherwise. Innocent people would have been hurt. We blew through the flimsy structures like they were made out of popsicle sticks. Wood chunks, jewelry cases, T-shirts, and all sorts of knick-knacks and debris went hurtling through the air. A piece of canvas from one of the structures completely obscured the front windshield. I caught a glimpse of Santa holding onto the back of the front seat like he was about to go down the first hill of a roller coaster, gun still in his hand. Rudy, up front, was shaking his head, dazed.

We slammed into something solid and came to a stop. I flew forward and then backwards with the impact and took advantage of the crash to throw the rear door open and roll out onto the pavement. I was up and running north in seconds. Behind me, I could hear the engine of the Ford still racing and Santa screaming curses. I didn't turn to see if anyone was after me.

I reached the Casino building, ran up the stairs, flew past the Funarama arcade. I passed a few people as I went, but I was moving so fast they didn't have time to do or say anything except jump out of my way.

Just short of the shooting gallery, about midway into the Casino, I banged a left and ran through the inside of the building. I raced by Ashley's General Store and came out at the back parking lot. I saw my goal across the street—the one-story Hampton Police station. I ran down the long flight of stairs, across the parking lot, and stopped when I was directly in front of the police station. I looked behind me, saw no one following. I bent, put my hands on my knees, and tried to catch my breath.

It was then that I heard the sirens. Two police cars pulled out of the station. A half-minute later, a fire engine and a rescue truck pulled out of the adjacent fire house. They all blew past me, sirens wailing.

Usually on Hampton Beach sirens are as common as fireworks on the Fourth of July. Funny thing though, you almost never know what they are for or where they are going. This time I knew both.

Chapter 11

I DIDN'T BOTHER going inside the police station. There wasn't any need now. The two thugs apparently hadn't followed me and I was sure they were long gone, with or without their car. As far as me getting tied in with the car crash, I was hoping I could avoid that. Questioned, I would have been honestly vague about what had happened and why, and I was certain that would have only fueled Gant's paranoid idea that I was involved in something very big and sinister on the beach, including Evelyn Kruel's murder. It might have even helped him convince others he was right. So instead, I started to walk south on Ashworth Avenue.

It was too early for my shift to start at the Tide, and besides, I had to get home and change out of my jogging gear and into my work clothes. Still, I wasn't in any hurry to get back to the cottage. For all I knew the two goons would be there waiting for me. After a few blocks I turned up the street that led to the High Tide. When I reached the back of the building, I entered through the rear door.

I walked down the short corridor into the brightly lit kitchen. Dianne and Guillermo were there as usual. Dianne, also as usual, was doing prep work on the speed table. She saw me first.

She looked at me quizzically. "Dan? What are you doing here now?" She glanced at the wall clock, then at my jogging clothes.

I walked up to her, didn't say anything. Guillermo turned from the fryolators he was fooling with and said hello in his accented English. He went immediately back to what he had been doing.

I was close to Dianne now and she got a better look at my face. She put a hand over her mouth. "What happened?"

I ran my hand quickly across my face, glanced to see if there was blood there. There wasn't. My face did sting in a couple of spots but I had hardly noticed it until she'd said something. I had more serious things on my mind.

"Let's go out there, talk." I pointed toward the dining area.

"Again?" she asked. I nodded.

Dianne put down the chopping knife she'd been using, wiped her hands on the stained, white apron she wore, and pushed a curl of soft black hair out of her eyes. "Come on," she said. I followed her through the swinging doors that led into the dining room. I watched her from behind as she walked. Even in my condition, with a lot on my mind, I couldn't help myself. She went to the same back booth we had used yesterday and slid in. I was just about to sit opposite her when I heard a noise from the bar area.

"One sec," I said.

I walked around the partition that separated the dining room from the bar area. I didn't even glance at the large fish tank sitting on top of the partition this time. Sitting on a stool at the bar was Shamrock.

He heard me coming and looked up from the newspaper he had spread out on the bar. "Danny," he said. "What the hell are you doing here?" Before I could answer, he said, "I can't win a goddamn thing in this." He thumped the newspaper with his fingers. "I think the fix is in. Not like the Irish lottery. Now that's a real lottery. On the up and up, too."

"I told you it's a waste of money, Shamrock. Just another tax." I didn't give him a chance to respond. "You got a minute? I have to talk to you and Dianne. She's over there in the back booth." I motioned with my thumb over my shoulder.

"Sure, Danny Boy, sure." He quickly pushed away from the bar and headed in Dianne's direction.

Before I followed him, I scooted behind the bar and took a quick peek over all the liquor bottles lined up there. I could see in the long bar mirror that I had two red welts on my face— one on my forehead, the other on a cheek. There were no cuts.

When I reached the booth, Shamrock was opposite Dianne, chattering away about something as he usually did. The man was quite a conversationalist. I slipped in beside Dianne. Shamrock stopped talking and he and Dianne both looked at me.

"Has something happened already, Dan?" Dianne asked.

I told them about the two thugs and the car crash.

"I heard all of them sirens," Shamrock said. "I poked my head out the door. A guy walking by from that direction said someone slammed into the stalls up at Rexall. Hit and run. He got away."

"I didn't hear anything," Dianne said. Then she added, "On the other hand, you hear sirens so much around here." She reached over and touched my face gently with her hand. "Are you all right?"

"I'm fine," I said.

She withdrew her hand.

"You wouldn't be if you got that pistol-whipping," Shamrock said, nodding his head gravely. "I seen those on the late movies. They aren't good."

Dianne winced. "I was going to tell you when you came in later—*I* found out some information." She looked back and forth between the two of us before continuing. "I remembered something I'd heard at one of the Chamber of Commerce meetings. So I called a friend. I guess Evelyn was having a lot of trouble with a guy named George Ransom. You know him? Owns a motel on Ashworth Avenue. I guess he was anxious to turn his motel into contels. That's where they make all the motel units into little condo rooms and sell them off one by one. I imagine he could have made a lot of money, gotten out of the motel business, and retired. Problem was parking. His building is real old, not much space for cars. He needed to buy the empty lot next to his motel to make the deal work."

Shamrock interrupted. "I'll bet Evelyn Kruel owned it and she wouldn't sell. Am I right? Am I right?"

Dianne let out a sigh. "Yes, Shamrock. Maybe she had plans for the lot herself. I guess Mr. Ransom wasn't happy. They say he's not a very nice man and I was told the contel deal meant a lot to him."

"Hmm," I said. "That's interesting, Dianne." I had no idea if it would lead anywhere, but at least it was an avenue to investigate.

"I found out something too, Danny," Shamrock said.

"Boy, you people are fast." I waited.

They both blushed lightly and smiled. Shamrock grabbed an ashtray, spun it. "I picked up a little dirt." He hesitated.

"Well?" I said.

This time his face turned bright red. He shot a glance at Dianne, looked back at me, stalled, then cleared his throat. "It's about a woman. Marcy Wade's her name." He hesitated again, looked around.

This time Dianne said, "Well, Shamrock, what is it?"

"Well, this Marcy is Evelyn Kruel's secretary. And I guess... well, it's a rumor, mind you. Ahh..."

"*Shamrock?*" I was getting a bit irritated.

"Oh, all right." He looked around again. "They was lezzies."

"Who?" Dianne said, leaning back. "Evelyn Kruel and her secretary?"

Shamrock nodded, still blushing.

"Are you sure?" I asked.

Shamrock held up both his hands. "Like I said, it's a rumor. So I don't know for sure."

"Hmm," I said again. It was becoming one of my trademark sayings.

"I never heard that," Dianne said.

"Me neither." Then I nodded at Shamrock and added, "But we don't hear half the things on this beach he hears."

Shamrock sat up in his seat and beamed.

"But that doesn't have anything to do with murder," Dianne said. "Everybody has a right to their own lifestyle."

"Yes, they do," I said. But still, it was another name thrown into the mix.

"What are you going to do now?" Dianne asked.

I shook my head. "Not sure. But at least now I've got some places to start, thanks to both of you."

"We didn't just do it for you," Dianne said, looking from me to Shamrock and back again. "We have a stake in this, too."

"That's right, Danny," Shamrock chimed in. "Besides, that's what a best friend and..." he stumbled, "...two best friends do."

Dianne and I looked at each other and we both chuckled. Pretending around Shamrock was ridiculous.

"It's okay, Shamrock," Dianne said. "*You* can say it."

Shamrock looked relieved. "Significant other," he said.

He said it so seriously that Dianne and I both laughed, loudly this time. Shamrock looked at us for a few seconds and then joined in.

When our laughs died out, Dianne glanced up at the clock. "Oops. I have to get back to work. Anything else I can do, Dan?" she asked as I stood to let her out.

She brushed against me as she squeezed by and I caught her scent. "Not right now. I'll let you know if I need any help."

She waved her finger as she walked off toward the kitchen. "You'd better."

When she was gone, I said, "I hate to ask you for something else, Shamrock, but..."

He interrupted. "Danny, like you know...you're my best friend. I'd do anything for you." Then he added, "Dianne would, too."

I felt a tinge of embarrassment. I knew it was true. They had both proven their loyalty a long time ago. Back when I was the owner of the High Tide. Back before I drove the place into the ground. Back when I was a good businessman, a good man for that matter. Back before I threw away my family, my two beautiful kids. Everything that meant anything to me. Back when I came close to throwing away my life, too. Dianne and Shamrock hadn't given up on me even when I'd done all those horrible things.

Dianne bought the Tide just before the bank got it; she kept me on as bartender. She and Shamrock got me through some of my blackest days. They pulled me back from the edge just before I went over. Without them, I wouldn't still be around. It was still a daily struggle but I was determined to win. They both thought I could; I hoped they were right.

"Danny?" Shamrock said.

I pushed my thoughts aside. They weren't good thoughts for someone like me to dwell on. "Could you check on Eddie

Hoar and Derwood Doller?" I said. "See where they live? I don't think it has anything to do with the Evelyn Kruel thing, but I have to find out what those two nitwits have gotten me involved in. I want to get that squared away quick. I can't be dealing with two gorillas chasing me around the beach while I'm trying to get a handle on her murder."

"I can do that, easy."

I glanced up at the clock. "Jesus, I got to get home and change and get back here." I slid out of the booth. "I'll talk to you later, Shamrock."

"You will, Danny. And I'll get that information for you, too. You'll see."

I went home the back way, along Ashworth. I wasn't sure what had happened to the two goons, Rudy and Santa, and if they were still around. But I got home without incident and after scouting my cottage to make sure they weren't waiting for me, I was able to get ready for my shift. I hoped the rest of the morning was less eventful than the beginning. I had already had enough for one day.

Chapter 12

NOTHING OUT OF the ordinary happened during my shift. Until it was over, that is. I had been going over in my mind who I was going to approach next on my list of suspects and how I was going to do it. I had come to the conclusion that it didn't matter who I talked to first. As for how—I just had to screw up my courage and do it. About the time I started counting my tips, preparing to hand over the bar to my relief, I looked up and saw Steve Moore come through the door. He gave me a nod, just stood there. I finished up and came around the bar.

"Can we talk?" he asked.

"Sure. Where?"

"Not here."

I was glad he'd said that. I wouldn't have been comfortable talking to a Hampton detective here at the Tide, not now. Too much had happened since the last time we'd spoken. Now the situation seemed more ominous. I realized that Steve must have felt the same way about talking to me.

When we were outside, I asked again, "Where do you want to go?"

"How about the White Cap?"

"All right. Where's your car?"

"Over there," he said, pointing across Ocean Boulevard to the municipal parking lot. "Let's walk."

We walked the short distance silently. Inside the Cap we took a table that looked out onto the side street.

A waitress came up. She looked young enough to be in high school. She handed us menus, glanced at the gun on Steve's hip, didn't react. Then she said, "What can I get you, gentlemen?"

"Coke, please," Steve said. The waitress frowned.

I don't drink much when I go out but I had a feeling I might need it today. "Heineken." She gave me a smile and walked away.

"She probably thinks I'm a cheapskate," Steve said.

"She saw your gun. Probably knows you're on duty."

"Yeah, I guess so."

"How's Kelsey?" I asked.

Kelsey was Steve's adopted son. He was a boy I'd helped when his mother had been killed on the beach a while back. He was a good kid. Steve told me he was doing fine. We talked about him for a bit.

"Why don't you come by and see him, Dan?" Steve said. "I know he'd like to see you. Still talks about you all the time."

"I've seen him around the beach a few times. He looks like he's doing good."

"He is. But come by and have dinner. It'd be good for him. You too."

I felt uncomfortable. How could I tell Steve that sitting there at dinner with him, his wife, and Kelsey would just remind me of my own kids and what I'd lost?

I was about to say something lame when the waitress returned and delivered our drinks. She took out her order book and pen. "What can I get you?"

Steve waved his hand. "Nothing for me, thank you."

She frowned again, then looked at me. I'd already eaten at the Tide for half price. Our meals used to be free, until one worker had taken advantage of Dianne and ordered a steak dinner every shift. She had changed it to the half price deal. I didn't blame her; I would have done the same, I guess. No one had pulled that trick when I had owned the Tide, though.

"Large side of french fries," I said.

She didn't frown at me but she wasn't jumping up and down either. She said, "Thanks," and walked away.

"Might as well bring the check, too," Steve called after her.

We sat there silently for a short minute. I poured my beer into the glass, took a sip. Nice, like the first one always is. Finally, Steve got to his reason for wanting to talk to me. "You want to tell me what happened this morning?"

"How do you know about that?"

"How do I know about it? Everybody on the beach knows about it. It isn't every day that a runaway car takes out half the stalls beside Rexall. Those stalls've been here longer than we have. Well, me anyway." Steve grinned. "What you really want to know is how I know you were involved. Right?"

"And?" I asked.

"Someone who will remain anonymous saw you running from the car. What the hell was it all about, Dan? People could have been killed, for Chrissake."

I already knew from the talk at the High Tide that no one had died. Miraculously, no one had been injured either. At least no one that anyone knew about. The two goons had fled the scene in the car. And it was dumb luck that a large beach towel from a display had been wrapped around their rear bumper, obscuring the license plate.

I didn't say anything. Steve sighed. "Come on, what happened?"

I told him the whole story.

Steve shook his head sadly. "Hoar and Doller, huh? Boy, if they aren't a pair of beauts. You got to be careful who you hang out with, Dan." He smiled.

I took another sip of beer, almost cracked my tooth on the glass. "I told you...I got stuck with the boobs for an hour or so, and the two goons who grabbed me today must've seen us together and thought we were best friends."

"You didn't recognize them?"

"No. They did use names though." I looked at Steve warily. "Santa and Rudy."

Steve's eyebrows connected. "You're kidding, right?" I shook my head. "All right," he continued, "I'll see if I can come up with anything on a Santa and Rudolph."

"It's not funny, Steve."

"Sure it is," he said. "Still, I'll see if I can find out anything on two guys with those names. Maybe there's been an escape from a local mental institution I didn't hear about."

I ignored the comment and gave him their descriptions even though Steve hadn't asked. He took out his pocket notebook and wrote it all down.

When he was done scribbling, I said, "Ahh, can you keep Gant from knowing about this?"

He made a face as if that was a tall order. "That I might not be able to do."

I must have looked like I suddenly felt because he added, "I believe what you told me and I'll tell him you were just a victim."

"He won't believe you. It'll be just one more bullet in Gant's Dan Marlowe gun."

Steve chuckled. "You're right, but at this point it won't make much difference."

I took another sip of beer, careful not to bang my teeth this time. "You haven't heard anything unusual about Hoar and his friend, have you?" I asked.

Steve shook his head, stirring the straw in his coke. "Everything is unusual about them. But no...nothing except small-time shit." He hesitated for a few seconds, looked like he was remembering something. "One of the funniest things I think ever happened on the beach is the time those two birdbrains burglarized the Funland Arcade. They had a car backed up to the rear door and had loaded the trunk with sacks of quarters. The coins weighed so much that driving down Ashworth the car's ass scraped on the pavement, making more racket than a steel mill." Steve laughed. "Sparks were flying everywhere. The goddamn car caught on fire and was a total loss. The bums were gone before we showed up but the quarters were still there."

"I remember reading about that in the *Union*," I said. "That was Eddie and Derwood?"

Steve nodded, a big smile on his face. "An informant told us it was them, but we could never prove it. They stole the car, a real crate, from someplace over in Seabrook. Our man said all they got away with were the quarters in their pockets."

I had to smile. "I can just see the two of them running down Ashworth trying to hold up their pants. Christ, what idiots."

We both laughed. Just then the waitress returned, dropped off the fries, and put the check on the table in front of Steve. "Thanks," she muttered and left. There were other tables that were vacant, thank God; otherwise, I would have felt even worse than I already did for tying up her table for one beer, one coke, and french fries.

I decided to take advantage of our meeting. "Have you had any luck with the Evelyn Kruel investigation?"

Steve grabbed a fork, speared a couple of french fries. "If you mean are you still at the top of the suspect list, you are. At least with Gant."

I cleared my throat. "Have you looked into Marcy Wade and George Ransom?"

Steve furrowed his brow. "We know about them. We don't think they had anything to do with the murder." He looked at me suspiciously. "Why? I hope you're not nosing into this." When I didn't answer, he said, "You aren't, are you?"

"Just a bit. I have to. If I don't, Gant'll hang this on me."

"Dan, for Chrissake. You're going to make the situation worse."

I wanted to cut this part short, so I said, "Do you know about Tiny Bastards?"

"Artie Neal? What the hell's he got to do with it?"

"He was fooling around with Evelyn Kruel."

"How do you know that?"

I didn't want to tell him Paulie, the mailman, told me. I knew how ridiculous that sounded. "I heard it somewhere."

"Somewhere? That sounds reliable." He shook his head, took a sip of coke, set the glass down. "And even if he was, so what? The beach is like Peyton Place. You know that. Getting a little on the side is a football field away from murder."

I had my hands on the table, opened them up. "You could look into it."

Steve snickered. "Sure I could. If I wanted to be the next public servant mauled on Neal's talk show. No thanks. Even if the fooling around were true, it's not illegal. And I don't think a guy like Neal would murder someone. Come on. He's got too much to lose."

"But if his wife was going to find out?"

"Dan! Drop it. And stay out of it."

I felt my blood pressure rising. "Well, aren't you looking at anybody?" When he didn't answer, I threw in, "Just me, huh?"

"No, not just you as a matter of fact. We're looking at her brother, too." I could tell the minute he said it, he wished he hadn't.

"Morris Kruel? Why?"

"Ahh," Steve said. "Forget I said that."

"He's her heir?" I said, feeling stupid I hadn't thought of that angle before.

"I can't be telling you that, Dan."

"You don't have to. Who else would be? She wasn't married and didn't have any kids."

Steve got up quickly. "I have to go. I'd advise you to stay out of this, Dan."

I stood up quickly, too. "And then what happens? Gant hangs me and maybe my friends for something I didn't do?"

"You're going to make it worse."

"I don't think I can."

Steve shook his head again, turned, and headed for the door. "See you later."

When he was gone, I sat back down, finished my beer. I didn't like conflict with Steve. I considered him a friend. I didn't want to lose that friendship. I would have to tread carefully.

One good thing had come out of my talk with Steve though—Morris Kruel. I could add him to my suspect list. Would someone actually kill their sibling for money? Of course, some people would. Whether that included Morris Kruel, or not, I didn't know.

Chapter 13

THE NEXT DAY I was more determined than before to find out what happened to Evelyn Kruel. There were only two ways to go. After mulling them both over, I guess I chickened out and took the less threatening—deciding to visit Evelyn's secretary over motel owner George "Not a Very Nice Man" Ransom. I left the cottage, glanced at the black sky, hopped in my car, and headed to town. That's where Kruel Realty Trust, Evelyn's business, was located—in the middle of the small downtown area on Route 1. I was lucky to find an open parking space just steps from her building.

I jumped out of the car, dodged raindrops, and dashed the few yards to the door. I opened it and stepped into the vestibule. The names of a half-dozen businesses were listed prominently on the wall. I assumed that Evelyn Kruel had been the landlord here as she had been at so many other places, anything else would have been poor business. She certainly hadn't been a poor businesswoman. The real estate office was located on the second floor. I went through an inner door and took the stairs up.

Kruel Realty Trust was displayed in large letters on the first door I came to. I opened it and walked in. If I hadn't known better, I would have thought that Evelyn Kruel was in the back office, alive and still running her empire. Seated behind a desk, banging away on a keyboard, was a woman I assumed was Marcy Wade. I remembered the rumors Shamrock had mentioned but I didn't observe any hint of masculinity. Just the opposite. She was very good looking. A blonde, around middle age. Marcy Wade looked like she took care of herself. She had what you'd have to call a *hot* tan. I had no idea if it was true that Evelyn had found her attractive, but I was sure that most men did.

She didn't acknowledge my presence immediately, so I glanced around the room. The wall to my right was plastered with real estate awards and degrees. The wall to my left had framed photos of Evelyn Kruel with various dignitaries. I spotted the governor in one photo and did a double-take when Donald Trump's hair jumped out from another. Apparently, Evelyn had been well connected. Or at least had wanted people to think she had been.

Finally Marcy Wade turned her head, looked up at me over her glasses. She continued typing. "Can I help you?" Her voice was very attractive and feminine.

I stepped closer to the desk. "My name is Dan Marlowe. I'm wondering if I could talk to you about Mrs. Kruel?"

Her expression didn't change but her fingers froze over the keys. After a few seconds, she turned from the computer to face me over her desk. She folded her hands like she was praying and rested them on the desk. She wore more than one ring and they looked expensive. None of them resembled a wedding ring or band. From what I could see—the waist up—she was dressed like any executive secretary would be. As if Evelyn Kruel would walk through the door at any moment. The white blouse she wore was buttoned to the neck. It was made from some soft material I couldn't identify.

"Have a seat," she said.

I sat in one of the two upholstered barrel chairs facing her. When I was situated, she said, "What can I do for you?"

I cleared my throat. "I was hoping you could tell me what you might know about Mrs. Kruel's death?"

She straightened in the chair. My eyes were glued to her face but I couldn't help notice the material of her blouse tighten across her chest. "And what business is that of yours?"

That was a good question. It was none of my business. I was just a bartender for God's sake. The only way I could think to play this little game of mine was straight, so I did.

"The police think I'm mixed up in it somehow, Ms. Wade. I'm trying to clear my name."

She removed her glasses, set them on the desk. She instantly went from very attractive to very, very attractive. "The police think *you* killed Mrs. Kruel and you think I'm going to help you?"

She had me on the defensive now. "I'm just trying to find out who really killed her. Was she having a problem with anyone?"

"What did you say your name was? I want to make sure I get it right if I decide to call the police."

I didn't like repeating my name, but I did. "Dan Marlowe."

She looked at me with fiery blue eyes. "Well, *Mr. Marlowe,* if that's your name. Mrs. Kruel didn't have any enemies if that's what you're asking. She was loved by all."

I remembered what Dianne had said about Evelyn refusing to sell George Ransom the land he needed to make his contel project happen. "I would think a landlord as big as she was would've stepped on a few toes through the years?"

"No. She was an excellent and aboveboard businesswoman. She followed all rules and regulations to the letter."

"All right." I wasn't sure what to ask next, and before I could figure something out, she jumped in.

"I think that's about enough of this, Mr. Marlowe."

It was over that quick. I'd blown it.

Not quite. She hesitated, then said, "What have you found out in your unofficial investigation? Just so I can tell the police who else you're harassing."

I didn't like the sounds of that, but still it was an opening. I took it. "Artie Neal. I'm not harassing him, but do you know him?"

Color seeped into Marcy Wade's cheeks. "The talk show host? I know who he is. Everyone does. *I* would never listen to his show."

"Was Mrs. Kruel having an affair with Neal?"

She leaned toward me. I could see her makeup; there wasn't much of it. "Evelyn...ahh...Mrs. Kruel wouldn't have anything to do with a man like that! How dare you even say it. I think you..."

I interrupted. "He lived just a few homes away from *Evelyn.*" I emphasized the name.

"I don't care where he lived. You're just starting a vicious rumor. I'll report that to the police, too. Now get out of this office." She stood up quickly, pointing toward the door. She wore a tight skirt and her bottom half was as appealing as the top.

I got up slowly from my chair, lobbed one more grenade before I left. "How about her brother Morris and a business-man named George Ransom? Did Evelyn have any friction there?"

"I wouldn't know anything about that." Her face seemed to relax just a bit and I could see her wheels spinning. She seemed to want to continue this part of the conversation, though evi-dently thought better of it. "Go," she said, reaching for the phone, punching in numbers.

I walked to the door, let myself out. I left it just an inch ajar behind me. I stopped, listened. She didn't speak. I heard her set the phone back in its cradle.

On the drive back to the beach, I thought about what had just happened and if I had learned anything valuable. The only nerve I'd seemed to hit with Marcy Wade was when I mentioned the rumored affair between her boss and Artie Neal. I think she would have scratched my eyes out if she could have. Was the anger just because I had sullied Evelyn Kruel's name by linking it with Tiny Bastards? Sure, that could have been it; I could believe that. Or was it more? I remembered again what Shamrock had said about Evelyn and Marcy being a number. Visualizing Marcy in my head, *that* I had trouble believing. Or was I just displaying a little prejudice myself? Possibly.

I had gotten the feeling Marcy had wanted to talk about Morris Kruel and George Ransom when I had mentioned them. Why? I'd made a mistake not pushing harder. Steve Moore wouldn't have made that mistake. He was a professional after all. I was an amateur and didn't know what the hell I was doing. And it showed.

I'd better learn fast. Marcy hadn't dropped a dime on me but sooner or later someone would and then Gant would know that I was nosing around. He wouldn't be happy, not that he was anyway. I wasn't sure what he would do, but I was sure it wouldn't be good. I didn't have much time. I had to move and move quick.

I stepped on the accelerator and sped along Winnacunnet Road toward the beach. I passed a radar cop hidden on a side street on the way. I was lucky I wasn't stopped. That would've *really* spoiled my day.

Chapter 14

THE DAY WAS still early so I decided to make one more stop. I couldn't waste time. I didn't know why Marcy Wade had hung up that phone without talking to the police, but if she changed her mind again and did make that call, Gant would be after me faster than a bloodhound behind an escapee from a chain gang.

On Ashworth Avenue I pulled the car into the parking lot of the Waterview Motel. I chuckled at the deceptive name. You couldn't get a look at the ocean from here if you had binoculars and were standing on the chimney. I guess the name referred to the marsh out back but tourists who booked from out of state didn't know any of that. Anyway, I was lucky I knew where it was; the sign was resting face down on a small strip of dirt just beyond the asphalt. Probably brought down in a nor'easter and hadn't been replaced yet. I guess the owner figured the summer crowd hadn't arrived yet, so he wasn't in any hurry to get the sign back up. Talk about cutting it close.

I parked my car beside an old beat-up Buick parked near the "Office" sign. I got out, took a look around. The view wasn't the only thing missing at this place—there wasn't any class either. It was a two-story, red-and-white horseshoe-shaped structure that encircled a very small parking area. Not enough parking for today's zoning, but the place had probably been here so long that it was grandfathered in. There were a series of numbered room doors on both levels. A new paint job would have helped the building's appearance, but not much. The place was too far gone. There were only a few cars, mostly crates, scattered about. Most of the winter people were probably already gone. This little motel provided some of the cheaper accommodations for summer tourists. Still, their rate was too high for the off-season tenants. They'd be back in September.

I took the two steps up to the office door. Both steps creaked under my feet. Once inside I closed the door behind me and glanced about. I was inside a room that looked like the nor'easter that had taken down the sign had gotten in here, too. The place was a mess. Papers were strewn across a waist-high counter directly in front of me. A sofa to my left resembled something that probably had been purchased at a yard sale. A blind man must have hung the few cheap pictures on the wall and the last time the floor had been swept must have been the same year the Casino was built. And that wasn't in this century.

I walked up to the counter, banged the bell a couple of times. I could smell cigarette smoke and mold, a sickening combination. My throat tickled—my standard reaction to cats—and I wondered where the felines were. Just then a door behind the counter opened and in walked a man who fit the motel better than the president fit the White House.

He was taller than me and had a toothpick stuck in his mouth. He had a face like one you would see on a wanted poster. He was entirely bald—shaved, I figured. There was a gold hoop earring in one ear. He wore a white wife-beater T-shirt that stretched across his massive chest. I pegged him as late 40s. When he leaned against the counter, I instinctively pulled back. I knew he didn't have to hire anyone to take care of evictions.

"Yeah? Whattaya want?" As he spoke, the toothpick floated around in his mouth.

I knew I wasn't looking at the most formal of innkeepers; still, the rudeness surprised me. "Just wondering about your motel here." I raised my hand, looked around the room.

"Ya wanna room?" He put both his hands on the counter. They were scarred and the knuckles were hairy.

I began my spiel. "No. I heard that you might be interested in turning your motel into contels."

Immediately he looked like he wanted to change into a business suit. He stood straight, pulled in what little belly he had, and put his hands down by his sides. He removed the toothpick from his mouth and deposited it somewhere out of sight. He then walked around the counter.

His manners improved, too. "Have a seat, Mr...? Right here. My name's George Ransom." He pumped my hand as he directed me to the couch, removing the debris littering the cushions so I could sit. I prayed he didn't sit beside me. He was intimidating enough from a distance. Fortunately, he chose an easy chair adjacent to the couch, a chair I assumed had more farts in it than there were fish in the ocean.

"Excuse how I look. I've been working out back." He brushed something that I couldn't see from the front of the wife-beater. I noticed his English had moved from Hell's Kitchen to Park Avenue. "You have something to do with motel conversions or real estate?" He stared at me like a kid gazing into a candy store window.

"Well, I do have an interest in it." No lie there. I did have an interest in beach real estate. Just as a curious observer though, not as a landlord, let alone a developer. I knew about the abhorrent level of aggravation inherent in owning beach rental property. Because of that and my aversion to putting the business end of a gun in my mouth, I had stayed clear of owning rental property even back when I'd been doing well. "I heard you were considering turning your motel into contels."

He spoke gingerly, choosing his words carefully. "Well...I have been giving it a little consideration. Only because I'm not as young as I used to be. The motel business is a young man's game." He hesitated, looked around at the ceiling. "It would break my heart to give up a business like this, though."

I tried to hold the laugh in; I couldn't. Between his statement and the invisible cats causing my eyes to water and my throat to tighten, something between a snicker and a gag came out of my mouth. I did my best to disguise the sound as a cough. I don't know if I succeeded.

"Are you all right, Mr... What did you say your name was?"

I gave my throat one deep clear; it opened enough to talk. "Must be the sea air," I deadpanned. "I'm Dan Marlowe."

"Well, Mr. Marlowe. There's been quite a boom in contels on Hampton Beach. As you know, with a fine property like this, contels can be quite lucrative."

I wasn't going to learn anything playing footsie with this guy, so I said, "Some people say the boom is just about over."

He shook his bald head. "No, no, no. This is a wonderful vacation area. People are fighting to buy contel units. I've got friends here on the beach who sold all their units before the conversions were even started. With a property like this, there would be a rush to buy units."

His nose didn't grow, but I could clearly see the deceit in his eyes.

"Have you had any interest from other developers, Mr. Ransom?"

"Yes, I have," he said, straightening himself proudly in his seat. "I haven't accepted any offers yet though."

"Not interested, huh?"

"Oh, I'm interested," he quickly said. Then he slowed down a bit and appeared to regroup. "None of the developers seemed up to my standards. That's all."

"Was Evelyn Kruel one of them?" I asked.

His eyebrows shot up. I could hear his brain clicking. Finally he said, "Mrs. Kruel was very interested in helping with the project. Unfortunately, as you probably know..." He stopped. I nodded and he continued. "We didn't have time to finalize anything before she died. She was very anxious to though."

I still didn't see any lengthening of his nose. I decided to keep the pressure on. "How about parking?"

Now it sounded like the cats were getting to *him* as he cleared phlegm from his throat. I watched as he swallowed. "Parking will be adequate."

"You have the required number of spaces?"

The color of his face told me his blood pressure was rising. "Well, no. But I'm in the process of acquiring it. Possibly from Evelyn Kruel's estate, as a matter of fact."

"There will be no problem there?"

He shook his head; a bead of sweat flew off. "None. I'm good friends with her brother." Apparently regretting what he'd just said, he quickly added, "Evelyn was anxious to make property available for parking anyway."

"And you say Morris is agreeable also?"

For the first time he looked at me suspiciously. "You know him?"

I realized I had gone too far. On the other hand I'd done pretty good, considering my lack of experience. "I've heard of him."

Ransom's black eyes narrowed. "What's the name of your company, Mr. Marlowe?"

Caught and captured. "I don't actually have a company. Kind of do this as a sideline." No lie there. I was talking about detecting crime, not real estate development. He didn't know that though.

He stood quickly. "I think I better get back to work." He held his hand out. "Do you have a card? I could call you later?"

I shook his hand as I stood. He squeezed a little too hard and I flinched. "Not with me. I'll call you."

"Ahh, yeah sure," he said. He looked as suspicious as a beach store owner after twenty high school kids had just trooped in.

Outside in my car, I grabbed some tissues from the glove box, gave my nose a good blow. I wished I could have taken my eyeballs out and given them a vigorous scratching. Just before I backed the car out of its spot, I noticed a slat in an office shade open a crack. When I had the car set to move forward, the slat was back in place. I was sure Ransom had my license plate number. I wondered if that would cause me a problem.

On the short drive to my cottage, I went over what I had learned and decided the information was a bit more helpful than what I had gotten out of Marcy Wade. Even though he'd tried to hide it, there was no doubt Ransom wanted out of the motel business in the worst way. With the place he had, who could blame him? Anybody would want to cash out of that shit hole. Downplaying Evelyn Kruel's lack of interest in the project could have been nothing more than a shrewd business move to not scare away developers. You certainly wouldn't want it to get around that someone with a reputation for good business deals, like Evelyn Kruel, had wanted no part of his contel project.

Mentioning that he was good friends with Morris Kruel could mean something, though. Put together with what I knew about Evelyn refusing his offer meant it would be very beneficial for George Ransom to have Evelyn out of the picture and her brother taking her place. I would have to look into that little insight. How, I didn't know.

Chapter 15

THE REST OF the day went by quickly, like days tend to do sometimes. I filled the time with errands and some odds and ends I'd been putting off. By nighttime I'd just about driven myself batty trying to make sense of everything and everyone—Artie Neal, Marcy Wade, George Ransom, and Morris Kruel. Truth was I was lost and I wasn't doing anything but torturing myself. Enough was enough.

I threw on a windbreaker and decided to take a walk up to the White Cap. Some fresh air and a new scene might help me come up with something. At least I wouldn't have to worry about running into Eddie and Derwood. The Cap would be the last place they'd show up knowing those two goons, Santa and Rudy, were after them. On the other hand, I would have loved to bump into them myself. I had a few questions I wanted to ask those two lamebrains.

Outside, I zipped up the windbreaker. It was an unseasonably chilly night. The wind was blowing hard and gray clouds streaked across the sky. Occasionally a raindrop splattered on my cheek. There was a big storm passing offshore, but they'd predicted we'd miss the worst of it. I hoped they were right.

I turned onto Ocean Boulevard. Being pre-season and with threatening weather, there were only a few cars on the street and no other foot traffic close by. I'd only walked a short distance when a shadow darted from between two cottages up ahead. I knew instantly something was out of place and froze. It was a man, I could tell that much—stocking cap pulled down, jacket, white pants. He had a large object clutched in his arms, about the size of a small suitcase, a bit fatter.

I couldn't make the object out and his next move didn't help. He turned and started moving away from me, across Ocean Boulevard. For a moment I wondered if I was witnessing a B&E getaway. But it was raining harder now. He might just be hurrying to get out of the rain. I watched as he moved quickly down N Street and out of sight. I started walking again but by the time I reached the corner, I could see no sign of him.

I put it out of my mind and resumed my walk to the White Cap. I'd only gone another block when I noticed some type of commotion farther ahead. I hurried across the municipal parking lot to the boardwalk. The railing that ran almost the entire length of the beach, and the beach itself, was to my right. Police lights flashed up ahead and figures moved back and forth, some on the sand. I forgot about the White Cap and picked up my pace. Beach people are a curious lot. We don't like to miss any action, although usually disturbances like the one I was headed for turned out to be the smallest of incidents, maybe a sprained ankle or a couple of teenagers caught with beer. By the amount of sirens, rescue lights, and gawkers you'd think the Casino was on fire. I picked up my pace even more.

When I finally reached the area where the action seemed to be taking place, it was a madhouse. It was just short of the beach playground. Police cars, a red rescue truck, and two fire engines were on the scene. Another police car skidded to a halt, almost slamming into the playground fence just as I arrived. Two uniformed cops jumped out and ran down one of the sets of concrete steps that led to the sand. I found a small open space on the railing between two people and shouldered my way in. The rain had diminished to a very light sprinkle.

There was a lot to see down on the sand, although nothing showed clearly. Beams from flashlights bounced around, dark figures raced about, and a constant stream of unintelligible shouts filled the air. My first thought was that someone had foolishly gone out to surf the large waves the storm was tossing on the shore—it had happened before. I could hear the surf breaking loudly on the sand. There was no moon, so what I could see of the ocean was just a black churning mass of water.

In these situations I hate asking, but I did. "What happened?"

I looked at the woman beside me. She had on a red slicker and a matching floppy rain hat. When she turned to answer, I noticed she looked familiar, but I had no idea who she was. On the beach that's common. You can see the same person over and over again, year after year, never knowing who they are or what they do, just that they aren't a short-term vacationer.

"I just got here," she said. "I guess they found something on the beach."

"A body?" I asked.

"No, I don't think so." She turned and pointed at the emergency vehicles. "The back doors of the rescue truck aren't open." She looked toward the man on my other side. "He said they haven't taken any stretchers down on the sand."

That told me that either someone wasn't too badly hurt or they hadn't found whoever they were looking for yet. After watching the scurrying figures on the beach for another few minutes, I discarded the idea that someone was only slightly injured. There wouldn't be this type of activity if that were the case, even in Hampton Beach. Someone had probably gone out too far in the treacherous water and they hadn't found the body yet.

There was a large stack of something on the sand that the emergency personnel seemed to return to every so often. Rescue equipment? The stack seemed to have grown in size since I'd arrived on scene. I was thinking about that when a voice spoke from behind me. I recognized it immediately.

Gant.

"I bet you're going to be crying in your beer tonight, Marlowe."

I turned to look. Lieutenant Gant stood behind me. In the harsh glare of the street light, his face looked gray and craggy. He had on a black leather car coat. His eyes drilled into me. Beside him was Steve Moore. He was wearing a short yellow raincoat and didn't look happy to see me. I said nothing.

The woman in red beside me must have recognized them as Hampton cops because she said, "What happened, officers?"

"We can't go..." Steve started before Gant cut him off.

"Why don't you ask your friend here?" he said. In the un-flattering light, his smirk looked evil.

She looked at me, then said, "Well, nice talking to you. Bye now." She hurried off in the direction of the Chamber of Commerce building.

Gant quickly took her place and faced me. Steve moved in close behind him.

"She was in a hurry," Gant said.

"I don't know who the hell she is," I said irritably. "She was here when I got here."

"And I bet you don't know anything about this either?" He tilted his head sideways toward the action on the beach.

I looked at him. "I have absolutely no idea what's going on down there. As I said, I just got here."

"Sure," Gant said. His tone was sarcastic, even for him. "You just happened to show up now."

"It's a small beach, Lieutenant. I saw the commotion. Where else was I going to go?"

"Yeah, maybe. But it seems odd that whenever something big happens on Hampton Beach, Marlowe, you—or your name—seem to always be right in the middle of it." Gant's eyes narrowed. "And where's your partners? The Mick and the broad who *owns* the High Tide."

That did it. This guy had it in for me and my friends, no matter what I said or did. There was no sense being civil to him. It wouldn't do any good. "You ought to check your medication level, Gant. I think it needs to be adjusted." I shouldn't have said it but it felt good.

Even in the poor light, I could see Gant's face darken. Before he could respond, Steve spoke up. "We've got a big problem here, Dan. A boat might have broken up off shore."

"Some fatalities?" I asked, wondering what Gant's crack about me had to do with that.

"We don't know yet. But the problem right now is what's washing up on shore...bales of pot."

Pot. I immediately remembered the man I'd seen running from the beach area with the large object on my way here. I knew now what he'd been carrying.

"How much washed up?" I asked.

Steve started to speak, Gant held up his hand to silence him. "That's none of your business, Marlowe. Inspector Moore told you too much already. I am happy to tell you, though, that the shipment you were waiting for won't be arriving." He snickered.

I looked at Steve; he rolled his eyes. I turned to Gant. "You got to be kidding me, right?"

"Do I look like a kidder?" Gant said.

I had to admit he didn't. His face was like stone.

"I didn't have anything to do with this."

"Just more coincidence, right?" Gant said. "The sister of someone you assaulted and threatened to kill shows up shot dead on the beach. And you supposedly find her." Gant laughed. "Then this stuff comes floating ashore on almost the same spot. And here you are again. And with your background to boot."

"I didn't threaten to kill him. And what the hell does one thing have to do with the other?" I said.

"You threatened to break his neck," Gant fired back. "That qualifies as a death threat in my book. You just took it out on his sister instead. She was the one who was causing you and your girlfriend problems. And as far as this," he waved his hand toward the beach, "having anything to do with Evelyn Kruel's death...it does. *You*. If you're not involved in both, I'll eat sand."

This confrontation couldn't do anything but deteriorate. If it did, I would be the loser. I pushed off the railing and started walking back the way I'd come.

I'd only taken a few steps when I heard Gant call, "I'll be seeing you, Marlowe."

I didn't answer or slow down, just kept walking. I had no desire now to stop in at the White Cap. Gant had spoiled that. I just wanted to get back to my cottage.

When I arrived, the first thing I did was grab a Heineken and a frosted glass from the fridge and occupy my easy chair. My anxiety level was at full throttle. I didn't take a pill though. I tried to do that as little as possible now.

I just sat there, drinking beer, wondering how the hell I could be in this position. The Hampton police, represented by Gant, seemed to believe I was involved in not only the murder of Evelyn Kruel, but what sounded like some type of pot smuggling operation.

And there wasn't just that to worry about either. Just like Gant, I didn't believe in coincidences. Within a couple of days, Eddie and Derwood, two characters who never had more than a couple of joints between them, had tried to sell me a few pounds of weed; Santa and Rudy had almost pistol-whipped me looking for their *merchandise;* and mysterious bales of marijuana had started washing up on the beach. Whatever those two nimrods had done, the goons thought I was involved, too. I had trouble coming at me from more directions than the Bird Man did seagulls at feeding time. Trouble I didn't deserve. And it wasn't coming only for me. Dianne and Shamrock were under the gun, too. There was no doubt about that now; Gant had made that clear. I would have to step up my game if I wanted to get the three of us out of this jam. And I did. The thing was, I wasn't sure anymore exactly what the jam was, or how to get us out of it. The only good thing I could see about all this was that it couldn't get any worse. Could it?

Chapter 16

THE NEXT MORNING I decided to take a drive up to the Casino and grab a coffee. Last night's storm had passed and the sky was clear. It wouldn't take long for the bright June sun to dry out the beach sand. The rain had left behind a sharp, clean crispness in the air. The sun seemed to help with that too. I had a couple of hours before I had to be at the Tide.

I'd just reached the Casino when I saw Morris Kruel come off the building's steps with a coffee and newspaper in his hands. I watched as he crossed Ocean Boulevard. There were two cars ahead of me and he didn't see me. He marched past the Seashell Stage benches, where I sat often in the summer to watch the free nightly bands, and disappeared around the entertainment building itself. This was a chance to save myself a trip.

I drove quickly past the Casino. A few of the parking spots facing the ocean were open. I pulled into one, hopped out, and headed back in the direction of the Seashell. When I reached the building, I looked around. It was quiet, with only a few people wandering around, not like during the crowded, hot days of July and August, that was for sure.

I continued around the building in the direction of the ocean and there he was. Morris Kruel was seated on a bench facing the water, reading a *Boston Herald*, and sipping his coffee.

I walked up to him. "How are you doing, Morris?"

He looked up, startled. When he recognized me, he drew back on the bench a bit. "Do not start any trouble, Marlowe."

"I don't want any trouble. I just wanted to give you my condolences."

He looked at me suspiciously. "Well...thank you, I guess."

"Do you mind?" I said, sitting beside him before he could answer.

"Now wait just a second. I said thank you on the condolences. That does not mean I want to be your friend."

Morris Kruel had short brown hair combed to the side, a pipe cleaner of a neck, and proper diction I found very irritating. He wore a red Ralph Loren polo shirt, cuffed powder-blue chinos, brown loafers, and no socks.

"I just wanted to ask you a few questions, Morris."

"Questions? Who the hell are you, sir, to ask me questions? After what you did to me."

I held down the urge to tell him he had deserved it and the simultaneous urge to do it again. After all, I was trying to accomplish something here.

"Do you know anybody who would want to harm your sister?"

"Are you crazy, Marlowe?" He started to stand and his coffee spilled on the pavement. "Get the hell out of here before I get the police."

"George Ransom, maybe? You two had some business dealings, didn't you? Do the police know about that?"

He sat back; I could see the wheels in his mind spinning faster than a pinball game at Funarama. "So what? We *are* businessmen after all. And what the hell is going on here, anyway? You're a bartender, for God's sake. What business is my sister's death to you?"

"The police think I had something to do with it. That's what business it is of mine."

He looked surprised, then looked down his long nose at me. "I suppose that's quite possible, now that you mention it."

I ignored that. "Did you know your sister was having an affair with Artie Neal?"

"Neal? The talk show host? I don't believe you."

I couldn't tell if he was lying. "They were."

He rolled the newspaper up, began slapping it against his thigh. "I'm not going to allow you to dirty my sister's name, Marlowe."

"That's not what I'm trying to do. I want to know who killed her."

"Why?"

"I already told you. I don't like to be accused of a crime I didn't commit."

Morris stuck the rolled-up newspaper an inch from my nose. "Unless you did do it and this is your way of trying to make people think you didn't."

I shoved the paper away. "What do you know about Marcy Wade?"

"Evelyn's secretary? She's been with...what the hell am I doing? I'm not talking to you anymore. Be on your way." He fluttered his hand like he was a king dismissing a subject.

"Was there something going on between them?" I continued.

He gave me a shocked look. Again, I couldn't tell if it was feigned. "What are you insinuating?"

"Nothing." But I wanted to push him, so I added, "What do *you* think I'm insinuating?"

He almost bit but held himself in check. "You're lower than I thought, Marlowe. My sister was a wonderful woman.

A pillar of the community. A successful businesswoman. She had nothing off-color in her private life. And I won't let you tear her sterling reputation down after her death. I'll stop you; I'll defend her with my last breath. Everyone cherished my sister."

Nice speech though I didn't believe a word of it. "I'm not out to defame anybody, Morris. But someone didn't think so highly of your sister. And as long as the police think it's me, I'm going to be trying to find out who really did it. I thought you would be, too."

That caught him off guard. He sputtered. "Of course, but I...I...I'll let the police handle it. And you...you." He pointed the paper at my face again. "It may very well have been you. *You!* With your reputation?"

I snatched the newspaper from his hand and tossed it over the railing onto the sand. Seagulls hopped out of the way.

I stood up. "I may want to ask you a few more questions, Morris."

"Are you insane? I'll have the police on you, Marlowe."

Everybody was threatening me with the police. As far as I knew, no one had called them yet. I wondered why.

I gave Morris Kruel one last look. "I'll talk to you later."

I turned and walked away. I could feel his eyes boring into my back. When I started to round the corner of the building, I glanced over my shoulder and saw I was right—he was still looking in my direction.

On the short walk to my car, I thought about what I had just learned and decided it was next to nothing. I couldn't tell if Morris Kruel had anything to do with his sister's death. I wasn't a trained investigator. Maybe he was putting on an act; maybe he wasn't. How the hell could I tell the difference? I couldn't. And I wasn't happy about that.

There was one thing I was happy about though. I had paid visits to Artie Neal, Marcy Wade, George Ransom, and now Morris Kruel. I had stirred the pot with all four of them. They knew I was determined to find out who killed Evelyn Kruel. I was hoping at least one of them didn't want me to succeed. If that was so, that person might make a move—and I had to hope—make a mistake too. It was risky, but that was all I had going. I'd have to keep my fingers crossed.

Chapter 17

LATER THAT MORNING, during my shift at the Tide, the conversation amongst the bar regulars had shifted from the murder of Evelyn Kruel to the events down on the beach last night. Again, the Manchester and Boston media trucks were across the street just like the day I'd found Evelyn's body. Again yellow police tape curled around the beach railing as far as you could see in both directions. By the chatter along the bar you would think that someone had won the lottery. And the speculation was that maybe more than one someone did.

Eli was holding court. "I'm tellin' ya, there was people down on that beach fishin' packages out of the water at least an hour before the cops came. That's what I heard and I believes it, too."

I thought back to the figure I'd seen running down N Street the night before with the large package in his arms. I wondered if there had been others just as lucky.

"Are they saying how much they found?" Paulie asked the bar in general.

"Five hundred pounds I heard," someone piped in.

"Five hundred pounds," Paulie repeated dreamily. "That's a lot of money." He stared off into space, blowing cigarette smoke.

"Forget that," Eli said, his voice echoing off the ceiling. He was standing on the leg supports of his stool again. "The cops'll burn that. What about the dope people got away with before they come? Huh, what about that? That's a nice early Christmas present for somebody. That's for damn sure."

Mel, one of the regular gang, was seated at the other end of the bar. He was old—if he'd ever seen marijuana, I figured it was back when the stuff was legal. "How much do they get for those bales anyway?" he croaked.

Eli and Paulie glanced in my direction. I looked away even though I was used to my old baggage following me around.

Finally, Eli stubbed out his cigarette like he was mad at it. "I ain't sure, but it's got to be plenty. I wish I found one. Yeah, I sure do."

Paulie feigned shock, choking on his beer. "You wouldn't know what the hell to do with it, old man."

Eli shook his head angrily. "I'd find out pretty quick." He grabbed his draft, took a swallow, slammed the glass down on the bar. "And you're right—I ain't no kid. I been around. I know a lot of people. You'd be surprised."

"You ever smoke it, Eli?" Paulie baited.

Eli flushed. "Well, never you mind."

"You don't put it in your ear, you know," Paulie said. The bar exploded in laughter. I started to smile, turned away.

"Ha, ha," Eli said.

Just then the screen door opened and into the bar walked Hank Fuller. He was dressed all in black again and had his beret cocked jauntily on his head. He didn't have his walking stick. He stopped for a moment, probably to adjust his eyes to the dimmer light. Many older customers did. When he saw me he gave a nod and walked up to the bar.

"Hank," I said. "Thought you never got down this way?"

He boosted himself gingerly onto a stool. He had a wide smile on his face. "I usually don't, Dan. But I thought I'd drop in and see you." He glanced around. "The place hasn't changed much. Don't remember the fish though." He pointed a thumb behind him in the direction of the aquarium.

"They've been here maybe ten years," I said. "Knick?"

"You carry it?" He looked surprised.

"Sure do. Probably the only place on the beach that still does."

I grabbed a sixteen-ounce bottle from the chest, placed that and a frosted glass in front of him. I took a moment to watch him pour a perfect head.

"Menu?" I asked.

He shook his head. "No, thank you. Just came to have a beer and a little chat with you." He nodded toward the front window. "What's going on over there?"

Before I could answer, Eli jumped in. "Five hundred pounds of pot, that's what. Washed up on the beach. Some's missin' too."

"Oh," Hank said.

"That's right," Eli said, spinning on his stool to face Hank. "The stuff's worth lots of money, too. How much you think?"

"I wouldn't know," Hank answered.

"I'll tell you then," Eli continued. "Plenty. That's how much."

"I'll bet," Hank said.

Hank started to speak to me, but Eli tried to reel him back. "People was scampering away with those things like full lobster traps had broke their moorings. I seen that happen before on the beach, too. Christ, one year after a big storm, the 'Brookers' were down there with pickup trucks snatching the traps up as soon as they came ashore. Sometimes they wouldn't even wait, just wade right out in the water, clothes and all, and pull 'em in. I'll bet some of those Seabrook people were here last night too, gettin' them bales. Those people can smell money, believe me." Eli nodded.

"I'm sure," Hank said. He turned to me.

"Something you wanted to talk about, Hank?" I asked.

He took a long drink of his beer, let out a satisfying sigh, and smiled. "You can't beat that first one." Then the smile faded. He looked quickly at Eli who looked like he was just waiting to yak again, then turned fully to me. He drew closer, lowered his voice. "Well, there is something I thought you might be interested in. Probably nothing, but..."

I held up a finger. "Give me one minute." I went up and down the bar, refreshing anyone's drink that needed refilling. When I was done, I returned to Hank.

I put my hands on the bar, kept my voice low. "Something to do with Evelyn Kruel?"

He still spoke softly. "I'm not sure, Dan. It's about those people I told you about. You know the ones with the Dobermans."

Out of the corner of my eye I noticed Eli still looking in our direction. Probably wanted in on the conversation. I gave him a look; he turned away.

"What's going on?" I asked.

Hank fingered the beer bottle sitting in front of him, spun it a little. "That's just it...nothing really."

"What do you mean?"

"Well, after talking to you, I got to thinking. It's probably nothing. Just an old man with too much time on his hands."

"What old man?" I said, smiling.

He chuckled and continued. "Well...it kind of dawned on me. Except for that incident with you there's been no sign of those dogs. Before...before Evelyn Kruel was killed I'd see them almost every day. It's almost like all of a sudden the owners are being good neighbors and not letting their dogs run loose."

I thought about it for a short minute. "Well, maybe they are."

Hank shrugged. "Maybe...and..."

"Something else?"

"I don't know why I didn't mention it before. Probably didn't seem important—or maybe a senior moment's more likely—but the last time I spoke to Evelyn, she said some things that I've been thinking about."

"Things?" I asked. "What things?"

"Well, she said she was going to go up and confront those dog owners once and for all. Said they'd be sorry when she got through with them. And by her attitude, I believed they would be." Hank stopped, took a swallow of beer, then continued. "I didn't even think of it when she got killed. But after my talk with you, I remembered it."

"You think the reason the dogs haven't been around is that the owners are trying to maintain a low profile?"

"Maybe. The police have been asking questions of her close neighbors. Not everyone though. Maybe not them."

"Hmm." It wasn't much. Evelyn Kruel threatening to read the riot act to some dog owners, the dogs scarce on the beach after her murder and...and that was it? Who would kill a woman because she told you to keep your dogs tied up? No one that I knew.

"Who are they, Hank?"

"I don't know. Two gents, I heard. Never seen them."

I looked down the bar. Both Eli and Paulie were looking in our direction. They both quickly looked away. They weren't used to not having my full attention and they especially weren't used to me whispering to a stranger out of their earshot. I knew it made them both feel put out. But this was more important.

I wanted Hank to think the information he had brought might be worthwhile; I didn't want him to think he'd wasted his time. So I said, "You think they might have something to do with Evelyn's murder?"

He shrugged. "I have no idea. It does seem odd. Maybe just coincidence."

Yes, it did seem odd. But there were more than a few odd things happening on Hampton Beach. If odd was a crime, half the residents on the beach would be locked up. And as far as that other word—coincidence—went, there was a lot of that going around the beach lately. People believing in it, too. Lieutenant Gant had a bad case of the coincidences. He couldn't seem to shake it.

Now I was starting to feel like I'd caught the coincidence bug, too. I had to make sure that the rather dubious information Hank Fraser had told me was just that—coincidence—and nothing more. If I discarded any information, any possible clue, that information would probably turn out to be the one piece of the puzzle that wasn't a coincidence.

"Have you told the police?" I asked.

He shook his head. "What would I tell them? A couple of dogs haven't been around for a few days? Or that I thought Evelyn might have been killed over a dog dispute? No, I don't want to be laughed at or cause trouble for anybody. They might be very nice people for all I know."

"They could be. Anyway, thanks for the information. Maybe I'll go back, look into it." I pushed myself away from the bar.

He held up his glass, tipped it toward me. "Be careful, Dan."

Yes, I'd be careful. As careful as I could.

Chapter 18

"I FOUND THEM, Danny." It was Shamrock. I had just stepped out the back door of the Tide following the end of my shift. He had walked out behind me.

"That was quick," I said. We were alone, standing beside the dumpster.

"It wasn't easy." He had a pained look on his face. I didn't see that kind of look often on Shamrock. "I had to take a little advantage of a lassie down at the Crooked Shillelagh."

I must have looked surprised because he quickly added, "No, no, no. Not that way. Her boyfriend...well..." He lowered his voice. "He sells a little coke and I knew that Eddie Hoar was one of his customers. So I figured...I bought her a few drinks, Danny, and pumped her a little."

I had to say it. "Pumped?"

"Ha. You have a dirty mind, lad. Anyway, I was right." His freckled face beamed. "Her boyfriend had delivered some coke to Eddie that day. Did you know their business was off?"

"The coke guy's business?"

Shamrock shook his head disgustedly. "Nooo, Danny. The Shillelagh, for the love a Jaysus. She was telling me that this was one of the worst off-seasons they've had in a long time. I guess..."

I cut him off. "Where are Hoar and Doller, Shamrock?"

"Seabrook."

I wasn't surprised. I knew there were areas in the town of Seabrook where Eddie and Derwook would fit right in. "Whereabouts?"

"I wrote it down."

"Got it with you?"

"I do."

"Can you go now?"

"I can. I punched out."

"Let's go then."

Thirty minutes later, Shamrock and I were in my car, in Seabrook, trying to locate the address where Eddie Hoar and Derwood Doller were supposedly holed up. I was surprised by what we'd found so far—a well-kept mobile home park. I had expected to find the pair living in a dilapidated trailer with pit bulls out front that I would have to kill before I could get to the door. The only pet we'd seen so far was a white miniature poodle being walked on a leash by a plump retiree who looked like he'd just returned from his Florida winter home.

I inched the car along asphalt streets that ran like a maze around the community. The roads were so narrow, Shamrock and I could have leaned out our windows and touched homes on both sides. I had hoped to come up on their hideout undetected and maybe send Shamrock up to the door to get them to open up. If they saw me, they might not be anxious to let me in. But the layout of this community would make it impossible to conceal my car and myself. So I dumped that idea.

Shamrock held the paper with the address in his hand, and as we poked along, he kept staring at it like something might have changed since the last time he'd looked. Every so often,

he glanced up from the paper and studied the numbered mailboxes as we went by.

"Stop," he said, his voice loud enough to make me jump.
We had just rounded a corner and were facing a lone home
at the end of a little cul-de-sac. It was slightly more isolated
than the others. "That's got to be it, Danny." He pointed at the
trailer directly in front of us.

Unlike the other mailboxes, I couldn't see any numbers on the
one that went with this mobile home. "Are you sure?" I asked.

He nodded at the house on his right. "That's thirty-six,"
he said, then looked past me at the home on my side. "That's
thirty-eight." He pointed again at the one in front of us. "That
has to be thirty-seven."

Shamrock had to be right. Eddie and Derwood had probably
either removed or hidden the street number on the mailbox.
A useless ploy but it did show how paranoid they were. The
place looked nothing like what you would expect those two to
be calling home. I had to give them a little credit; it was a good
disguise. Just not far enough away from Hampton Beach.
Though I had to admit, this mobile home was probably as
far out of town as they'd ever been. They didn't look like the
traveling type.

"How do we do this, Danny?"

I looked around. There was only one place to park the car—
in their tiny driveway, the only empty spot around. Apparently,
they'd been smart enough to ditch the Cadillac. My plan about
sending Shamrock to the door alone was still out. They could
easily spot me sitting in the car.

"Go right up to the door and knock, I guess."

I pulled the car up and parked in the little driveway.

Shamrock and I walked up to the front door. The outside
of the home was in pristine condition. It was a light green

color with white trim. There was a well-kept postage stamp-size lawn and each of the three windows had a window box with brightly colored flowers. I couldn't tell if the flowers were real.

I rapped on the door. The windows had lace curtains and all the shades were down. The shade at the farthest window was pulled back a short inch for a long second, then dropped back into place. I waited a bit more.

When I realized they weren't coming to the door, I gave it a good pounding with my fist. I waited again; not as long this time.

I pounded again. "Eddie, open up."

Shamrock looked around nervously. I hoped my banging and yelling was having the same effect on those inside, too.

I was in the middle of repeating the racket when the inside door opened. It was Eddie Hoar; he looked pale. "Jesus Christ. Keep it down, will ya?" I could see his pupils were pin points as his gaze shifted back and forth, checking out the area behind us.

"Eddie, we want to talk about..." I began.

"Yeah, yeah," he interrupted. "Get in here, will ya?" He swung the screen door outward, pushing me into Shamrock. I regained my balance and squeezed past Eddie, getting a whiff of that odd smell meth users sometimes have, somewhere between cheap cologne and body odor. Shamrock must have been wrong about the kind of product they'd purchased.

When Shamrock and I were both inside, Eddie locked the two doors behind us. He went immediately to the closest window and peeked around the shade. "You weren't followed, were ya?"

I could tell *this* was going to be fun. "No, we weren't followed."

Eddie turned from the shade. "How'd you find us?" His voice quivered.

I looked at Shamrock; he shook his head. "Never mind," I answered. "We're here. That's all that matters."

"Sit down," Eddie said. "You're making me nervous." He then added, probably not out of politeness, but more out of a need to keep moving, "I'll get you beer." It didn't matter that he hadn't asked. I had a feeling we would both need a cold one anyway before this talk was over. At least I knew I would. I felt my anxiety going up and took a deep breath. It didn't help.

With Eddie off like a roadrunner, headed for what I assumed was the kitchen, I took a quick look around and spotted Derwood Doller. He was sitting in a chair in what was apparently the living room. His frame was so large I couldn't even tell what color the chair was. The place was a mess. Certainly the same person who took such meticulous care of the outside of the home wasn't responsible for this manmade disaster inside. It had to be these two clowns. A coffee table and assorted end tables were littered with beer cans and used ashtrays. There was a large pizza box, half the pizza still in it, sitting in the middle of the floor. There was a couch beside Derwood's chair and another chair near the far end of the couch.

I wouldn't have had to see all that debris to know what was in the room though, the smell would have given it away. The aroma of stale pizza, butts, and beer—not to mention the sickeningly sweet smell of a meth junkie's body odor—was enough to make me lightheaded. I needed a seat.

Shamrock and I both nodded at Derwood. He nodded back. Then we made a dash for the couch. We pushed newspapers and magazines aside so we could find room to sit. I picked up an opened *Penthouse* gingerly with two fingers and deposited it on the coffee table. We sat.

Eddie returned with four cans of beer. He set a lite beer in front of both Shamrock and me. The cheap stuff was about as far away from Heineken and Guinness as you could get. We looked at the beers, glanced at each other. This beer was going to be no help.

Eddie handed a can to Derwood, then sat in the vacant chair and slurped beer from his can. "So what are you guys doing here? Huh, huh?" He bounced up and down in his seat like his ass was being pinched. Derwood rolled his eyes, looked away.

I got right down to business. I leaned forward, rested my arms on my legs. I was closest to Eddie and I got that odor from him again. I sat back. "I'll tell you what I'm doing here, Eddie. Two guys took me for a wild ride and almost gave me a pistol-whipping the other day. The same guys who are looking for you two." I tilted my head toward Derwood.

Eddie's voice shook and he turned a lighter shade of pale, a complete lack of color I'd only seen once or twice before. On dead people. "A pistol-whipping?"

"Your hearing's good, Eddie," I answered. "A pistol-whipping."

"You don't look like you got no pistol-whipping to me," Derwood said. He didn't look wired like Eddie but he gulped his beer just the same.

"That's only because I was able to get away from them... barely. A few businesses on the beach weren't as lucky."

Eddie's eyes popped. "The car crash up near Rexall? That was you?"

"Yeah, it was me," I said, "and the two goons, too. *And* they were after you." I shook my finger at Eddie. "What I want to know is—what the hell have you got me involved in?"

Eddie's tongue darted in and out as he licked his lips. "They said my name?"

"Yes, they said your name. Your's too." I looked at Derwood. He gulped beer again.

"Jesus Christ, Eddie," Derwood stammered, looking at his partner. "This is bad. They might have followed these guys here."

"Shut up, Dumwood. Let me think."

"Don't call me that, Eddie. I don't like it."

If I waited for Eddie to think, we'd be here until Christmas. "Forget what you two don't like. You got me and my friends involved in something. Something dangerous. I want to know what it is."

"Nothing. It's nothing." Eddie looked at the door. "What was that?"

I hadn't heard anything.

"Stop it, Eddie," Derwood said, staring at the door. "You're scaring me."

"This isn't getting us anywhere," I said. "Come on, Shamrock. I guess I'll just have to tell those goons where these two are."

"Whoa, whoa, whoa," Eddie said, looking at me and holding his hands up like he was stopping traffic. "Okay, okay. I'll tell ya. Just don't do that, please. This is my aunt's place. Besides, you'll get us killed."

I heard a whimper from Derwood.

Shamrock and I were both half out of our seats; we sat back down.

Eddie continued to lick his lips. "We kind of misplaced something that belonged to those guys."

"Yeah, merchandise," I said. "I know that. What kind of merchandise?"

Eddie looked around, sniffled.

"Come on, Eddie," Derwood said. "Tell him. We need help."

"Yeah, tell him, Eddie," Shamrock tossed in. "If you know what's good for you."

"All right. All right," Eddie said. "Pot. We kinda owe 'em for some pot."

Shamrock cleared his throat.

Pot. Of course that was what I figured it had been. I'd just needed confirmation. "How much?" I asked.

"Three hundred," Eddie answered.

"Three hundred bucks?" I said. "You got to be kidding? Pay them, you dumb shit."

Eddie looked nervously at Derwood; they both swigged beer.

"What?" I said.

"Three hundred pounds, Dan," Eddie said sheepishly.

Three hundred pounds! The first thing that flashed through my mind was who the hell would be stupid enough to front two mental midgets like these three hundred pounds of marijuana?

I looked at Shamrock. He looked dumbstruck.

"These characters gave you three hundred pounds of pot?" I said doubtfully. "On the arm?"

"Well...," Eddie said. "Not exactly."

"What's that mean?" Shamrock asked.

"Tell 'em, Eddie," Derwood said. "Maybe they can help us get out of this jam." The big lummox got out of his chair. "You guys want another beer?" He looked at me and Shamrock. We shook our heads; neither of us had touched our first one yet. He headed for the kitchen.

"I...I guess they think we stole it," Eddie said, as if the thought of him stealing was as unlikely as seeing black snow.

"You stole three hundred pounds of pot from those guys?" I said. "That wasn't too bright, Eddie. Where'd you steal it from?"

Eddie fidgeted in his chair. "It was their own fault. They just left it out in the open."

"Left it out where in the open?" I asked.

"Hampton Harbor. Me and Derwood, we go down there once in a while at night. You know..." Eddie raised himself in his chair and tugged his shirt down. "See the boats."

"Sure, see the boats," I said. "Don't you mean, see what you can steal off the boats when no one's around? What the hell can you get off those things, anyway? Some old fishing gear and warm six-packs?"

Eddie got indignant. "You'd be surprised."

Then I remembered we were talking about three hundred pounds of pot and realized for once he was right.

Derwood walked back in and set a beer on the end table beside Eddie. He carried another over to his chair and sat down. The chair groaned. "You tell 'em, Eddie?" he asked.

Eddie grabbed the fresh beer, took a swig, wiped his thin lips with the arm of his shirt. "I told them."

What he had told me was enough. I had the general idea—he and his partner had been on one of their sleazy little night-time harbor rip offs when they'd stumbled on three hundred pounds of marijuana that someone had left unattended on a boat. And they made off with it.

"Then what?" I asked.

Eddie looked quickly at the door again, then at me.

"There's no one there," I said. "Then what?"

Eddie kept glancing at the door as he continued. "We gave it to these big dealers to sell for us."

"Not we, Eddie, you," Derwood spit out. "You said they was okay."

"How was I supposed to know they'd gone sour?"

"I didn't want to do it," Derwood said. "I told you that."

"Yeah, you told me," Eddie said. "Your bright idea was to sell it all in ounces. You know how long that would have taken, Dumwood?"

Derwood started to get up from his chair. "I told you not to call me that, Eddie."

I jumped up, held my hand up in front of Derwood. "Get back in your chair if you want our help." He eased himself down. I glared at Eddie. "Both of you knock it off. We didn't come here to watch you two tangle."

Derwood shifted in his chair; it groaned again.

I sat down. "So let me guess," I said. "They took off with your pot. Didn't pay you."

"They gave us a few grand," Eddie said. "That's all gone."

I looked from Eddie to Derwood and back again. They were both staring at the floor. "Any chance of getting the pot back or the money?"

Eddie shook his head slowly. "They're long gone. Nobody knows where. We'll never see them again."

He was probably right; whoever "they" were, they'd never be back. Unless maybe someday in the future the money from the three hundred pounds ran out. Then they might come back to find two new saps like Eddie and Derwood. But that wouldn't do us any good now.

"How do the guys you ripped-off know about me?" I asked, looking at Eddie.

Derwood jumped in, his words rushed. "The night we brought you home. They must have been following us. When we left your house, they tried to run us off the road. They would've got us, too, except we got across the bridge just before the gates came down. They didn't make it."

"Thank God," Eddie said. "I always hated that bridge. I seem to catch it open every time. This time it saved our lives, though. I love that bridge now."

Derwood nodded his big head.

So that was how Santa and Rudy had found out about me—
it made sense. They'd seen me dropped off at my cottage by
Eddie and Derwood. Must have been watching us back at the
White Cap. Had it looked suspicious, me talking to Eddie and
company that night? Maybe, but it didn't matter now. Looking
at the two partners seated in front of me, I could understand
why Rudy and his friend figured someone else must be involved in the rip-off. I didn't think Eddie or Derwood had
enough brains between them to steal a free game of skee-ball
at Funarama.

I almost asked how they'd been found out. Then I remembered the pair setting up the bar at the White Cap, spending
money like crazy, and the new Caddy. They'd probably flashed
dough at every bar on the beach except the Tide, which they
had been barred from. So they obviously hadn't been hard to
find. They'd hung a sign on themselves—*We Stole Your Pot!*
Half the people on Hampton Beach had seen it.

Shamrock spoke. "You could always pay them."

I looked at him to make sure he was joking; he was.

Eddie didn't know it though. "Three hundred grand? That's
what they told somebody they want. We ain't got that kind of
money."

"We ain't got any kind of money," Derwood added.

We were all silent for a couple of minutes. Except for
Eddie's fidgeting and Derwood swigging beer, there wasn't
much movement either.

Finally, Derwood said, "Can you help us, Dan?"

I had no idea if I could help them. In fact, under normal
circumstances, I wouldn't have wanted to. If these two didn't
deserve to be dropped off a boat halfway out to the Isle of
Shoals on a January night, I didn't know who did. But it wasn't

that easy. The pot's owners thought I was tied up with Eddie and Derwood. To help myself—and Dianne and Shamrock—I'd have to assist these two pitiful fools. I consoled myself by thinking that maybe they could contribute something to all of us getting out of this, though I wasn't confident of that at all.

"Maybe," I said. "Are you two going to stay here for a bit?"

"Yeah," Eddie said. "My aunt's still in Florida. She won't be back for a while. Found a boy-toy or something. She hasn't owned this place for long, so no one knows about it. Except you guys." The minute he said that, I could almost see the dim lightbulb go on over his head.

"I wouldn't let anybody else know where you are, Eddie. You already let enough people know. Hopefully, the guys looking for you don't know any of those other folks. Nothing we can do about that now. Just keep our fingers crossed."

"I told you not to tell anybody where we was," Derwood bellowed. "You and your dope. I ain't going get a wink a sleep here now."

"Give me your number," I said.

Eddie sprang up and fast-walked to the kitchen. He was back in less than a minute, handing me a piece of paper.

I put it in my pocket and stood. Shamrock stood too.

"You two sit tight here until you hear from either me or Shamrock."

They both agreed.

Outside in the car, I said, "Can you imagine those two clowns trying to get rid of three hundred pounds of pot?"

Shamrock quickly turned to look out the passenger window. "Nope," was all he said.

Shamrock usually had a lot to say. I realized he had said next to nothing in the little mobile home and didn't seem to want to contribute anything now. I was about to ask about that when I saw the shade peel back on one of the windows. I waved; the shade snapped shut.

After backing out of the tiny driveway and maneuvering down and out of the mobile home park, I headed back toward Hampton Beach. On the drive we were both silent. I thought about what I had just learned about the stolen pot, the reason the two goons had grabbed me. That was something. It also dawned on me that I wasn't mired in just one predicament anymore, I was stuck like quicksand in two. A suspect in the Evelyn Kruel murder and also a suspect in the theft of three hundred pounds of marijuana owned by Rudy and Santa.

What I was going to do about extricating myself, Dianne, and Shamrock from these unfortunate circumstances was a rock-hard conundrum. I hoped I'd be able to crack it.

Chapter 19

WHEN WE GOT back to the beach, I treated Shamrock to dinner and a couple of beers at his favorite watering hole—The Crooked Shillelagh. After that I dropped him at his place and returned home. When I opened the outer screen door, a sheet of paper floated out. I picked it up, couldn't read it in the dark. I fumbled with the keys, let myself in, flicked on the light, and read the note without sitting down.

Marlowe—keep your fucking mouth shut and your nose out of other people's business. Or you'll wish you had. And your friends will sure wish you had.

It had been typed on plain white paper. There was nothing that I could see to distinguish it. I read it a few more times. Only one part of it scared me—the last sentence. "Friends" meant Dianne and Shamrock. I was sure of that.

I didn't have time to wonder about the threatening note because just then the phone rang. It was Dianne. I didn't like the sound of her voice.

"Dan, can you come up here right now? Please."

"What's the matter? Are you all right?"

I could hear noise in the background; I could tell she was at the Tide.

"Please?"

"I'm on my way."

Something was up. I grabbed the .38, stuffed the note in my pocket, and drove like a madman to the High Tide. Out front were Hampton police cruisers, a rescue truck, and a fire engine. All had their flashers on. I found a parking spot on a side street, left the gun in the car, and hurried up to Ocean Boulevard. There was a large crowd around the Tide's front door. I elbowed my way inside.

Pandemonium greeted me. Police and firemen milled about. Some of the night regulars were standing near the bar, drinks in their hands. No one was sitting. The dining room tables were empty. I could see right away what the commotion was all about—the aquarium on top of the partition that divided the bar area from the dining room had shattered. A few of the tables right under the aquarium had been soaked. Large shards of glass glittered on those same tables, along with various species of fish, a few of which still flopped about. The dining room floor was flooded.

"Dan."

It was Dianne. She had on her white apron and her hair was up. She looked frazzled.

She came up to me and I grabbed her elbows. She was trembling. "Are you all right?"

"I'm fine. I'm fine." She pulled away from me, pointed at what was left of the aquarium. "Do you believe this?"

"Did anyone get hurt?"

She shook her head. "No, but, my God, people could have been killed." Her eyes filled with tears.

I thought she was overreacting and tried to calm her down. "You can always get more fish and another aquarium, honey. It's not that big a deal."

She looked at me like I was dense. "Not a big deal? Someone could have been killed, Dan. I was walking by when it happened."

That's when I looked up and noticed Steve Moore and Lieutenant Gant over in the bar area, inspecting the big picture window that looked out on Ocean Boulevard. I could see two holes with spiderwebs in the window.

Someone had taken a couple of shots through the front window and shattered the aquarium.

I was stunned. "I didn't know it was a gunshot." My mind flashed back to the note I'd just found at my cottage.

"Well, it was," she said. "More than one, too. Who would have done this, Dan, and why?"

I must have given something away in my face because she shook her head, said, "No, it couldn't be because of...?"

"I don't know, Dianne." Then I remembered what she'd just said about walking by the aquarium just as the shots were fired. My stomach sunk faster than the price of clams during a red tide scare. Could the bullets have been meant for her and not the aquarium? I didn't mention that—she was scared enough. "You're going to have to be extra careful for a while."

"Extra careful? Dan, I'm too busy to be extra careful." She looked around at the mess on the floor. "How am I going to explain this to my insurance agent?"

"I'm sure they've heard everything."

"I'm sorry I called you like that." She was wringing her hands, something unusual for her. "But when it first happened, I was scared to death. People were running out the front door." She stopped talking and I could practically see her mental wheels spinning. "Some probably left without paying."

"Insurance might cover that, too. At least no one got hurt and you're all right." I reached for her hand.

She didn't let me take it. "Oh, Dan, not now." She seemed flustered. "This is horrible and it's because of..."

A fireman called her name, waved her towards him.

"I have to go," she said.

"Dianne, please be careful. I'll find out who did this."

She turned and walked away.

I noticed Guillermo standing near the swinging kitchen door. He was surveying the dining room with a concerned look on his face. I could count on one hand the times I'd seen Guillermo in the dining room.

I felt a tug on my arm. "Sweet Jaysus, Danny, was anyone hurt?"

Shamrock stood behind me in his restaurant whites.

"No. You got here fast. How did you hear about it?" Then I remembered the little police scanner he had at his place. "Never mind. I'm glad you're here. Look." I took the note out of my pocket and handed it to him. "I found it tonight wedged in my door."

He read it at least twice.

"This ain't good, Danny. Do you think...?" He looked around the restaurant.

"Come on, Shamrock. How often does someone take pot-shots through the window of the High Tide?"

"Never," he said.

"You're going to have to be careful, Shamrock. You and Dianne are the *friends* in the note, that's for sure."

"Do you think it was Eddie Hoar?"

"No. He wouldn't have a reason. He's hoping we can help him out of his own jam. Besides, you saw the condition he was in today. He couldn't hold his cigarette steady let alone a gun. I don't think he's the type anyway."

"Who then, Danny?"

"I don't know. But I'm going to find out who did it. And fast." I took the note back from Shamrock, shoved it in my pants pocket.

Shamrock shook his finger at me. "*We're* going to find out who did it?"

I hoped at least one of us was right.

Chapter 20

AN HOUR LATER I was still at the Tide. I was seated in a booth with Lieutenant Gant across from me. Steve Moore was beside him. They both were reading the threatening note. When they were finished, they looked up at me.

"Where'd you copy this from?" Gant said. "A 1940s crime novel?"

"I told you it was stuck inside my front door."

"Yeah, that's what *you* say," Gant said. "*I* say, how do we know you didn't do this yourself?"

"Because I didn't. I suppose you think I did this, too?" I waved my hand around the dining room.

Gant snorted. "With the business you're in, Marlowe, I'm sure you don't have the most savory associates."

I sat back and threw up my hands. "You've got to be kidding. Why the hell would I write this?" I tried to grab the note from Gant's hand. He pulled it away, stuffed it into the pocket of his black leather car coat.

"I'll keep this for now," he said.

I was fuming, but I continued. "And why would I take pot shots at the business I work at?"

Gant shrugged. "Who knows how you think, Marlowe? So far, you haven't been too smart. You've proven that."

I looked at Steve. He looked like he wished he were some-where else. "Whoever killed Evelyn Kruel was behind this," I said.

Gant straightened up in his seat. "That's just what I think. And I hear you're going around harassing people, too. Trying to pin the murder on someone else. Get yourself off the hook. You're upsetting a lot of people, Marlowe. I don't blame them. *And* you're upsetting me."

"I don't care who I'm upsetting." Gant really steamed me. "I'm not going to jail for something I didn't do or have my friends sharing a cell with me or maybe being hurt."

Gant leaned across the table and pointed a ramrod straight finger at me. "Look, you piece a shit, you keep out of this and stop bothering people or I'll get you locked up on charges, yesterday. I won't wait for the main event. That'll come soon enough anyway."

Gant got up and stepped out of the booth. He looked at Steve. "Talk to him," Gant said like I wasn't there. "See where he was when this happened. I've got some other things to deal with."

Steve nodded. We both watched Gant walk away.

Finally, I said, "Well that was fun."

"You shouldn't be wise-mouthing him, Dan. This is serious. You're in a lot of trouble." He was staring at me with a look of genuine concern on his face.

"What, do you think I did this too?"

Steve sighed. "Dan, come on. Give me a break. You know I don't. But I have to ask you because he's going to ask me."

I glanced around the restaurant. Most of the firemen and policemen were gone now. Shamrock and a few waitresses and busboys were cleaning up the mess. At the bar a few regulars were still drinking and chattering away. Otherwise, the place was empty.

"I was at my cottage," I began. Steve took out his small notebook and a pen and scribbled. "Shamrock and I had been up at the Shillelagh for supper. After I dropped him off at his place, I went home and found the note. That's when Dianne called and told me to come right up. I didn't know what had happened 'til I got here."

"Were you alone at the cottage?"

"Who else would be with me?"

"I have to ask. So that means no one?"

"Of course it does."

"Look, don't get mad at me. If I don't ask, then Gant'll be at your house tomorrow at seven a.m. to ask you himself."

I tried to cool down. None of this was Steve's fault, I had to remind myself. In fact, he was going as easy on me as anyone could.

"Anything else?" I asked.

Steve shook his head, put the notebook and pen back in his shirt pocket. "Not right now."

I decided to try to get something out of this little powwow. "I found out what kind of merchandise Rudy and Santa were after."

"Oh?"

"Pot." I didn't feel like I was ratting on Eddie and Derwood. The pot was long gone so I knew they couldn't be charged with that. And as far as the theft went, well, no one was going to press charges on that either. "I guess Eddie and Derwood ripped them off and they found out it was them."

Steve made a sour face. "Sounds like a lot of trouble to go to for some pot."

I watched for his reaction as I said, "It was three hundred pounds, Steve."

His eyes popped. "Three hundred pounds?"

I raised my eyebrows. "Yeah, can you believe it? Those two chuckleheads finally made a big score. But now they're in deep trouble because of it."

"Why don't they just give it back. Better to be broke and alive than dead and rich."

"They fronted it out, according to them, and got ripped-off themselves."

"They could pay..." Steve caught himself. "No, that wouldn't work. They probably haven't got two dimes to rub together."

"You haven't tied anyone to the pot that washed up on the beach, have you?"

"No." Steve took a drink from a glass of water. "You think that could be Rudy and Santa?"

I shrugged. "Maybe indirectly. I'm not sure they're bright enough to put together a smuggling scam."

Steve looked like he was thinking for a moment, then said, "There was a Fed on the beach a while ago. Some of us were notified he was going to be around. We were told to stay out of his way. Haven't seen or heard anything about him lately. Figured nothing came of it. I thought it was probably heroin or crank, but now, after what you've just told me and the pot on the beach..."

"So you don't know if there's any bust coming down on whoever he was after?"

"No. Why, what do you care?"

"Well, I don't need Rudy and Santa chasing me around the beach while I'm trying to deal with this Evelyn Kruel situation. I also told Eddie and Derwood I'd help them get out of their trouble. It's my trouble, too. So if Rudy and Santa got taken off the streets, that'd help me with both of those problems."

"Why are you helping the two knuckleheads anyway?"

"Like I said, it's my trouble, too. Have you found out anything about Santa and Rudy?"

Steve blew a long raspberry. "A little. The unusual names helped. Rudolph Valentine and Santo Gorrassi. Both got felony records. We're still checking them out."

I could tell he wasn't going to offer any more. "Have you had any luck with anyone else who could've been involved in Evelyn's death?"

"Not really." Steve furrowed his eyebrows, cocked his head. "What about *you*?"

I realized I was caught, but I tried playing innocent anyway. "What do you mean?"

"No use pretending you're being a good boy, Dan. Gant knows you've been going around the beach asking questions again. Everybody on the beach probably knows. You're going to get yourself in a lot of trouble."

I could hear my voice shake. "I can't just sit here and not do anything." I glanced around the restaurant. "Look."

Steve didn't look. "It might be better for everybody if you back off and let us handle it."

I shook my head hard. "With Gant in charge? No way. What about Evelyn's brother? If he's her heir. She was loaded so that's a good motive for murder."

Steve looked like he was about to tell me my best friend died. "It was. Until about six months ago."

I was afraid to ask, but I did. "What happened?"

"She cut him out of the will." He said it like he had just dropped a thirty-pound rock on the table. That's what it felt like, too.

I grabbed at a straw. "Marcy Wade?" I asked.

"Nooo, not Marcy. Mrs. Kruel left all her dough to a trust. It's going to be doled out to charities. Handled by a bank. Her will is out of the picture as far as motive goes."

"Morris couldn't have been happy about that."

"Probably not. But it wouldn't make any sense to kill her. If it was me, I'd do everything I could to get her to change it back. That'd be the smart thing to do."

I had to agree. "And Morris knew about the new will?"

"We think so."

"Marcy," I said quickly. "Maybe she thought it was all left to her."

"Now you're reaching. Anyway we went over to tell her. Get her reaction. We were lucky we caught her. She was on her way to Jamaica for a vacation. She didn't seem surprised to hear about the will. Probably already knew."

"Jamaica in June? How do you know she wasn't pretending she knew that it was going to charity?"

"I don't think she's that good an actress."

"There's still Artie Neal. Have you looked into him?"

"Very carefully," he began. "But I got bad news for you there, too. Neal's wife filed for divorce three months ago. Named Evelyn Kruel as the other woman."

My heart sank. I knew what that meant.

Apparently, Steve could read my face. "That's right. He wouldn't have any motive to kill Evelyn Kruel if his wife already knew about her and was divorcing him anyway."

"And George Ransom?"

Steve gave me a pitying look. "Morris Kruel and he had worked some deal out before Evelyn was shot. Morris had the authority to do it. So Ransom wouldn't have any reason to kill her, either." Steve threw up his hands. "We're going to keep trying, but..."

"Trying what?" I said. "Finding the killer or hanging it on me?"

"That was uncalled for, Dan." He didn't sound angry, just disappointed.

"I'm sorry. It's just that I'm worried." I looked at Steve; he looked at me. "Dianne," I said. "And Shamrock too. They're in bad danger, Steve. I know it."

Steve chewed at his lip for a moment. "I'll dig into it more. Try and turn Gant around."

"Good luck with that." Then I decided to be honest with Steve. "I'm going to have to go full out looking into this. It's the only thing I can do. I don't have a choice."

He held up his palms. "Don't tell me about it. I don't want to hear it."

"I have to," I said. "I might need your help."

"Great."

"I'll let *you* know everything I learn."

"I'll probably hear about it anyway when you're arrested. Dan, I'm not..."

I interrupted him. "How's Kelsey?" Sure, it was low, reminding him how I had helped save the life of his adopted son, but I had no choice. I had to get Dianne and Shamrock out of this mess and I needed Steve's help.

He looked at me, blew air out of his mouth. "All right. I'll help you if I can. It better stay between you and me though."

"That goes without saying. But Dianne and Shamrock are involved too. They might have to know."

"If word gets out that I'm giving you a hand, Dan, no matter from who...I'm blaming you." He wagged his finger at my face. "And I do want to know if you find out anything."

I forced a smile. "Absolutely, Steve. We'll get to the bottom of this together."

"I hope so," was all he said before getting up and walking away.

I sat there and went over what I'd just learned. It was worse than bad—I didn't have a damn suspect left. I was back to square one.

Chapter 21

THE NEXT MORNING I got up late after a lousy night's sleep. I was worried sick about Dianne. I wasn't sure whether the shooter last night had been trying to kill her or just scare her.

I'd wanted her to stay here, or for me to stay at her place, but she wouldn't allow it. *No one's going to scare me*, she'd said. But I could tell she had been frightened and who wouldn't be? Anyway I took her home, saw her in safely. Steve told me the police were going to watch her place for the night, just in case.

The High Tide was closed for the day. Dianne had a commercial cleaning company coming in to clean up the mess. That gave me the day off, with lots of time to worry. After last night, I had no doubt that all three of us—Dianne, Shamrock, and I—were in physical danger. I had to move fast before whoever was behind all this had another chance to take a shot at one of us. The next time it might be more than a few fish who didn't survive.

I had coffee and a bagel and called Shamrock. I made arrangements to pick him up that evening. The rest of the day I did next to nothing. I tried to lose myself in a paperback and a mystery movie on TV. Nothing worked to ease my mind. So it was a long slog before the time came to pick up Shamrock.

When the time finally arrived, I threw on a light coat, more to carry a couple of things than because of the temperature, and grabbed the .38. Outside, the sun was just sinking below the dunes. I hopped into my car and backed out of the unpaved driveway. When I pulled up in front of Shamrock's place down off of Ashworth Avenue, I gave the horn two quick blasts. Within seconds he came out the front door. No restaurant whites today. He was dressed in jeans and a shirt with a big green shamrock on the front. Perfect.

When he was in the car, I pulled back out onto Ashworth. I made the turnaround just before the bridge and headed north on Ocean Boulevard. I was in a foul mood and drove right up the ass of the car in front of me. He slowed and I had to jam on the brakes. The tires squealed. Shamrock almost put his foot through the floorboard.

"Did you have your coffee today, Danny?" he asked in a shaky voice.

I let out a rush of air, stepped slowly on the gas. "Sorry. Last night's got me worried."

"It is bad, Danny. Very bad, that's for sure. My God, if anything had happened to..." He trailed off, glanced at me, and dropped it.

I drove for a few more minutes.

"Where are we going?" Shamrock asked.

I pulled the car over to the side of the road near Boar's Head. You couldn't see the ocean; a seawall was beside us. I wasn't sure what we'd be getting into, so I wanted to give Shamrock a chance to bail out if he wanted. I hoped he wouldn't though. I might need backup.

"There's a house up on Plaice Cove that I want to check out."

"Tiny Bastards?"

"No."

"Evelyn Kruel's?" he guessed again.

"No."

He looked at me quizzically. "Whose, Danny?"

I told him what Hank Fuller had told me at the Tide.

"That doesn't seem like much of a reason to kill somebody," Shamrock said.

"No, it doesn't. But there's a couple of things I'm curious about." I hesitated, said, "We'll probably have to break in. If you want out, I wouldn't blame you."

Shamrock shook his head. "Forget that, Danny. I'm going. Nothing scares Michael Kelly." He paused, then added, "Ahh... dogs, Danny. I don't like dogs. Especially vicious ones like you say these are."

"Hank said they haven't been around."

Shamrock swallowed hard. "All right, then. Come on. Let's go. What are you waiting for?"

I smiled and resumed driving.

We'd only gone a short distance when Shamrock said, "Hey, where you going? You just went by Plaice Cove."

I pointed with my chin. "It's up here," I said.

"That's North Beach, Danny." Shamrock gestured back over his shoulder with his thumb. "*That's* Plaice Cove back there."

Was I the only one on the beach who didn't know that? "How did you..." I caught myself, remembering who I was talking to.

I pulled into the small unpaved parking area I'd used the last time I'd been here. It was deserted. "I think it's best if we leave the car here and go in the beach way."

"Aye."

Shamrock and I trudged up the tiny hill that led to the beach and came down the other side. It was almost dark now.

The moon was out, reflecting enough light off the water that we could see most of the beach spread out in front of us. Except for the pounding of the surf, the only other sounds were our footsteps on the hard sand.

"Which one is it?" Shamrock asked after we had walked a bit.

"Up there," I answered, pointing a few buildings ahead of us. Even in the semi-darkness I could see the large antenna looming over our destination.

We turned at an angle and in a couple of minutes were at the foot of a rickety staircase that led up to our target. I could just make out the concerned look on Shamrock's face as he looked up the stairs.

"You sure about those dogs?"

I held my finger to my lips. "That's what I was told," I whispered. "If we hear dogs, we'll split."

"All right. I guess."

I began the climb up the staircase, Shamrock behind me. The wood creaked as we moved. At the top, we stopped, frozen to the spot. We listened. I could feel my heart beat and hear Shamrock's rapid breathing. Apparently, Hank had been right about the dogs; there was no sign of them. After a minute, I looked at Shamrock. He nodded rapidly.

We moved toward the building and I got a better look at the place. It was just an old one-story wood-shingled cottage. There were a couple of windows and a door on this side. I tried the door. It was locked. I moved to one of the windows. Shamrock followed me like a shadow. The window was locked, too. I checked the other window. Ditto.

I motioned for Shamrock to wait there and I walked back toward the staircase, looking at the ground. There was no shortage of rocks, and it only took a minute to find what I wanted. Back at the window, I looked at Shamrock, gave him a shrug. I took the large rock I'd just picked up and tapped it carefully against the pane near the window lock. It took three taps, each a bit harder than the last, before the glass gave with a little tinkle. I dropped the rock and carefully removed the glass shards from the window. When I had all the glass out of the pane, I stuck my hand through and released the lock.

Whoever the occupants were, they would know someone had been there. My plan was to take something of little value, maybe booze, a VCR, or something else minor. That way the break in would be chocked up to neighborhood kids or junkies. There were a lot of those breaks on the beach, so it wasn't an unreasonable assumption.

We both piled through the window. Inside, Shamrock and I stood there. We were in total dark. I took a flashlight from my coat pocket and turned it on. We were in the kitchen. There was nothing for us there. We moved into the adjoining room. It was a living area—a couch, couple of chairs, table, lamps, and a fireplace. Nothing out of the ordinary here either.

To our right were three doors—number one, number two, and number three. I hoped one of them would be the lucky door. I opened door number one and played the flashlight around inside it. It was a bedroom. I stepped in, followed by Shamrock. The bed was made. I walked past a television on a stand and approached a bureau. I held the flashlight in my mouth and proceeded to go through the drawers. There was nothing of any use in there, just a man's clothing, and that was a bad sign. It meant someone was planning on coming back.

Back out in the main room, I turned the knob on door number two and pushed it open. I could feel Shamrock's hot breath on my neck. This was a bathroom; evidently, the original. Everything very old. I opened the medicine cabinet, played the light. I picked up a prescription bottle. There was no label.

I opened the bottle and saw familiar pills. Tranquilizers. I was tempted to take some but Shamrock was practically sitting on my shoulder. Besides, I didn't want to take the chance the owner would notice a few missing and realize he'd had adult company—kids would've taken them all. I returned the bottle to the shelf and moved on.

Behind door number three I found what I was looking for. I moved the light around the room. Shamrock stepped up beside me. "What is it, Danny?" he whispered.

"A radio room," I whispered back.

We bumped shoulders and got stuck as we tried to step into the room at the same time. I shook myself free.

"Sorry, Danny," Shamrock said.

Finally in the room, I danced the beam of light around. Against the far wall was a long table. I walked up to it. Shamrock came up beside me. On it was what appeared to be some type of ham radio equipment. There were more dials and knobs than a jet's cockpit. There was a microphone on a stand and a set of headphones on the table. I pegged the radio as a transmitter/receiver combination. There were other, smaller electronic devices on the table, too. I had no idea what they were. On the edge of the table sat an ashtray with more than one cigar butt crushed in it. The butts gave off a strong unpleasant odor that was vaguely familiar.

Shamrock reached over to the radio, played with a dial.

"Please don't do that," I said. "I don't want them to know I'm interested in this."

"Sorry." He withdrew his hand. "This stuff looks awful expensive, Danny."

Shamrock was right—it did look expensive. I put the light on the wall above the radio. There was a map. It showed all of North and Central America. Small round stickies of various colors dotted the map. I let the light dance around the wall some more, then looked closer at the table. An operation of this type generally required some kind of license. I was hoping to find it along with the name of who it was issued to. I had no luck though.

I did see a spiral notebook resting on the table. "Hold this." I handed Shamrock the flashlight as I thumbed through the notebook. He focused the beam on the pages as I read. It was some type of log record. There were entries dated on consecutive days, some repeated for a couple of weeks. There would be a lapse for a few months and then the same entries would start up again. There was a handwritten list of what appeared to be radio frequencies with a random word beside each. In each section there was also a list of male first names with another name beside it.

"What's it mean, Danny?" I jumped. Shamrock's mouth was an inch from my ear; his whisper sounded like a shout.

"I'm not sure, but I'd like to know." I tapped on the notebook with my fingers.

"Take it then."

"No, Shamrock. Kids wouldn't bother stealing this and I don't want anyone knowing we were here."

I turned to the back of the notebook. Plenty of blank pages; there was no way one would be missed. I pulled the last sheet out slowly, then sat in a swivel chair in front of the radio and rummaged around the desk for a pen.

"You aren't going to copy the whole thing, are you?" Shamrock asked.

"No. Just enough so maybe we can figure out what it is later."

I'd just found a pen and was about to start copying from the notebook when I heard a car pulling into the driveway out front. Headlights illuminated the front room. We both froze.

"Oh shit," Shamrock hissed.

I grabbed the flashlight from Shamrock. I shoved it and the blank paper in my jacket pocket. "Come on, quick. We got to get out of here."

This time we made it through the door without getting stuck. We dashed across the living room, into the kitchen, made it to the window. I forgot about taking something to make the break look like a kid's job; it was too late for that.

"You first," I said.

Just then two car doors slammed and I heard the bark of a dog.

"Sweet Mother of Mercy, Danny. The dogs."

Even in the darkness I could see the look of terror on Shamrock's face. He wasn't alone; my heart was going like I'd just inhaled amyl nitrate.

"Hurry, hurry," I said. Shamrock crawled through the window. I gave him an extra push and he crashed to the ground. I followed him through. I turned and raised my arms to close the window behind me and just as I did the front door opened and the light went on. I was blinded and couldn't see who was there, but they must have seen me.

Someone shouted, "Hey, what the fuck?"

I dashed for the staircase that led to the beach. The moon gave off enough light that I could almost see where I was going. Still, I couldn't see or hear Shamrock; I assumed he was already down on the sand.

I reached the staircase and went down as fast as I dared in the semi-darkness. Behind me I heard the rear door of the cottage open followed by shouts and the beam of a flashlight skipping about. I had just jumped off the last step and landed in the sand when I heard the dogs barking. There was more than one and they'd been released. I ran in the direction of the car.

"Shamrock, Shamrock," I called in a muted shout. I was sure he was ahead of me.

Behind me I could hear the dogs' toenails scraping on the wood staircase as they scrambled down it. When the scraping stopped, I knew they had reached the sand. I was halfway to the car by that time. I expected a dog to leap on my back at any second. My senses were wired, so when the screams started my nerves jumped like I'd mainlined espresso.

"Ahhh! Help me, someone. For the love of Jaysus, help me."

Shamrock! Behind me! I turned and raced back toward the stairs. In less than a minute, I could just about make out the stairs we had come down. I didn't see anything human in the vicinity.

I didn't have any trouble finding Shamrock, though. I just headed for the screams and the barking dogs. Shamrock was backed against a rock wall about fifty feet from the staircase we'd used. Apparently, he'd gone there to hide instead of heading for the car. Bad move. When I got close enough, I could see the dogs were doing a job on him. One of the Dobermans snapped and gnashed at his leg. His pant leg was torn and the animal had drawn blood. The other beast had latched onto his left arm. Shamrock swung the arm, trying to throw the dog off. Every time he did, I thought I could actually hear flesh rip. I hoped it was only his shirt.

Just as I ran up, Shamrock lost his footing and tumbled to the ground. He landed on his side. Both of the animals were still latched onto his clothes, shaking their heads furiously, trying to tear off whatever they had in their jaws. I couldn't tell if it was Shamrock's skin or not.

I ripped the .38 from the back of my waistband. Of course, I couldn't try to shoot one of the dogs—they were on top of

Shamrock. I raised the gun and fired into the night sky. Both mutts yelped and jumped off Shamrock. They didn't run. Instead they turned and stood side by side, facing me. Both dogs bared their teeth and growled.

I held the revolver in a two-handed grip and pointed it at them. If they charged together, I'd never get both of them. I'd have to fight the second one with my bare hands. I didn't fancy that.

They were still too close to Shamrock for me to risk a shot, so I raised the gun over my head and let off two quick shots. I was in luck—the dogs turned tail and bolted. They headed for the staircase and I could hear their nails scratching on the wood as they scrambled up.

I went over to Shamrock and knelt beside him.

"Danny, Danny," he moaned. "Thank God, it's you." He rolled over and got himself into a sitting position. He moved his face close to his leg so he could inspect his wounds in the dim moonlight. From the little I could see, they didn't look good but I didn't have time to make a prognosis. I didn't hear the people from the cottage, but they could come down the staircase any second.

"Can you walk?" I put the gun away.

"Do I have any choice?"

At least he still had his sense of humor; that was a good sign. "No, you don't. We've got to get the hell out of here."

I could feel sticky blood on my hands as I grabbed under his arms and struggled to get him to his feet. I kept my arm around him as we stumbled along the sand. I could hear him breathing heavily. I guess I probably was too. When we finally reached the car, I opened the front passenger door.

"I'll ruin your car, Danny," he said.

"Get in," I said. I helped him, pushing his head down like a cop shoving a criminal into a cruiser.

When I got in the driver's seat, I flicked on the overhead light and got a better look at his wounds. I didn't like what I saw. I hadn't seen a lot of dog bites, but I'd seen some. Shamrock's were the worst I had ever seen, bar none.

"Take me home, Danny. I need a Guinness. Maybe two."

I knew I wasn't going to be able to do that. I wasn't an expert but it didn't take expertise to know these wounds needed medical attention and quickly.

"Sorry, Shamrock. I'm going to have to take you to Exeter Hospital."

"Ahh, Jaysus. Not there, please. I'll be all right. Take me home."

I wondered for a moment if he was in shock. "I don't think so. Some of those bites aren't going to stop bleeding by themselves." Blood dripped onto the seat.

Shamrock must have realized I was right about the hospital; he didn't give me any more trouble.

I drove fast. On the drive, I thought about what the hell I was going to tell the doctors and nurses about a man coming in at night with wounds that looked like he had been mauled by a she lion protecting her cubs. Everything I came up with sounded ridiculous. Still I couldn't tell the truth, one of the tales spinning round in my head would have to do. So I decided the old-fashioned way—*eeny, meeny, miny, moe.*

Chapter 22

THE NEXT DAY started with a slight hangover. You know, the type where the symptoms fortunately aren't major, but nevertheless, you never feel yourself the entire day. The night before, after all that had happened, there had been no way I was going to sleep without a few; so that's what I had—a few. Now I was guaranteed my day would never get above a six, on a one-to-ten scale. It could have been a lot worse though.

At Exeter Hospital they had stitched Shamrock up, given him a shot for tetanus and another for pain. When I told the doctor about Shamrock taking a night stroll on Hampton Beach and being attacked by dogs, she didn't try to conceal her alarm. She wanted to call in the police right then and there. I cut that off at the pass by convincing her we'd stop at the police station on the way home. Of course, that was a lie.

We were at the hospital for a few hours. When we left, Shamrock had a prescription in his hand as he walked shakily to my car. We filled the scrip on the way home. Shamrock had refused my invitation to stay with me for the night, so I had helped him into his small studio apartment, propped him up in a chair in front of the television, and brought him two cold Guinness before I left.

Now, awake and not refreshed, I decided to check into something that I felt had to be looked into. Something I felt I could handle with my slightly diminished capacity. I had the day off from my bar duties, so I had a muffin, coffee, showered, dressed. I grabbed both the .38 and the Xanax to bring with me. I don't know why I took the pills; just that I didn't feel right, I guess. I stepped outside into drizzly weather.

I hopped into the green Chevette and headed for Hampton proper. When I reached the town hall, I pulled into a parking spot and walked into the building. I didn't have to check the office locations on the foyer wall to find out where the assessor's office was located—I'd been there before. When I reached the correct room, I opened the door, went in.

A short cotton-headed woman was behind the counter. I had seen her before. She'd been there almost as long as the building.

"Can I help you?" she asked in a pleasant voice that couldn't completely hide the amount of times she had asked that question.

I reached into my pants pocket, pulled out a slip of paper, and handed it to her.

She slipped the glasses that hung on a thin chain around her neck up onto the tip of her nose. She gave the paper one quick glance and dropped it on the counter. I thought for a moment that she might already have the information in her head, but of course, I was wrong. Even she hadn't been here long enough for that.

She opened one of three large heavy albums resting on the counter and leafed through it. It only took her seconds to find what I was looking for. She spun the book around, pushed it in my direction. She leaned closer and I could smell perfume like my mother used to wear.

"This is it," she said. She tapped on the page with a gnarled finger that looked like it must hurt for her to do so.

I wasn't really surprised when I read *Kreul Realty Trust.* At least I wouldn't have much of a drive. I said thank you and goodbye to the woman and returned to my car.

After a couple of minutes I pulled into a spot directly in front of the Kruel building. Inside, I went to the second floor and turned the knob on the office door. The second I realized that it was locked, I remembered that Steve Moore had told me Marcy Wade was in Jamaica on vacation. Odd that they weren't still open. With both Evelyn dead and Marcy gone, maybe they didn't have anyone qualified to watch the store. But with the beach busy season right around the corner? Strange. Almost as strange as going to Jamaica in June.

Back in the car, I headed for the beach. I wasn't giving up. Now that I knew who owned the cottage with the ham radio and the dogs, I wasn't going to give up on following that lead. No matter how many people were on vacation.

I got as far as Boar's Head, the peninsula at the north end of Hampton Beach proper that juts out into the Atlantic. A one-way road ran up and around the length of the peninsula. On the left side of the road, the inner side, were modest homes without ocean frontage. On the right sat the oceanfront homes, some facing south toward Hampton Beach; Newburyport, Massachusetts; and Boston beyond. The homes on the opposite side of the peninsula faced north toward Hampton's North Beach, Portsmouth, and beyond that, Maine. One estate at the tip was graced with one hundred eighty degree views. I drove past that mansion and pulled into a driveway farther down the Head.

I'd stopped at an older home, probably an easy seventy- or eighty-years old if I had to guess. The outside of the structure and the grounds were both immaculately kept. I knew this was where Morris Kruel lived. The house had been pointed out to me somewhere along the line. I didn't know if he or his sister owned it.

Before I went up to the front door, I stood along the side of the house, looking at the ocean. The homes were situated up high, and even with the drizzle, the views of the Atlantic were breathtaking. I could see north along the New Hampshire coast and the Isle of Shoals off shore. Of course you had to leave the Head to get to the beach. And you had to drive or take a very long walk to get anywhere else, but the scenery made up for it. Oceanfront on Boar's Head was unbeatable. The houses on the inner side, not so much. Little or no views, a walk to the beach, and longer walks, or a drive to get anywhere else. Walk across a thin little street and properties went from a ten to a five in desirability. At least in my book they did.

After I got my fill of the view and sucking in the salt air, I marched up to the front door and rang the bell. Morris Kruel answered the inner door. His preppy clothes were wrinkled.

"Marlowe," he said. "What the hell do you want now?"

"I want to talk to you for a minute."

I expected him to slam the door in my face; he didn't. That definitely meant something. I didn't know what.

Morris glanced out onto the street and looked both ways. He was a very nervous man indeed. He could have used one of my pills. "I'm only letting you in so you'll stop bothering me once and for all."

That was unlikely but it got me in.

He opened the screen door for me and I followed him into the house. He led me into a room that was old but quite cozy. Nautical knickknacks and paintings covered three walls. They reminded me of my own home, although his decorations were much more expensive. The part that didn't resemble my cottage at all was the large picture window that looked out over the Atlantic Ocean. The view was gorgeous.

"Sit down," Morris said like I was a brother-in-law who had dropped by to sell him something. He pointed at a chair that looked old, antique-old that is. I sat gingerly; the chair was not comfortable. He sat across from me in a chair that looked very comfortable.

I expected Morris Kruel to offer me something. When he didn't, I decided to let him start talking first.

Neither of us spoke for a minute. Finally, Morris said, "All right, Marlowe. What is it you want this time?"

"I want to ask you about a property."

He grew indignant. "You came here for that, Marlowe? You want to rent," he looked at me disdainfully, "or possibly buy, go over to the office. They can take care of you there."

"The office is closed. You must know that. *And* Marcy's in Jamaica." Something registered on his face; exactly what I couldn't be sure.

"Well, wait till they reopen."

"I can't. I want to know about a cottage up on the water at Plaice...North Beach. Just past Plaice Cove. It's the one with the huge ham radio antenna." I took the slip of paper out, read him the address.

That look on his face again. Surprise? Fear?

"I don't know about any property like that. And the address doesn't sound familiar."

"I've been over to town hall, Morris. *Kruel Realty Trust.* That's you, right?"

"My sister." He glanced around, probably looking for a way out. "Could be a mistake," he finally said. "Maybe we used to own it. Properties change so fast on the beach." His voice shifted to a friendly tone. "You know that, Marlowe."

I wasn't going to give this guy any breaks. "I know just the opposite. Things are slow now. You'd know about any property that your sister had dumped recently."

He sat up straight, suddenly angry. Or was he feigning it? "We don't *dump* property. Besides, the address and house you describe doesn't ring a bell at all."

I didn't believe him. Even if the address really meant nothing to him, he still would have been familiar with the antenna. You couldn't ride up 1A without seeing the monstrosity.

There was silence for a minute. Finally he spoke with a voice so sweet I thought he'd been eating cotton candy. "Why are you so interested in that property, Marlowe?"

I decided to have some fun. "Why are you so interested in why I'm interested?"

He sputtered. "Because...well...because I'm curious, just curious. And for all I know, you may be trying to sully Evelyn's name again—somehow—with this."

"Or are you worried about your own name?" I said.

"What do you mean by that?" he said. Before I could answer, he jumped up from his seat. "Get out, Marlowe. And don't come back. Or I'll call the police."

I stood. "Didn't you ever hear the story about the little boy who cried wolf, Morris?" I headed for the door. I could hear him following me.

When I stepped outside, I looked over my shoulder. "I'll be back when I have some more questions," I said.

"You...you do and I'll have the law on you."

"Everybody keeps saying that, but so far I haven't seen any cops." I gave him my biggest phony smile and walked to my car. Behind me I heard the door slam.

As I backed out of the driveway, I saw a curtain move in one window. I was seeing a lot of that lately too—people peeking out of windows at me. For some reason that made me feel good.

Chapter 23

AFTER LEAVING Morris Kruel's, I stopped on Ashworth Avenue and made a call from a pay phone to the number Eddie Hoar had given me.

"Hello," Eddie said in a poor singsongy imitation of an elderly woman's voice.

"Eddie, it's Dan Marlowe."

"How'd you know it was me?" he asked in his normal voice.

"Never mind that now. I'm coming over. I want you to take a ride with me."

"What's wrong? Is there a problem?" His voice shook.

"No problem at all, Eddie. I just want to check some things out. Might help us both."

His voice still shook. "All right. As long as you're sure there's no problem."

"No problem. I'm leaving the beach now."

On the drive over the Hampton Bridge, I didn't even glance at the nuclear power plant off to my right like I usually did. I was lost in thoughts currently more important than the possibility of a nuclear accident.

My mind was tangled up in a jumble of suspects—all with a reason to kill Evelyn Kruel. Or have her killed. There was

Artie Neal, although he didn't look quite as promising now that I knew he was already separated from his wife. And that his wife had already known about his dalliance with Evelyn to boot. No need to silence Evelyn there. Still, maybe a lover's quarrel?

And what about Marcy Wade? The rumors of a gay liaison with Evelyn? Marcy certainly didn't look gay, whatever the hell gay looked like. Could Marcy have been jealous about Evelyn and Neal? Or were the gay rumors just malicious? And what about the will? Was Marcy in the will at one time? Was she angry because her name had been removed?

Morris? He certainly had a lot to gain by his sister's death. The will...wait a second. Steve said the will had been changed to name charities as the beneficiaries and that Morris knew about it. But what if Steve was wrong? Maybe the will hadn't been changed, or maybe it had been changed back, or maybe Morris didn't know about the changes after all. Or maybe he had another reason.

Then there was George Ransom. Evelyn wouldn't do a deal for the parking he needed. If she were dead and Morris ended up in charge, well, that could be a different story. But hadn't Ransom and Morris already had a deal before Evelyn's death? Had Evelyn nixed it or was the deal a lie to begin with? And would Morris go so far as to let Ransom kill his sister? Certainly there wasn't enough money in the deal to justify fratricide. Still, George Ransom seemed as shady as a giant redwood forest.

I couldn't forget the two goons either—Santa and Rudy. The distinctive cigar butts in the ashtray had told me that they were the tenants at the ham radio house. And that connected them to Evelyn Kruel—she'd been the landlord. But that was a stretch, I knew. After all, she'd been the landlord for half the people on the beach. On the other hand, those two were the ones with the definite tendency to use violence. They'd proven that when they picked me up and almost pistol-whipped me. But why would they want to kill Evelyn Kruel? The dogs? So they wouldn't have to pay their rent? Those scenarios were both less than not likely. Or was there something else going on up there besides ham radio chats?

I was about as mixed up as the Jesus freak who strolled up and down Ocean Boulevard every summer with the fire-and-brimstone sandwich board hanging from his shoulders. At least he was sure who the main player was. In my case, I had no idea.

By the time I pulled up to Eddie's aunt's mobile home, I was thoroughly confused. In disgust I pushed all the confusion out of my mind and decided to concentrate on why I'd come to get Eddie.

I gave a light tap on the horn. He must have been waiting at the door, because it opened immediately and Eddie stepped out followed by Derwood Doller. Eddie stopped to lock the door and Derwood banged into him. Eddie grabbed a railing and caught himself before he fell down the few steps. He pushed Derwood past him down the stairs, locked the door, and they both trooped over to my car. Derwood slid in back; Eddie hopped in beside me. I maneuvered the car along the narrow roads and out of the mobile home park.

Eddie spoke first. "So what's up? Did you square it away already?"

He spoke rapidly and his eyes were dilated. I also noticed that sickeningly sweet aroma again. "I'm not a magician, Eddie. There's just something I want to check out." I glanced into the rearview mirror; Derwood's head was scraping the ceiling.

"You both didn't have to come."

"I wasn't gonna stay there alone," Derwood said.

I looked at the big man again to make sure he wasn't kidding. He wasn't.

"Where the hell are we going?" Eddie asked. He was chewing and snapping gum as he spoke. It was irritating; I could have snapped his neck.

"We're going over to Hampton Harbor."

"Hampton Harbor?" Eddie said, flailing his arms. "I don't wanna go near Hampton, let alone the harbor. Take us back."

I gave Eddie a quick glance. Beads of sweat stuck out on his pockmarked face. "You're going," I said. "You don't have to like it, but you're going. Unless you want me to forget about helping you."

"But jeez, man," Eddie said. "Hampton Harbor? That's where this whole thing started. I dunno."

Derwood leaned over the seat; I got a whiff of pepperoni as he spoke. "We ain't got a choice, Eddie. We gotta let him help us. Besides, they won't bother us in broad daylight down there. It's too crowded."

"He's right," I said.

"I must be out of my mind," Eddie said.

I agreed but I didn't say it.

Derwood sat back and shortly we were going over the bridge into Hampton. I took a left on the far side and went down a road that led to the harbor and the docks.

"Where?" I asked Eddie.

He directed me and told me where to park.

"Come on," I said, opening my door and sliding out. Derwood climbed out of the back. Eddie's door didn't open.

I leaned back in. "Come on, Eddie, get out." He didn't move. "If you don't, I'll take you back to your place and you'll be on your own."

Derwood opened Eddie's door and Eddie slowly climbed out.

"Hurry it up, will you?" I said. "Which way?"

Derwood led the procession. I followed. Every so often I had to reach behind me, grab Eddie by the arm, and hurry him along.

Derwood led us onto a dock with a variety of boats bobbing beside it. He stopped, turned to me.

"That's it. It's still here." He pointed toward a beauty moored out on the water. I didn't know much about boats, but I could see that it was a very large sailboat, not a power boat like most of the others in the area. There were a few people working on nearby boats, but I couldn't see any activity on the one Derwood had pointed out.

"How'd you get out to it?" I asked Eddie.

"We borrowed a little boat."

I smirked and said, "Come on."

Eddie was behind me. "You're going to go closer?" he asked as if there were a pride of lions guarding the boat.

"No, we all are." I pulled his arm and we all walked along the dock toward the sailboat. I was leading the way now, Derwood behind both of us.

When we reached the end of the dock, we stopped and looked out toward the sailboat. I couldn't see anything unusual from where I stood. For a moment, I considered renting a rowboat. But there were too many people around, and I realized anything that would have been helpful would probably have been removed long ago. I made note of the name on the stern, turned, and headed back the way we'd come.

Eddie was right beside me this time. "We're going?" he asked.

"One stop," I answered. I pointed at a small white building with a door marked *Office*. When we reached it, I opened the door, stepped in. Eddie and Derwood remained outside.

Behind a wooden counter was a grizzled old man in a black captain's hat with a shock of white hair protruding out from under it, navy kerchief, and a blue denim shirt. Pleasantly sweet pipe tobacco scented the air.

"What can I do for ya?" He rested his hands on the counter. They were deeply tanned and aged, with painful-looking cracks in the skin.

I pointed out a side window in the direction of the sailboat. "I'm wondering what you can tell me about that sailboat. *The Technology Geek*?"

He waved at me. "Not supposed to give out any info on our lessees, mister. Policy. Sorry."

"Can you tell me who owns it?"

He shook his head. "Like I said, I can't. Policy. Sorry."

I took my wallet from my back pocket. I don't know why, except I figured I had nothing to lose. I removed a ten-dollar bill, placed it on the counter between his sore-looking hands.

He looked at it, then at me. "Don't insult me."

I almost took the ten back and then realized maybe I wasn't interpreting him correctly. I still had the wallet in my hand so I took out another ten and placed it on top of the first one. He looked at it, smiled, and went over to a small filing cabinet. He had his back to me as he rummaged through the contents.

"That mooring's leased to *Technology Geeks, Inc.,*" he said. "It's got an address. Want that too?"

"Yes," I told him. I grabbed a pen from a small cup on the counter and pulled a piece of paper from my wallet.

The address was a post office box in Portsmouth.

When he turned and stepped back to the counter, I decided to see what else I could find out for twenty bucks. It wasn't going to be much.

"Can you tell me about any of the people you've seen on her?"

He didn't speak. I opened my wallet, and not wanting to insult him again, dropped a twenty on top of the tens. He looked at the money on the counter like it was a hot fudge sundae.

"Not much to tell," he began. "Young guys mostly. Twenties, thirties maybe. Had her out for quite a while recently. Just got her back a bit ago. Somebody says one of them is some big tech mogul. Computers or something. I don't understand none of that stuff."

"Know any of them?" I asked.

"Nope." Then his brow furrowed. "They did have one visitor I know, though. Well, don't know him really. I was over getting some fireworks for my grandson, getting ready for the 4th, you know. And I seen this guy that was here once. He owns the fireworks store."

"The one on 1A?"

"Yeah, that's it."

"What was he doing on the sailboat?"

"Beats me. Maybe the boat people were looking into having a party and buying fireworks or something." His face screwed up. "I hope they ain't thinking of doing that here. I didn't think of that before. Our other tenants wouldn't like that." He hesitated, then added, "Maybe one of them is his kid."

"Maybe," I said. But I strongly doubted it.

"Thanks," I said.

"Anytime." He hadn't touched the money, just watched me as I left.

Outside the three of us headed back toward the car. Eddie sat up front again. "What'd he say? Huh? What'd he say?"

"Not much," I answered. There was no sense in mentioning the corporation to Eddie or Derwood. They didn't travel in corporate circles.

After we were back in the car and had closed the doors, I said to myself, apparently loud enough for Eddie to hear, "Why would they have Mexican weed in a sailboat?"

Eddie looked at me and snapped his gum. "It wasn't Mexican. It was super Jamaican. Kinda tight press, though. But, Jesus, was it strong. Right, Derwood?"

"That's right, Eddie."

Jamaican? I had assumed it was the Mexican pot that was common on the seacoast. Made sense though. Most Mexican was trucked to New England. Jamaican? That country's name had come up recently. I mulled that over along with what I'd learned from the dock master as we crossed the Hampton Bridge headed back toward Seabrook.

"You takin' us home now?" Derwood asked from the backseat.

"Of course he's taking us home, Dumwood. Where else would he be taking us?"

"I keep telling you not to call me that, Eddie. I don't like it."

Eddie held his hand up and waved it. "Ahh, can't you take a little joke?" Then to me, he said, "Can you pull in somewhere so I can get some beer to take home, man?"

"You're not going home yet. We've got a stop to make first."

"Where?" Eddie said.

I didn't answer. Instead, I took a peek at him. He looked like he wanted to jump out at the next light.

"Why?" Derwood asked.

I didn't answer him either. I looked in the rearview—he looked like he'd jump with Eddie if he got the chance. They grumbled for the rest of the short trip. I tuned them out.

Chapter 24

I'D DECIDED TO stop at the fireworks store the dock master had mentioned. I had to go by the place anyway to take my two passengers home. I don't know what I expected to gain by the visit, but I couldn't leave any stone unturned. If nothing else, I'd be able to grab some firecrackers just in case the danger I was in resolved itself and the kids came for a visit over the holiday.

When I pulled the car into the parking lot of 1A Fireworks, there were only a couple of cars in the dirt lot. I pulled up close to the store. The dock master had said the owner visited *The Technology Geek*; I had to find out why. The only way was to approach the owner directly and see if there was a reasonable explanation for his visit or if I'd been handed false information. I could have stopped in later by myself, but like I said, it was on our way.

The second Eddie saw where I was planning on going he went into a tirade. "I ain't goin' in there." His voice squawked like a little girl's. "No way. Get out of here now or I'm staying in the car. That's for sure."

I turned the car off, looked at Eddie. "You know something you're not telling me, Eddie?"

"Yeah, I do." His voice was shaking now. "The dude that owns this joint is a mean mother." He pointed his thumb at Derwood in the backseat. "We got enough trouble as it is. We don't want none with him. Right, Derwood?"

"He's right, Dan," Derwood said. In the mirror I could see his face. He wasn't as frightened as Eddie, but he wasn't jumping with joy either. "I heard he cut up a biker's face with a busted beer bottle over at some strip joint and..."

Eddie grabbed my wrist. "Yeah and I heard that the biker gang decided not to come after him. That tells me more than I want to know."

I didn't know how much was true or if the story was just an exaggeration to talk me out of the visit. Wasn't going to work. Now I had more of an interest in seeing this character and— from what I'd just been told—I might need backup. "It tells *me* that you either go in, keep your mouths shut, and let me do all the talking or I'll let you out here and you can walk home. *And* that'll be the end of the help you get from me."

"Jesus, man," Eddie said.

"Jesus is right," Derwood echoed.

"Don't worry. There won't be any trouble," I said. Still, I was reassured to feel the .38 digging into the small of my back. "All you two have to do is stand there."

I looked from one to the other. "Come on. Let's go."

They followed me reluctantly out of the car, across the few yards to the entrance door, and into the fireworks shop. The first thing I noticed was the odor of gunpowder. I was happy that this place wasn't any closer to the nuclear power plant.

The second thing I noticed was a man with his back to me standing at a group of display tables. He was holding up a long rectangular red, white, and blue package with the words *Stars & Stripes Assortment* on it in bold letters. What looked like a mother with two teenage boys was listening as he gave his sales spiel. His voice sounded vaguely familiar.

Every time she didn't jump at the price he mentioned, he dropped it ten dollars. In the short time I stood there watching, he dropped the price thirty dollars. It seemed like fireworks had a very good margin.

Finally the woman nodded and the man turned to head for the register. That's when I realized why the voice had sounded familiar. It was George Ransom, owner of the Waterview Motel. Looked like he owned this place, too. He glanced my way, recognized me. His face darkened. I stared back at him, then looked over my shoulder. Eddie and Derwood were over at a far table going through a stack of novelty fireworks. Eddie was holding one of those little tanks that you light; the ones that move along the ground and shoot out fireballs from the gun turret. He studied the tank like it was a rare gem. Derwood held up a variety box and seemed to be counting the items inside. It was a poor attempt to appear they weren't with me. And it wasn't going to work; I'd make sure of that.

I joined them at the table. "Find anything interesting?" I said.

"No, matter of fact we were just going over to another table," Eddie said. He grabbed Derwood's arm, tugged.

I seized Eddie's hand, pulled it free. "You aren't going anywhere."

I could see the expressions on Derwood's and Eddie's faces change before I heard the voice behind me.

"What the hell do you want?"

I turned and faced George Ransom. He wasn't wearing his wife-beater shirt this time. Instead, he wore a black T-shirt stretched tight across his huge chest and arms. Stenciled across the chest in white was the business name, *1A Fireworks*. He didn't look happy.

"We want to ask you some questions," I said. I heard some shuffling behind me.

"Look, Marlowe, I'm trying to run a business here. I treated you nice last time. Since then I've found out you're nothing but a bartender. So I don't feel so generous now." He jutted out his chin and his bald head glistened. "What's with them?" He looked at my two companions.

"They're with me," I said.

He wasn't impressed. "You must be back on the stuff, hanging out with those two." He let out a deep laugh.

I looked behind me. Eddie and Derwood were back at one of the tables, studying the wares as if they were coin collectors trying to price a valuable collection.

I turned back to Ransom. "What do you know about *The Technology Geek* over at Hampton Harbor?"

Bingo! His face gave him away. After taking more time than a game show contestant, he answered, "I don't go over there." He was a lousy liar. "And do I look like I know anything about technology?"

The answer was obvious, so I ignored the question. "You've been seen over there, Ransom."

"Maybe I like to look at the boats."

He wasn't making a move to toss us out, so I continued. "Boat, singular. What's your connection to that specific boat?"

He shook his head. "I don't have any connection to any boat. If I happen to be over there, I sometimes check them out. Maybe I'll buy one someday."

Somehow I'd gotten him on the defensive, so I decided to keep pressing him. "First you said you don't go over to the harbor. Now you go over, but you don't visit *The Technology Geek*. I have witnesses that have seen you on that boat."

His mouth grew tight. Finally he said, "Witnesses? Who do you think you are, Marlowe, some type of cop or something?"

I heard the warning bell on the door tinkle and turned to see Eddie opening it. "Eddie. Get back in here," I said. He looked at me sheepishly and walked back to the display that Derwood was going over for the umpteenth time.

When I turned back to Ransom, he was smiling; his smile wasn't the friendly type. "You sure know how to pick them. You would've been better off bringing Barney Fife. Now get the hell out of here." He wasn't smiling anymore.

I had one wild card up my sleeve. I didn't know if it would do any good to mention it and on the other hand it could be dangerous. No matter. Dianne, Shamrock, and I were in a boatload of danger already, and if I didn't get this pot boiling and overflowing soon, one of us was bound to get hurt anyway. So the sooner I could get someone to make a hasty move, and maybe make a mistake, the sooner I might have a chance to wrap this thing up. "I heard that *The Technology Geek* has been making trips to Jamaica."

That stopped him cold. He didn't say anything and his face turned to stone. "Get the fuck out of here, Marlowe."

He started moving toward me. I was just about to reach for my gun, when he veered off and headed in Derwood and Eddie's direction.

"I seen that little weasel in here once trying to clip stuff," he said as he walked past me.

Eddie saw him coming and heard what he said. He jumped behind Derwood. "I didn't steal nothin' from you. Don't let him get me, Derwood."

"Bullshit, you little punk. Now I'm going to give you a good ass-kicking right out the door."

Derwood stood up straight, his fists balled. "Don't you hurt, Eddie," he said. He was a big man, too. I had no idea if he was a powder puff or not, though he talked like one sometimes. I knew Ransom wasn't, that was for sure.

Eddie crouched down, peeking from behind Derwood's waist. "We don't want no trouble," Eddie said. His voice shook. Whatever stimulant he had in his system was really kicking in now.

Ransom got up close to Derwood and said, "Get the fuck out of my way."

I wondered how far Ransom was going to carry this. The few other customers scattered around the store were watching the action. Was this his way of changing the subject? If it was, it certainly worked.

"Don't you touch him," Derwood said. He had a look on his face I'd never seen on him before. It reminded me of a brave kid confronting a schoolyard bully.

Ransom gave Derwood a hard push. Derwood stumbled backwards, almost tripping over Eddie.

"Ahh," Eddie screamed.

I was shocked by what came next; I think Ransom was too. Derwood steadied himself, let out an animal roar, and barreled into Ransom, taking him to the floor. He'd caught Ransom off guard and now that he was on top, he was getting in some good head punches.

Eddie duckwalked to the front door and disappeared outside. I jumped out of the way as the two big men got to their feet and bulled their way into a display table. The combined weight of the men collapsed the table like it had been made of paper. Ransom was yelling a string of obscenities. Behind me I heard a woman scream.

They were back on the floor exchanging blows, some connecting solid. I was surprised to see that Derwood seemed to be getting the best shots in and decided not to intervene. I wasn't sure if I could anyway. Out of the corner of my eye I could see the woman herd her two teenage boys out the front door, quickly followed by the other customers. I could also see Eddie peering in through the plate glass window farthest from the door.

The two men were still on the floor grappling with each other. Derwood still had the upper hand. Until Ransom savagely jammed his thumb into Derwood's eye. Derwood let out a roar of pain.

Ransom took the opportunity to break free. He got to his feet and stumbled toward the checkout counter. Blood streamed from his nose, coloring the white letters on his T-shirt red. When he reached the counter, he reached down and came out with an automatic in his fist. My heart lurched.

He moved toward Derwood, still on the floor clutching his eye. "I'm going to beat your brains in, motherfucker," he said, raising the weapon over his head.

He was just about to slam the gun down on Derwood's head when I came up behind him and jammed my gun hard into his right side. "You do that and you're going to be minus one kidney, Ransom."

Ransom was breathing hard. "You...don't have...the balls, pussy."

I aimed the gun a few inches from his foot and fired. The slug tore into the floorboards. Ransom jumped; so did Derwood. I poked the gun into his back again.

"All right," Ransom said. Now it was his turn to have a shaky voice. "Easy. Easy."

I reached around and pulled the gun out of Ransom's fist; he didn't object. "Get over there." I shoved my gun hard, pushing him toward the counter.

"Are you all right?" I asked Derwood as Ransom pressed his back against the counter. Derwood just moaned.

Just then the door tinkled and Eddie hurried in. "Good job, Derwood," he said, helping his partner to his feet. "Of course, I had your back. If you couldn't handle him, I would've taken him out." Derwood let out a groan.

"That'll teach you," Eddie said, waving a finger in Ransom's direction. "Don't mess with us."

Ransom ignored him. He wiped the blood from his face with paper towels from a roll on the counter. "I'll get the cops on you for this, Marlowe. You can't come into a place of business and do something like this. You're screwed."

"Sure, call them. Join the club." Everybody had been threatening to call the cops on me lately. But so far no one had—as far as I knew. That in itself was interesting. I wondered what Ransom would do.

The three of us headed out the door—Eddie first, of course, me helping Derwood.

"What about my gun," Ransom snarled.

"It'll be in there." I nodded toward a rubbish receptacle outside the door. "Don't come out to get it until our car's out of sight." I dropped the gun in the waste can as we passed it.

With Derwood stretched out on the backseat and Eddie seated beside me, I backed the car out and then pulled onto the road. As I did, I could hear sirens. One of the customers must have called to report the brawl.

"I'm going to take you over to Anna Jaques, Derwood. It's closer than Exeter," I said. "That eye doesn't look good."

"Ahh, he don't need that," Eddie said. "Do you, Derwood?"

Derwood let out a deep groan.

On the drive to the Newburyport hospital, I kept going over in my mind what it might mean that George Ransom owned not only the Waterview Motel but 1A Fireworks as well. I came up with no answer. And what was Ransom telling the police right about now? Whether he'd spill the beans on me or not would tell me something. Wouldn't it?

Chapter 25

THE THREE OF us spent a few hours in the emergency room. When we left, Derwood had a patch over his eye. The doc said he was lucky he hadn't lost it. The patch made him look like an overgrown kid at Halloween.

I drove to a pharmacy where Derwood filled the prescription for pain pills the doctor had given him. On the way to their house, I had to listen while Eddie tried to pry some of the pills from Derwood. By the time we reached the mobile home Eddie had more of the pills on his person than Derwood did.

"I'll call you if I need you again," I said as the two of them climbed out of the car.

"Jeez, don't do us any favors," Eddie said.

I laughed. "You need favors, Eddie. A lot of them."

Eddie started to say something. Derwood grabbed his arm. "He's trying to help us, Eddie." Then he bent over and looked in at me with his one good eye. "It wasn't your fault, Dan. We'll be here if you need us. Right, Eddie?"

"Do we got a choice?" Eddie snapped

I nodded to the two buffoons and left.

On the ride back to Hampton I went over a couple of ideas I had in my head. After a short internal debate, I decided to put everything off until tomorrow. I'd had enough excitement for one day. Some beers were in order; I deserved them.

I parked the car in my driveway, walked up the steps onto the porch. That's where they were waiting for me, crouched down, out of sight. The two men popped up on both sides of me like jack-in-the-boxes.

I felt something jab into my right side. "Get your keys out carefully and open the door," the one sticking me with the gun said. I did as I was told.

Once inside, he turned to his partner. "Close the shades and turn on a light."

I didn't have to be introduced. My nostrils were treated to the putrid stench of cheap cigars *and* I recognized the voice— a voice that made Louis Armstrong's sound feminine.

Santa and Rudy.

They didn't give me a chance to turn around and face them. As soon as the light was on, Santa stepped over and gave me a monster shove. I went sprawling across my easy chair, face down.

"You fuckin' wise guy. Let's see how wise you are now."

When I regained my breath, I struggled to my feet and turned around. Rudy stood smiling, holding a gun on me. My old friend Santa, who'd almost pushed me into Tuesday, wasn't smiling. Instead, he let go with a right hook directed at my jaw. I ducked. The blow slid past its target and caught me hard on my right shoulder. I flopped back into my chair again, ass first this time. I rubbed my shoulder. It was plenty sore but I knew I was lucky. A blow like that would've broken my jaw if it had connected.

It looked like I wasn't out of the woods yet. Santa stepped over, grabbed me by the front of my shirt, and pulled me to my feet. He balled his big fists. "You almost killed me in that car, smart ass. Now see how you like this." He cocked his right fist and I knew he wasn't going to miss this time.

Fortunately, Rudy intervened. "Hold it, will ya? Can't you even wait a few minutes, you big ox? Remember what we got planned?"

Santa stopped. His fist lowered in little jerky motions and a frightening smile spread across his face. "Yeah, that'll be nice to watch."

I didn't like the sound of that one bit. "What do you two want?" I asked, more to get my imagination off what they might have planned than to actually get an answer.

"We told you before what we wanted," Rudy said. "You didn't listen. Now it's too late."

I didn't like that *too late* part, either.

"You got anything on you I should know about, Marlowe?" Rudy asked.

My .38. It was still in the small of my back, covered by my windbreaker. "No," I answered.

"Check him," Rudy said.

Santa's big hands fanned out on me. He looked like he'd rather beat me to death than pat me down. He should have, too, because he wasn't good at a pat down. His hands did all my pockets, down my pant legs to my socks, and back to my waist. His hands stopped inches from bumping into my gun.

"He's okay."

"All right, Marlowe," Rudy said. "Give me your keys."

I pulled them out of my pocket, handed them to him. He tossed them to his partner. Then Rudy waved me toward the door with the end of the gun.

I glanced toward the bedroom and could almost see Betsy under the bed staring back at me with her two round black eyes. If I'd only been inside with her when these two had shown up, things wouldn't have turned out this way. Now I'd have to wait and hope I could get a chance to use Betsy's little cousin nestled against the base of my spine.

Outside, Santa headed toward my car in the driveway. Rudy shoved me in the opposite direction. We trudged through the sand, walking around my cottage. We came out on the neighboring street. A late model car was parked at the curb.

He handed me the keys. "You're driving."

I got behind the wheel. He rode shotgun, holding the pistol on me.

"Where are we going?" I asked.

"You'll see soon enough. Just drive up Ocean Boulevard until I tell you different." He wiggled the gun. "Try the demolition derby again and I'll have three slugs in your side before we hit the curb."

I looked at his face and the gun and believed him.

I wasn't really surprised where we ended up—the ham radio house at Plaice Cove. Rudy's obnoxious cigar had tipped me earlier to the identities of the two reclusive tenants. Why we were there now, I didn't know. I did know it couldn't be good. My car was already there when we parked in the driveway. Rudy slipped on black gloves.

"Get out carefully. And walk in," he said, sneering. "You know the layout. You been here before."

He marched me at gunpoint up the walkway and through the door. We stopped in the living room. I didn't like what I saw.

Besides Santa standing in the middle of the room, I noticed two five-gallon red plastic containers. I didn't have to ask what was in them. There was a smell of gasoline. It was so strong it masked the odor of Rudy's cigars. My anxiety naturally decided to take the elevator up. I wished I had asked for my medication before we left.

"Get in the chair," Rudy said.

He pointed to a stiff-backed chair. I hadn't noticed it the last time I was there. It was very uncomfortable but that was the least of my worries.

I looked warily around the room.

"I guess I don't have to tell you what's going to happen here, Marlowe," Rudy said.

"Please do," I said, desperate to stall. I kept thinking of the gun jammed in my waistband, hoping I'd be able to make something better than a suicide grab for it.

"You were told to butt out of other people's business," Rudy began. "You didn't, stupid shit." He gave me a knowing smile. "And you found out about this place."

My face must have given my thoughts away because he continued, "Yeah, that's right. I recognized your ugly puss at the kitchen window when you were going out. And how's your buddy's ass, by the way? Get chewed up nice?"

Santa snickered. I noticed he wore gloves too.

"You won't have to worry about the dogs this time," Rudy said. "They ain't here. Only you'll be here when the action starts, tough guy."

His partner let out a cruel little laugh. The smirk on his ugly face matched his laugh perfectly.

"This is all about Jamaica, right?" I said.

Rudy guffawed. "Jamaica? Where's that?"

I gestured at the room I'd found the ham radio in; the door was closed. "They'll find the radio equipment." I glanced at the ceiling. "The antenna. They'll have questions. They'll put two and two together."

"Not too observant, are you, Marlowe? There's no antenna up there anymore and no radio in there." He pointed quickly at both locations.

"You're going to a lot of trouble just to get rid of me."

Rudy held the gun on me. "Not really. It's like getting two birds with one stone—you *and* any prints or other troublesome things we might unknowingly leave behind."

"So I'm right about Jamaica? This is all about some Jamaican connection."

"Shut up," Santa said, his voice deadly. "You're gonna get yours right now. What are we waiting for?"

"He's right, Marlowe," Rudy said, his eyes narrowing. "This isn't some cheap mystery novel where you ask us what's going on and we tell you just before the cavalry arrives." He gave me a mean little grin. "Nobody's coming to help you."

I had to keep trying to stall. What else could I do? "I don't know what you've already done and I don't care, but now you'll have a murder charge chasing you. You don't want that, do you?" I looked from one to the other and back again. It didn't seem to faze either of them. Matter of fact, they were both smirking.

"That I can answer, Marlowe," Rudy said. "In fact, I want to. There won't be a murder. You see...an angry arsonist will be found burned to death. Caught in his own fire. One of the cans must have had a tiny hole in it and gas leaked out on the floor." He nodded at Santa who picked up one of the gas cans by its handle, tilted it. I could see a small strip of gray duct tape. "We pull that tape off, gas leaks out. These arson investigators are good. They'll find it." His partner set the can back down.

"They won't believe it," I said in a higher voice than I'd meant to use. "Why would I do that?" I glanced at the gas cans.

"Because you've had a running beef with the owner's family," Rudy answered, a satisfied smile on his face. "Probably killed her, they say. Even used violence on her brother. Threatened to kill him, too. You being a junkie doesn't hurt either. Any way you look at it, you're a ready-made patsy, Marlowe."

My mouth was dry. The sound of the surf was very loud now. Could be the tide coming in. "Does Morris Kruel know about this?" I asked.

Rudy's free hand shot up, signaling his partner not to speak. "Like I said, this isn't some book or movie. You know enough already."

I had to keep trying to stall. As long as we were talking, I wasn't cooking. "I'm not going to just sit here while you light me on fire. And you can't tie me—arsonists don't tie themselves up. And if you knock me on the head, they'll find the wound no matter how bad I'm burned. You haven't thought it through, Rudy. You won't get away with it."

"We thought it through, Marlowe," Rudy said. "You haven't. You see we know about your nerve pills."

Not many people knew about the Xanax; at least I didn't think many did. "How...?"

Rudy interrupted. "It doesn't matter." I had to agree with him.

Rudy used his free hand to take an unlabeled vial from his pocket and held it up for me to see. "Again we get two birds with one stone—a way to knock you out now and the cops'll think you got sloppy and took a few too many of your nerve pills before you got here. 'Course, we'll still have to give you a little love tap. We can't wait for these to work." He jiggled the vial in his hand. "But with the pills in your system, some empty beer bottles around the floor of your car, the leaking gas can, they'll figure a drunken junkie like you fell and hit his head either before or after the fire started if they even notice it."

I stared at the vial and kept my mouth closed. I thought my jaw was as tight as an alligator's. I was about to be proven wrong.

"Pry his fuckin' mouth open," Rudy said.

Santa walked over, grabbed my face with gloved hands. I gagged at the stench of cigarette smoke and body odor. He tried to force my mouth open. I fought just as strongly to keep it closed. We struggled like this for a minute, my head thrashing back and forth.

"Get out of the way," Rudy growled. He stepped closer, pushed his partner aside, and placed the barrel of the gun against my head. "We can change the scenario to suicide if you want, Marlowe."

I opened my mouth. Rudy handed the gun to Santa who placed the barrel back against my head. Rudy opened the vial and dumped a generous amount of pills into my mouth. Looking down my nose, I could see the last one fall onto my tongue as he withdrew the vial from my mouth. They were the same Xanax as my prescription; I could tell by the look and taste. I choked trying to get them down, the gun still touching my temple. I couldn't be sure how many there were. It didn't seem like too many, but I gagged on them nonetheless.

Rudy walked to the kitchen, returned with a glass of water. He handed it to me. "Drink," he said. "Now."

I drank. I felt some of the pills getting unstuck from my throat and traveling free.

Rudy stepped back and looked at me like I was a painting in a museum. Santa still had the gun pressed against my head.

I jumped when one of the windows in the room exploded in a shower of glass and something large bounced off the floor. We all looked toward the window and the gun moved inches from my head. It must have been my survival instinct that caused my gaze to flick instantly right back to the two men in front of me.

I sprang up, and holding the water glass by its bottom, I slammed the glass into Santa's face. The glass shattered against his chin bone. He screamed and his free hand grabbed his face. Rudy stepped backward, his gaze going from the window to me to his partner's face and back again all in seconds.

Santa pulled his hand from his face. There was a deep cut on his chin. He looked at the blood on his hand, then me. He raised the gun over his head, took one step closer to me, and growled, "You mother..."

He must have forgotten about the broken glass in my hand. I lunged forward with the shard, aiming for no place in particular. I caught him in the throat. The jagged glass sank in like it was going into a giant marshmallow. He tried to scream; only a gurgle came out. I let the glass go and stumbled backwards, knocking the chair out of my way. Santa's eyes were as large as two manhole covers. The gun clattered to the floor. What was left of the glass protruded from his neck. His hands flew up and he grabbed the shard. He tried to speak, couldn't. He pulled the glass out in one bloody piece and dropped it to the floor. His hands covered the wound but I could see blood pumping out between his hairy fingers. It had a nice rhythm to it. I knew I had hit something vital—he knew it too. I could see the knowledge reflected in the horror on his face.

He looked at Rudy. Tried to say something again, but blood was all that came out. Rudy's face looked like he'd just donated all *his* blood to the Red Cross. I saw him glance at the gun on the floor but I had my .38 out now. He turned and ran for the door. I fired a shot at him. It splintered the door jamb above his head just as he passed though.

I ran after him but was pushed aside by Santa who must have been running dead; he just didn't know it yet. He went through the door after his partner. I followed. When Santa and I got to the driveway, their car was pulling away in a shower of gravel. I couldn't get a clear shot—Santa, with his cut throat, was in the way, chasing the car down the driveway and out onto the main road. It was a pitiful sight; I knew he wouldn't run far.

I went back into the house. That's when I heard someone come in behind me. I spun around. It was Hank Fuller. His eyes were wild and he had on his black beret.

"Dan, are you all right?"

Except for my heart pumping like a Texas oil well, I was and told him so.

Inside the main room, it looked like someone had tossed a can of red paint around. There were large splashes of blood everywhere. Hank gasped.

"Oh my God," he said. "I'll call the police."

"Yeah, you better," I answered. I watched as Hank reached for the phone, pressed buttons. I remembered something and added. "We won't be here when they get here, though."

He stopped punching buttons, held the phone away from his ear. "Why?"

"They shoved a bunch of tranquilizers down my throat. I don't think it was enough to kill me, but I'm not sure. You got to get me to Exeter Hospital."

Hank jabbed at the numbers a couple more times. After a few seconds he rattled off a shortened version of what had happened and where.

After he'd hung up the phone, he said, "Come on." He grabbed me by the arm and propelled me toward the door. Just before we went out, I looked at my hand. It was sticky with blood.

We took my car; the keys had been left in it. I shoved my gun under the seat. Hank drove what he must've thought was fast. It felt to me like we were almost going backwards.

On the way the pills began to hit me, pleasantly at first. My heart and breathing slowed and I began to relax. What had just happened back at the radio house was no big deal; about as serious as a winter cold.

That delusion didn't last long. By the time we reached the hospital, my brain had lost most of its IQ. "Juss pushh...car slotss...theeeer," I said, trying to point towards where I thought the parking area was. For some reason my arm wouldn't move; it was as heavy as a pullout couch. Through a fog I saw Hank scooting around the front of the car. He's coming to get me out, I thought.

That was the last thing I remembered until I awoke later in a hospital bed.

Chapter 26

THE FIRST THING I saw when I opened my eyes were my two favorite people staring down at me—Dianne and Shamrock. I forced myself to smile up at them. And not just because I was happy to see them, which I was, but I also wanted to relieve the concern I saw etched on both their faces. Dianne swallowed. I thought she was going to speak, but Shamrock beat her to it.

"You scared us this time, Danny. How are you feeling?"

"Thirsty, Shamrock." My mouth was as dry as a fisherman's hands in January. I hoped no one would get close to me. I was sure my breath couldn't be pleasant.

"I'll get it," Dianne said. She went to a little side table and poured water from a pink plastic pitcher into a matching glass. She didn't have to, but she put one hand behind my head, held the glass to my lips with the other. I drank. It felt awful good. The water and her hand.

When I had finished the glass, I pulled my head away.

"More?" Dianne asked. Her hair was down and I could tell she hadn't come from work. I didn't know about Shamrock—he was in his restaurant whites.

I shook my head, tried to sit up, and finally asked Shamrock to raise the back of the bed. He played with a small control panel and various parts of the bed moved. Finally he located the right button, raised the bed so I was sitting up.

"Tell us what happened, Danny," Shamrock said.

"Shamrock," Dianne said, "maybe he doesn't feel up to talking about it now." I could tell she hoped she was wrong.

"How long have I been here?" I asked, looking at one of those wall clocks that only hospitals and schools seem to have. It said 7:05. I wondered if it was a.m. or p.m.

"Since last night," Dianne said. She must have read my mind. She walked over to a window and opened the curtain. Sunlight poured in.

"So, tell us, Danny," Shamrock said again, "What happened?" There was apprehension in his voice and his brogue became thicker.

"Shamrock!" Dianne looked at him like she was a teacher and he was an unruly student.

I held up my hand, waved. "No, it's all right, Dianne."

She didn't argue. I knew she wouldn't. She wanted to know, too. And I had to tell them; we were all in this together.

I told them the whole story—about Rudy and Santa snatching me again and how they'd tried to burn me to a crisp at the ham radio house on Plaice Cove. How Hank Fuller had told me he'd seen my car, became suspicious, looked in the window and saw what was going on. How he'd lobbed a rock through the window just in time and how I'd taken advantage of the distraction and used a water glass on the bigger of the two goons.

I stopped the recital and looked from Dianne to Shamrock. "How is he, by the way? Santa? The one I cut with the glass?"

Shamrock looked at Dianne; she shrugged.

"We don't know, Danny," he said.

"I know," a voice bellowed from the open doorway.

It was Gant. He stepped into the room, Steve Moore coming in right behind him. A nurse dressed in blue scrubs followed Steve.

"You're awake, Mr. Marlowe. Too many people, though," she said. "You're not up to this yet, are you?"

I let out a sigh. I felt surprisingly good and told her so.

"Well, we evacuated your stomach," the nurse said, shaking her head as she spoke. "And the blood tests came back that the dose wasn't too high. Unless you hadn't made it here, then you would have had a problem. You should rest."

I knew I'd have to face Gant sooner or later; it really didn't matter which. In fact, I was anxious to get it over with. "I'd like to speak to these people," I said.

She looked around at all the faces in the room. "All right then...I guess. Not too many questions, officers. The man just came out of it."

"Mmm, sure," Gant said. Steve said nothing. Looked like he was calculating how long until his pension kicked in.

As soon as the nurse had left, Gant came right up to the bed, eyed Dianne and Shamrock. Then he looked at me. "Talk," he said. He glanced over his shoulder at Steve. "Notes."

Steve pulled out his famous notebook and pen. He must have gone through a lot of those notebooks since he'd met me.

I repeated the whole story again.

Surprisingly, Gant didn't interrupt, just listened. Steve scribbled.

When I was done, Gant frowned. "You're a lucky son of a bitch, Marlowe. If Henry Fuller hadn't backed up your self-defense alibi, I'd be taking you in for murder one right now."

I blinked, my mouth dropping open.

"Yeah, that's right," Gant said. "The guy you slashed with the glass made it almost a half mile down 1A before he collapsed in the street."

"Santo Gorrassi?" I asked.

Gant snorted. "That's him. After he went down, a truck ran over him. What's left of him isn't pretty."

Dianne gasped.

"The M.E. thinks he was dead before the truck hit him though," Gant continued. "He'll know for sure after the autopsy. But it looks so far like you killed him, Marlowe. And we'll see if Mr. Fuller's story holds water." He looked from Shamrock to Dianne, a satisfied expression on his face. "Seems everybody around you comes to a bad end."

I couldn't just sit there and let Gant try to hang another murder on me. "Those two came looking for me. They were going to burn me alive."

Gant's tone became fiery. "That's what you say. Sounds a bit melodramatic to me. You were told to stay out of police investigations and other people's business. You got more enemies now than a meter maid."

Now it was my turn to get fiery. Or at least as fiery as a man in a hospital bed who'd just had his stomach pumped and had awakened from a drugged stupor could be. "I had to get into it, Lieutenant. If I waited for you to solve Evelyn Kruel's murder, I'd be dead of old age."

"You piece a..." Gant began, then stopped himself. I could almost see him biting his tongue. "Bad enough you don't care about yourself or your family, Marlowe." He looked at Dianne and quickly back at me, scorn on his face. "You don't give a crap what happens to your so-called friends, either."

Before I could respond, Dianne jumped down his throat. "Look, Lieutenant Gant, you've got some nerve. Someone's been murdered on Hampton Beach. Dan's been trying to help find out who did it. Look what's happened to him because of it." She pointed a finger at me.

Gant looked at her. "Look, Miss, Mr. Marlowe here has been going around interfering in a police investigation. Not to mention he's been harassing citizens. He's been warned to cease and he continues to do it. He's got no one to blame but himself."

"You're the one who's been harassing him," Dianne said, her voice going up a couple of octaves. "You should be trying to find out about the people who want to hurt Dan and why." She glanced at me with pitying eyes. I didn't like that.

Gant's face turned red. "Look, I don't need any lessons about my job from a gin joint owner. And in regards to him..." he waved his thumb in my direction, "he's brought this all on himself."

"Danny didn't..." Shamrock began.

Gant cut him off. "No one's asking you, Kelly. Your hands are probably plenty dirty in this, too."

Dianne stepped up to Gant. She looked up at him; her pretty face inches from his. "You leave him alone. Who the hell are you to come into a hospital and bully people anyway?"

Gant stared at Dianne. His face looked as hard as a trigonometry test. "Where were you when Evelyn Kruel was murdered?" he asked.

I'd had enough. I leaned forward. "Get the hell out of here, Gant," I said. "Now."

Gant spun toward me. "You don't tell me anything, Marlowe. You killed a man. Maybe a fuckin' woman, too." He quickly looked at Dianne. "Excuse my French, but this boyfriend of yours seems to be connected to every major crime on the beach. And I'm going to get to the bottom of it all."

Steve finally spoke up. "This isn't getting us anywhere, Lieutenant. Why don't we talk to him later?"

Gant turned on Steve. "I've told you not to question me in public." Steve looked down at his notebook.

"I'm starting to wonder about you too," Gant added. "You may be a little *too* close to *Mr.* Marlowe." Then he glared around the room. "I may be visiting any of you at any time to ask questions. Don't think someone won't be keeping an eye on the bunch of you either."

I wondered if he was bluffing about that. The Hampton PD didn't have an abundance of manpower. More likely all he'd be able to muster was an occasional drive past our homes or the High Tide, just enough to keep us jittery.

"As for you, Marlowe," Gant's gaze lasered in on me. "Even if by some miracle you didn't have anything to do with the Kruel death, you'll still be looking at a nice assortment of charges you've racked up since." He gave me a smug look, turned, brushed Shamrock aside, and said to Steve, "Come on, we have work to do."

When they were gone, I eased myself back down on the pillows, let out a sigh. "Well that woke me up, that's for sure."

Shamrock forced a laugh; Dianne didn't.

"What the hell is the matter with that man?" she said, crossing her arms.

"He thinks I really did have something to do with Evelyn Kruel's murder," I said. I wasn't feeling top notch and that thought didn't help any.

"He's a crazy man," Dianne said. "Why would someone do *this* to you?" She uncrossed her arms and stretched them toward me, palms up. "Not to mention everything else that's happened?"

"The man just doesn't like you, Danny," Shamrock said. He furrowed his brow. "Or me either, I guess."

"I think he's in love with me," Dianne said.

We all laughed.

We went over what had happened, but got nowhere. Eventually, Dianne sighed. "I have to get to work. Shamrock's going to wait and see if they're going to let you out today. He'll drive you home in your car. Mr. Fuller left it." She stepped closer to my bed, took my hand.

Shamrock stood there looking at us, a smile as big as Ireland on his face. Then I could almost see the light bulb go off over his head. "Oh, yeah. I'll be right outside. I gotta find a coffee machine. You want one, Danny?"

I shook my head.

"Can you close the door, Shamrock?" Dianne said.

"Ahh, sure." A bit of red crept up his neck.

He marched out, pulling the door shut behind him. Dianne and I watched him go, then looked at each other. Dianne sat on the edge of the bed, leaned toward me, and rested her hands either side of my head. She tilted her head and looked at me like a nurse might have, although there was a little more to it than that. I could smell her perfume. I'd have to remember someday to ask her what kind it was. For now, I just considered it Dianne's scent.

"Don't come into work until you're feeling better, Mister," she whispered.

"I won't," I said, my voice cracking.

She lifted her right hand, ran it slowly through my hair, then brought her hand down against my cheek.

"That doesn't mean you should be out poking around either. You were lucky, Dan. If anything happened to you..."

"Nothing's going to happen," I said. I almost promised I wouldn't poke around anymore, but I couldn't. I think she knew that.

She got up, went to the door, turned the lock. She returned to the bed and sat down close to me. She placed both her hands back on the pillow beside my head now.

She stared into my eyes. I could see little flecks of gold in hers. Her hair swung down toward my face, her thigh pressed against mine.

I was breathing deeply now and I was coming alive. It would have been embarrassing if it was anyone but Dianne, knowing the sheet near my legs was slowly tenting. But it was Dianne, and I wasn't embarrassed and she wasn't either. Her left hand left the pillow, brushed my face, and moved to the sheet. She pulled it down to my knees. I had on only a white hospital johnny.

"Dianne, I can't." I was still not myself and this wasn't the time to make my hospital room *debut*. I didn't have to worry though; I wasn't going to have to do much of anything.

"I love you, Dan," she said so softly I think I just read her lips. She took her right hand off the pillow, began stroking the side of my face and my hair. Her other hand pulled the johnny up to my chest. No one would realize I wasn't feeling top shelf by what she found there.

I stared at her face, her tongue moistened her lips. Her hand on my face was as soft as a whisper and as arousing as a fetish. My eyes moved to half-mast as her hand ran gently up my thigh.

By the time she found what she was looking for, and had wrapped her hand around me like a velvet vice, all I could do was moan.

Chapter 27

IT WAS FORTUNATE I hadn't promised Dianne, or anyone for that matter, that I was going to stay out of the Evelyn Kruel affair because later that day I found myself jumping right back into it. I had way too much in the pot to fold now.

Shamrock had given me a ride home from the hospital in my car and walked home from there. I sat around for a bit. That lasted an hour or two before I started going stir-crazy. I didn't feel half-bad considering I'd almost been turned into a toasted human marshmallow, been stuffed full of tranquilizers, and had my stomach pumped all in the previous day. I decided to jump back into the fray. I didn't have the luxury of time to waste.

I hopped in the car and headed up Ocean Boulevard with Hampton center my destination. It was hot, the sun was out, and so were the tourists. They were on foot and in cars. I was distracted by a teeny bikini and had to stomp on the brakes just south of the Casino to miss hitting a family crossing the street. Parents and three small children headed for the beach. The father lugged a cart loaded with enough stuff for a weekend camping trip. They all jumped at the sound of my brakes. The father gave me a disgusted look, waved his hand, and yelled something I couldn't make out. He was right, of course. I felt like a jerk and mouthed an apology through the windshield. Then I forced my attention back to driving, determined not to hit any pedestrians during the journey.

When I reached the Kruel Building I wasn't as lucky as before in regards to parking. I had to park out back in the municipal lot and walk around the building to the front door. When I reached the second floor, I didn't knock, just opened the door and walked in. I was happy to see that Marcy Wade was sitting in the same spot she had been last time I'd seen her. She stopped typing and looked up at me. Her tan was darker than it had been.

"Mr. Marlowe," she said as if she wasn't really surprised to see me. "What do you want?"

I strutted right up to the desk, stood there looking down at her. Like I said before, she was a very attractive woman; she knew it too. If I hadn't been there for business, I might have...I might have nothing. I wasn't any good at that type of thing; besides I considered myself committed. So I shifted my mind back to the task at hand.

"Did you have a nice vacation, Marcy?" I asked.

I could detect just a touch of red creep into that bronze coloring. "My name is Ms. Wade. And that's none of your business, Mr. Marlowe." She spun her chair to face me. "Didn't I ask you to leave the last time you were here? Didn't I tell you I'd call the police?"

"Yeah, you said all that. Along with half the people on the beach." I sat down in the same chair I'd occupied last time.

"What do you think you're doing?"

"Getting comfortable for our conversation."

"We're not having any conversation." She grabbed the edge of her desk with hands that spent a lot of time in a nail spa.

The tan contrasted nicely with the gold rings she wore on each hand. "I *will* call the police, Mr. Marlowe. Don't think I won't."

"You and others have already cried wolf on that. It only works so many times."

She shook her head. The sun coming in the window behind her made the tint shift nicely even though her blonde hair was done up in a neat bun. "There's nothing I want to talk to you about."

"Oh, yes there is—Jamaica." I gave her my best phony smile. "Tell me about your vacation." I now had a good idea what was going on in Hampton Beach, at least part of it. How it all led to murder, I still had no idea. But if I splashed enough gas around, sooner or later someone's paranoia might ignite.

"I'm not telling you anything."

"You didn't stay long. An awful long way to go for such a short vacation."

She shifted in her seat. "It...it was a long weekend." Then she raised her voice. "And that's none of your concern either."

I forged ahead. "You've been there quite a few times on short visits," I bluffed even though I considered it a good guess. "They sound like business trips to me. Funny business, maybe?" I smirked.

It shook her. "I have no idea what you're talking about."

I leaned toward her and grabbed the edge of the desk. "What I'm talking about is a sweet little money-making operation, Marcy. One that was probably a pretty good thing until it got you mixed up in murder."

"Murder?" she croaked. Her tan paled three shades.

"Yes, murder." I leaned across the desk. Her perfume, different than Dianne's, smelled just as tempting.

She must have seen something in my eyes and decided to try to take advantage of it. She cleared her throat. "Dan, I honestly don't know what you're talking about."

Dan was it? "You don't?"

That was a mistake—I should have hit her with everything I knew right then. I'd thrown the ball back too quickly. This time when she spoke, the quiver was gone from her voice and her words were soft, low, and as hot as the soundtrack on a XXX movie.

"Dan, maybe we've gotten off on the wrong foot." She took her glasses off, placed them on the desk. She leaned back in her chair, placed her hands down low behind her back in a most un-secretarial way. "I know you're just trying to find out what happened to poor Evelyn," she continued. "But I'm struggling with it, too, and trying to straighten this business out for Evelyn's family now that she's gone. Maybe that's why I've been short with you." I was waiting for her to loosen her hair and shake it free. "Dan, I want to help you. Is there *anything* I can do," she breathed.

I gulped, cleared *my* throat, and squeaked out, "You can tell me who murdered Evelyn Kruel. Was it Artie Neal? Or her brother Morris? Or George Ransom? Or someone else? Or maybe you?"

The barrage of names threw her. She changed from being the most desirable woman in the world to an ax murderess within seconds. "Why you dirty little...you're accusing me of killing Evelyn?" She flew forward in her chair, again grabbing the edge of the desk. "You don't know what the hell you're talking about, buster. You're going to end up in a lot of trouble." Her face was as white as someone's could be with a tan like that.

"What about the others, Marcy? Maybe you were just in this to make some easy money. Now one of your accomplices has murdered somebody. You could end up doing life for that."

She jumped from her chair, shaking, almost hysterical. "How dare you. Get out of my office, you no good bastard. Now. Don't ever come back. If you do, I'll...I'll..." She looked half out of her mind. Her face was pinched and all screwed up. She certainly didn't look attractive anymore. "There's the door," she said, pointing. "Get out. Now!"

I got up and moved toward the door. I almost felt sorry for her. Almost. But I was more concerned about Dianne, Shamrock, and myself than Marcy Wade. I had to keep digging at her. As I stepped through the door, I turned. "The girls up at Goffstown will love seeing you brought in," I said, referring to the New Hampshire women's prison. "Some bull dyke'll be introducing you as her girlfriend within a week after you arrive."

Her eyes took on the look of an escaped mental patient, full of rage or fear or both. She grabbed a fistful of papers off the desk and threw them in my direction.

I closed the office door softly on my way out, just as she hurled a metal stapler at me. Her sobbing followed me down the stairs.

Chapter 28

BACK OUTSIDE in the municipal lot, I moved my car so I could keep a discreet eye on Marcy's car. Earlier I'd noticed the three parking spaces designated *Kruel Realty Trust*. Only one of those spaces was occupied, so I figured that had to be her car. I didn't have to wait long to find out I was right. Within a half hour she showed up, glanced around, and hopped into the car I'd been eyeballing. She took a right out of the lot. I let one car fall in behind her and then I pulled out. We didn't have far to go. After a couple of miles she reached the light at the real Plaice Cove. The same car was still between us. Her turn signal flashed left, and now I was sure where she was going. When the light turned green, our little parade resumed.

Sure enough, within a minute she pulled into Artie Neal's driveway. As I drove past I saw her car stop flush against the garage. I took the next left, a side street, and turned around at the head of the street. Both hands gripped the steering wheel as I stared down Ocean Boulevard in the direction of the talk show host's house.

I went over my options. I could sit here and watch. At least now I knew I'd hit a nerve and that she and Neal were involved together in shady dealings. If I did just plant myself and observe, that might be all I'd get out of my confrontation with Marcy Wade. That and a dollar would get me two hours of parking on Hampton Beach.

On the other hand, I seemed to be having good luck by going all in when I was holding nothing. These people were jittery. They all had something to hide. Confronted head-on, they might make mistakes. In fact, a couple of them already had. I stepped on the gas and pulled out onto Ocean Boulevard.

I wasn't shy. I pulled right into Artie Neal's driveway. It was all or nothing now. At the door, I pressed the bell, listened to the chimes play that tune I couldn't quite place. At first I thought he wasn't going to answer. So I gave the button a few rapid pokes, got the music dancing right along. Finally, Neal must have realized that ignoring me wouldn't make me go away.

The door opened and Artie Neal stood there, looking at me like I was a Jehovah's Witness. "You don't give up, do you, Marlowe?"

He had on a white terry cloth robe, cinched at the waist, with his initials stitched in blue on the right breast.

"I'd like to talk to you, Neal." I had no idea how he'd handle this but I was sure if he was squeaky clean, he'd give me the boot. He didn't.

"I'd like to talk to you, too." He turned and walked away from the door. I followed him into the great room with its huge fireplace. Marcy Wade was seated on a frail but expensive-looking straight-backed chair. Neal stood beside her. I took a seat in a fancy love seat directly across from them.

"I didn't say you could sit, Marlowe," Neal sputtered.

I ignored the comment. "What did you want to talk about?" I said.

Neal didn't answer my question directly. "Why don't you go first?"

We were locked in that childish game of who goes first. I stuck it out for a moment, then got sick of staring at Artie Neal, neither of us even blinking. "So you and Marcy are good friends?" I tipped my head at her.

Artie Neal's mouth hardened. "Ms. Wade is here because you've been harassing her, Marlowe. You've gone too far this time. You..."

I interrupted. "How well do you two know each other?" Marcy wasn't a good actress, she slithered around on the chair like it was a hot plate. The anger I'd seen just a short while ago at the office was gone, replaced by something resembling a panic attack—I was familiar with those.

"We're acquaintances, Marlowe," Neal said, anger in his voice. I couldn't tell how much of the anger was real or how much was a ploy intended to intimidate me. "That's none of your damn business, anyhow."

Marcy began to sob. Her head was down. I couldn't get a good look at her face, but I didn't think it was an act. Her emotions were volatile, that was for sure.

"Look what you've done now," Neal spouted. He leaned down to Marcy, put an arm around her shoulder. "Now, now, Ms. Wade. Everything will be all right. This *man* won't be bothering you anymore. Can I get you something to drink?"

She raised her head, shook it. Maybe I was wrong—I saw no tears. Her eyes were smudged, probably because her hand had been kneading them like she was working dough.

If this was some kind of acting call, I might as well audition, too. Marcy and Neal were such lousy actors, I might look good. Besides, I'd decided to stick to my aggressive tactics. "I know all about Jamaica, Neal."

Neal looked at me, his black eyes dead as coal eyes on a snowman. Marcy shook Neal's arm off her shoulder and sobbed again into her hands.

Neal stood straight, looking at me. He wasn't an actor, but he *was* one arrogant son of a bitch. He walked toward me, pointing his soft chin in my direction. "I'll sue you, Marlowe. I'll have you in court so much you'll have to rent a seat. I don't think it'll take too much to break a loser like you. And that won't be all. I've got very good connections in the law enforcement field. I'm sure someone like *you* has a lot to hide." The smirk on his face made him more unattractive than he already was. "I'll have you either in jail, or maybe on the dole where you belong with the rest of the welfare cheats and moochers."

"And their *tiny bastards?"* I said. Neal looked like if he'd had a gun he would have shot me.

I hadn't liked this guy even before I'd suspected he was involved in murder. He was a human waste product who made big money by fanning the flames of bigotry. How much he actually believed of the poison he spewed out on the airwaves, I'd never been sure. Now I knew—not only was he getting rich off of intolerance, the warped ideas were his own. The man had two big reasons to convert people to his way of thinking —money and he was a true believer. Unfortunately, he had a powerful media outlet he could use to spread his garbage. *That* made Artie Neal not only a grave danger to my children and everyone I loved but to my country as well. There was no way I was going to let someone like him intimidate me.

"You're forgetting a couple of things, Neal," I began. Marcy looked up. "I've got nothing to lose. You're not going to get blood from a stone. And as far as any crooked cop friends you might have, I've already got a murder frame around me. So I'm not too worried about what else can be cooked up."

"What about your family, Marlowe? They got anything to lose?"

I was out of my seat faster than a used car salesman behind on his bills. Marcy gasped. Neal stumbled back toward the large fireplace. His demeanor had changed instantly.

"You're threatening my family, Neal?" I said. My voice shook but it wasn't from fear. By the look on Neal's face he knew he'd gone too far. He glanced at a stand holding fireplace tools.

I stepped closer to him, hoping he'd go for it. He moved quickly for an out-of-shape dough boy. But my exercise regimen paid off—I was faster. He'd just gotten his soft little hand around the gold handle of a fireplace poker when I grabbed the front of his robe and pulled him toward me, poker still in his hand.

I cocked my right fist and drove it into his cheek as I held the robe tight in my other hand. His body rocked back but I didn't let him go. Marcy screamed and the poker clattered on the hardwood floor. I breathed heavily, studying Neal's face. A look of terror settled in his eyes and he whimpered like a child. His hands went up, trying to shield his face.

I let him have another right to the face, harder than the first. This time I let go of his robe the moment the blow landed. Neal went backwards, flailing his arms like a comic doing a pratfall. He fell into the fireplace, banged his head hard on the top bricks, and collapsed against its inner wall. A cloud of soot and dust puffed out into the room.

He wasn't out cold, but you wouldn't know that by the way he sat, like a Calcutta street beggar, his arms and legs spread out and useless. Blood gushed from his nose and there was damage to the side of his face; time would tell how much. He was lucky his show wasn't televised. He'd either have to take some time off or hire a top-notch makeup person. Neal wouldn't like that; he was known as being the cheapest talk show host in Boston.

I waited for him to say something. He tried. All that came out were unintelligible words and lots of blood. I turned to Marcy. I didn't have to wonder if she was acting now. She glanced back and forth between me and Neal, apparently in shock.

Neal rubbed his face, smearing it with soot and blood. He looked like a drunken Indian on the warpath.

"If anything happens to my family," I began so calmly I surprised myself. "I'll assume you were behind it, Neal. *And* I will kill you." I stared at him another minute, made sure the threat sank in. By the look on his face, I knew it had.

It was time to leave. I couldn't accomplish anything else.

"Don't bother getting up," I snarled at Neal. "I'll let myself out."

On the drive along Ocean Boulevard back toward the beach, I didn't bother dwelling on what I might have learned in this confrontation. Right now, I didn't care. I felt damn good about what I'd done. A lot more pleased with myself than I'd been in a long time. If anybody in the world deserved to end up sitting inside a dirty fireplace with his face rearranged, it was Artie Neal. And I'd done it.

Even so, I couldn't ignore the threat to my family. Whether he'd meant it or not, I couldn't be sure, but I had to assume that he did. I hoped he felt the same about my threat. Because I did mean what I'd said and Artie Neal could take that to the bank.

Chapter 29

THE NEXT DAY was the last Saturday in June. The tourist season was off to the races. It was also the one weekend a month I was supposed to have my children. They loved Hampton Beach and missed it. Now they would have to get used to spending the summer in a sweltering Massachusetts suburb. We all used to spend the entire season at the beach as a family, but since the separation and divorce, my kids were only allowed to stay with me a few weekends during the good weather. That wasn't long on the seacoast—maybe the end of June until Labor Day. Most beach attractions were only open during that ten-week summer time frame. So this was the perfect time for them to visit, and I knew they were looking forward to their first weekend of the summer on the beach.

That's why it broke my heart when I had to tell their mother that I couldn't let them stay overnight. There was no question in my mind that the situation was way too dangerous for that. I'd already had more guns pointed at me this month than Bonnie and Clyde on their last day alive. I couldn't risk anything happening to my kids. Ever.

Sandy, my ex-wife, wasn't happy when I told her a rabid raccoon had come down the chimney and contaminated the kids' beds before I returned from work and chased the animal out the door. It would take a week to get the mattresses disinfected. Even though the story had actually happened to a friend and sounded believable to me, I don't think she believed it. She hadn't believed much of what I'd said for a long time now. I didn't blame her. Finally, we agreed that I would just take them for the day. That should be safe.

I left early to pick up the kids so I didn't get caught in any traffic on the way back. We made the trip in good time. It was about ten a.m. and there was very little traffic as we came abreast of the nuclear power plant.

"Hiii, Hampton," David singsonged from the backseat as we crossed the Hampton Bridge.

"That's so weird," Jessica said. "Talking to a beach."

I glanced over at my daughter sitting beside me on the passenger seat. She looked over her shoulder at her brother seated behind me. Her nose crinkled. She was thirteen, only two years older than her brother, but in her eyes the age difference was probably as great as that between an infant and a nursing home resident.

She was a very pretty girl, tall and still gangly, with long straight black hair and a complexion that tanned easily in the summer sun. People said she looked like me. I hoped that was the only trait of mine she inherited.

David was shorter than his sister, but I knew somewhere along the line he would pass her in height and end up looking down on her. His blonde hair was cut short for the summer. He resembled his mother. That was a good thing.

"*You* used to say that every year too," I said to her. "And 'Bye Hampton,' when we left."

She looked over at me like I was not too bright. "Dad, I was a kid then."

I almost reminded her that was just a year or two ago, but I held my tongue. I missed them both badly and didn't want anything to upset the short time we had together.

Within minutes I'd pulled the car into the cottage driveway and we all hopped out. David ran ahead, leaping up onto the porch.

"Come on, Jess, hurry up," he said. "I want to see what the raccoon did."

Jessica looked at me, rolled her eyes. "He's such a child," she said.

I said, "Come on. Let's just have fun."

Jessica and I walked up the stairs to the porch and followed David into the cottage. He dashed into one bedroom and then the next, staring at the beds I'd stripped. "I don't see anything," he said.

"Well," I began, "we have to get the mattresses cleaned just in case he got in the beds."

"Gross," Jessica said. She didn't look in either bedroom.

I didn't want my little fib to turn against me and scare them away from future visits. "I don't think he went in your rooms. It's just a precaution."

"How come you can sleep in your room?" David asked.

My son was sharp. Fortunately, I was for once too. "Oh, my door had been closed. He couldn't have gotten in there. I'd left your doors open to air the rooms out."

To get off the uncomfortable subject, I changed it. "How about we go down to the beach?" It was a perfect beach day and I was hoping to be surprised. I wasn't.

David said, "No, let's go to the Casino."

I'd known he would want to go uptown first and hit every arcade on Ocean Boulevard. That was always a priority with kids his age. I didn't know about Jessica though.

I *was* surprised—and happy I guess—to hear her join right in. "Okay, come on." She was already heading out the door. Apparently she hadn't outgrown everything.

The three of us began the march up Ocean Boulevard. We'd gone this route more times than the mailman. I tried to bring up a few old memories as we passed the different venues— like the giant pirate at Buc's Lagoon Miniature Golf—but even David wasn't interested. The years had slipped by, and the kids had changed more than just a bit. Instead of moving along at a snail's pace with two little toddlers, I actually had to work to keep up with them. Arcades are like magnets to kids. Expensive magnets.

When we reached the first of the arcades, Funarama, located on the south end of the two-block long Casino building, I followed the kids inside as they made a dash for the machine that changed paper into coins. I slipped in two fives and gave each a handful of quarters, not that the money would last long. When they were very young, I could fool them into thinking that they were actually operating the game without putting in a cent. That honeymoon only lasted a year or two. Now they burned through the quarters faster than a five-alarm fire would burn through the century-old wood building we were in.

I could remember a time when I'd led them around at a slow pace from game to game. Now I had to race as they led me on a whirlwind tour of the premises. It was a tour I didn't really need—I'd been a regular at this arcade back when I was their ages and younger.

When the kids had finally donated all their quarters, I used lunchtime as an excuse to get us out of there.

As we walked down the steps of the Casino onto F Street, I said, "How about we go to the High Tide?" I figured there'd be no objection; they both had always loved the Tide and it *was* the best restaurant on the beach.

I was surprised when Jessica answered, "No, not there." Her tone seemed angry.

"I thought you liked the Tide, Jess?"

"Not really."

Why the change? I must have been dumb or naive. More likely both. We walked along Ocean, me on the outside, Jessica beside me, David beside her. We had to part every so often to let people by.

"Where then?" I asked.

"I don't care," she answered.

"What are you angry about?"

"Nothing."

"Davey," I said. "Where do you want to go?"

"The High Tide." He looked around his sister at me. "Do they still have the BLT's, Dad? And the spicy french fries?"

I smiled. "Yup, they got 'em both."

He beamed back at me. "Guillermo makes the best BLT's."

I looked at Jessica. I was less than a head taller than she was. She wasn't filled out yet, though. She was still a beanpole. An awfully pretty beanpole.

"What do you think?" I asked.

"Oh, all right," she said as if she were agreeing to go to summer school.

At the High Tide one of the waitresses greeted us at the door. She sat us at a booth in the dining area beside the fish tank. The aquarium had been replaced and was well stocked again. David started pointing at the various creatures inside.

"It's just fish, David," Jessica said. "Haven't you ever seen fish before? Jeez."

I opened up a menu. Just for something to do, I guess. I knew it by heart. The thing rarely changed. Only occasionally when Dianne, or myself before her, had been forced to raise prices because of increased operating costs. Jessica had her menu open as well, though she was spending more time watching the fish than looking at the menu. I smiled.

When the waitress came over, my son cut our chitchat short. "I'll have a BLT toasted with mayonnaise and crispy bacon. Can I get those spicy curly french fries, too, please?"

"You sure can, honey," the waitress said as she chuckled. "Jess, what can I get you?"

"Hmm, I guess a clam roll," she said. If I hadn't known how much she loved the Tide's clam rolls, I would've thought she was just going to give them a try.

"Spicy french fries?" the waitress asked.

"Oh, yes, please," Jess exclaimed, then caught herself. "I guess that'll be okay."

"Two cokes?" the waitress asked. She received two nods.

I gave her my order and she left.

The waitress had only been gone a minute when I heard a booming voice.

"Ahh, for the love of all that's holy. Look who's here." Shamrock came striding up to our booth from the direction of the kitchen. "And look how big everyone's gotten."

Two young faces smiled up at him, a blush on both of them. "Hi, Shamrock," they said in unison. The "Mr. Kelly" had been dropped years ago.

"And, Danny," he said, winking at me, then looking back at the kids. "Everyone's getting so old. Thank goodness we aren't aging a day."

"You're still the prettiest lassie on the beach, Jess," Shamrock said, continuing with the blarney. Her face turned crimson, but her smile was brighter than the lighthouse on the Isle of Shoals.

"And you, Davey." Shamrock pointed a finger toward him. "You've gotten so big. You must be playing football, I'd say."

David shook his head. "No, Shamrock. Baseball."

"Baseball? Now that's my favorite sport, after soccer, of course. What position?"

"Shortstop."

"Whoa," Shamrock said. "That's a hot position. Lot of balls hit there. You must be pretty good to play that position."

My son's face beamed like an airport beacon.

"What are you getting to eat?" Shamrock asked. And before they could answer, Shamrock held up his hand, then put his forefinger on his temple. "Ahh." Then he pointed his finger at my boy. "BLT, I'll bet."

David's head bobbed up and down.

Shamrock turned to Jessica. "Clam roll," he said.

She nodded, smiling.

"And you're both having the High Tide's famous spicy curly french fries. Am I right?"

David gave a thumb's up. Shamrock had a good memory; in fact, his memory was uncanny sometimes. Still, I figured he'd grabbed a quick peek at our slip hanging over the speed table on his way out of the kitchen.

The waitress returned with our drinks, placed them in front of us, and hurried off.

Just then Dianne came through the swinging kitchen doors. She had on a white apron over a print blouse, the apron folded in half at her waist, and jeans. Her hair was up and she wore no makeup. She headed right for us.

"Hi, everybody," she said when she reached the booth. She was smiling, but seemed a touch uncomfortable.

"Hi," David said, smiling.

Jessica played with the straw in her coke, studying the liquid patterns she was making. She didn't say anything.

"You guys remember Dianne," I said. David nodded; he was still smiling. He tried to look around Dianne and Shamrock, probably wondering where his BLT and spicy french fries were.

"Jess, are you going to say hi to Dianne?" I said.

"Hi." It came out as reluctantly as information from a mafia member.

Shamrock cleared his throat. "Well, I better get back to work or the boss'll get mad," he joked uneasily. He looked at Dianne and forced a little chuckle. She gave him a small grin. "Bye, kids. You have fun and don't eat too many spicy fries." He turned and walked quickly away, escaping back into the kitchen.

"Are you guys staying on the beach for a while?" Dianne asked.

"No," David answered. "We have to go home today."

"Oh," Dianne said. "That's too bad."

"Mmmm," came from Jessica.

Dianne snuck a look at me, grimaced. I raised my eyebrows. She tried again. "I bet you've already been to the arcade."

"Yep," David said. "Funarama." He pulled a long strip of tickets he'd won from his pocket and held them up for Dianne to examine.

"What did you play?" she asked.

He rattled off a list of games that apparently meant nothing to Dianne. She had no children and probably hadn't seen the inside of an arcade in decades.

"What about you, Jess? Did you play the same things?"

"I don't *play* anything," she answered, none too politely.

"Jess," I said.

Dianne looked at me, frowned. Her lips were tight. Then she tried once more. "What do you think of our fish?"

David's finger pointed up toward the aquarium. "What kind is that big black one?"

Dianne had a puzzled look on her face. "I don't know. We just got him. I'll find out for you, though." She hesitated, then added, "Do you want to name him."

"Okay," he answered. His light-colored brows furrowed and he studied the fish. Finally he said, "How about Blackie?"

"That's very good," Dianne said. "Fits him perfectly. Blackie it is." Then turning to Jess, she asked, "Want to name one, Jess?"

"No, thank you," she answered, making a face like she'd just graduated from finishing school. "I'm thirteen."

A little color crept into Dianne's face. She looked as uncomfortable as a bookie at a tax audit. I almost scolded Jess but held back for fear of making Dianne feel worse.

We were both rescued from the situation when the waitress came up with our meals on a huge tray that she set down on a small folding table.

Dianne used this opportunity to retreat. I couldn't blame her.

"Okay," she said. "I'm going to let you guys enjoy your lunch. Bye, Dan." She looked at David. "Bye, Davey. It was nice seeing you."

"Bye, Dianne," he said happily, not taking his eyes off his BLT.

"Goodbye, Jess," Dianne said, putting a lot of warmth into it. "It was nice seeing you, too."

"Goodbye." There was enough warmth in her response to freeze the ocean.

Dianne glanced at me before she walked away; I felt as bad as she looked.

We ate our lunch. I tried to keep everything on a happy note. For David it wasn't necessary; he was happy as a clam. For my daughter and myself it didn't do much good.

The rest of the day went like that. I tried to make the best of it. Of course, I knew what the problem was. I wasn't *that* naive or dumb. The kids knew about Dianne and me, probably from their mother. Jessica obviously wasn't happy about it. I couldn't fault Sandy though. It was no longer a secret and I would have had to tell them sooner or later. I really had no one to blame but myself. I probably should have been the one to tell the kids about Dianne.

I wanted to talk to Jessica about it, but I couldn't get her alone without shunting off her brother, which I couldn't do. There just wasn't enough time on this visit. I'd have to make time, though, and soon.

Chapter 30

IT WASN'T SURPRISING that after taking the kids home, I got back to the beach in a foul mood. My mood didn't improve any when I saw a car parked on the street in front of my cottage. I pulled up beside it, took a gander. A blind man would have recognized it as a cop car. The sun was just setting, so there was still plenty of light to study the dark-colored, full-size Ford, black wall tires, and pencil-thin antenna that stuck up about six inches on the trunk. The car had Massachusetts tags.

I pulled into the driveway. I could see someone up on the porch before I even got out of the car. He was sitting on one of the twin rocking chairs, rocking slowly back and forth. His head was turned in my direction.

I walked to the porch stairs, stopped, looked up at him. Though I still thought it was a cop car parked out front, I wasn't one hundred percent certain. "Can I help you?"

"Can we talk up here?" the man said. He leaned forward in the rocker, arms resting on the porch railing, looking down at me.

That didn't reassure me at all. "About what?"

He scanned the area. There were a few people walking by on the street, no one close enough to notice us. He removed a wallet, opened it, and flashed a badge. He hung his arm over

the railing so I could get a better look at it. I took a step closer
and squinted at the badge.

"I'm Bob Whitney, Special Agent with the DEA."

This information didn't make me feel any better; in fact, it
made me feel worse. I trudged up the stairs and looked down
at him. He was young, mid-thirties maybe. He also looked
like the government gave him a free gym membership as a
perk. Either that or he was helping himself to government-
seized steroids. His arms stretched the fabric of what even I
could tell was a very expensive brown leather jacket. His legs
did the same to his designer jeans. His straight brown hair
was stylishly long. His face reminded me of a cocky college
star quarterback. He certainly wasn't pretending to be a street
corner dealer. He looked like he'd fit quite comfortably in a
yuppie joint on Newbury Street.

He leaned toward me, extended his hand. I shook it.

"Can we talk?" he asked again, nodding toward the rocker
beside him.

"I have to use the head first." I took out the key, unlocked
the door. "Beer? Something else to drink?" I asked.

"Sure. A beer would be nice." He smiled, showing a set of
perfect white choppers.

I took a leak, returned with two Heinekens and one frosted
glass. I sat in the vacant rocking chair, set the beers and glass
on the white plastic table between us.

"Glass?" I asked.

When he shook his head, I took the glass and emptied a
bottle into it. I made my trademark foamy head and took a
drink that drained almost half the glass. He took one small sip
from his bottle, watching me as he did so.

"This is a beautiful location you have here." He nodded
toward the sand dunes.

He was right, but it was the last thing I felt like talking about now. "Mmm. What's this all about, Agent?"

"Call me Bob, Mr. Marlowe." He shifted in the rocker. His leather jacket opened a bit and I could see a weapon on his hip.

"Okay, Bob. And I'm Dan. Now what's this all about?" I wanted to get this over with quick. I wasn't anxious to have a long discussion with an uninvited visitor. Especially one who was a federal drug agent.

He set his green beer bottle on the table beside my half-full glass. "Want to get right into it, huh? Okay. That's fine." His face took on the look of a surgeon coming into the visitor's room after losing a patient on the operating table. "We've come across some unpleasant information about you and your friends." I expected him to say that he knew I was the modern-day *French Connection*—that was about all I hadn't been accused of lately. But that would have made him Gene Hackman and he certainly didn't look like Popeye Doyle.

"There have been some physical threats made against you." He stopped, waited for my reaction.

"I know that." Was he here just to tell me something I already knew?

"Do you know about a professional hit?" He studied me with the same look that Madame Stella, the fortune teller up on the strip, used with her customers.

"A hit?" I croaked. Suddenly, being accused of international heroin dealing seemed not so bad. I cleared my throat. "On me?" I asked stupidly.

"That's right," he said. "There's going to be another attempt on your life. But this time, *you*," he continued, pointing a finger at me, "have a little breathing room. It seems they're going to come at you from a different direction this time. Hurt one or two of your associates. Give that a shot first. If that doesn't get you off their backs, they've got someone from Boston all lined up to do the heavy work."

I didn't like that word—associates. There was something about it. Somehow it made me sound like I was The Man in regards to everything that went wrong on Hampton Beach. From rainy days to dead bodies.

"What associates?" I asked, even though I was sure I knew the answer.

I watched as he took out a pocket notebook, flipped through some pages.

"Dianne Dennison and Michael Kelly."

My stomach sank like an anchor. My anxiety skyrocketed. "You've got to be kidding," I said. Of course, I knew he wasn't. I reached for my beer. Killed it.

"It's no joke, Mr...Dan. This is as serious as a head-on collision."

I wasn't surprised by any of this; not with what had been going on lately. Still, a hired hit man? That seemed to make the situation a lot more serious. And, again, Dianne and Shamrock were in the mix. Because of me. My heart sped up in a raggedy fashion that was very unpleasant. My mouth was drier than an old Yankee's martini. The porch decking beneath my feet felt like the boards had suddenly turned to pulp. I thought about my pills in the cottage and wondered how I could get to them.

"How do you know this?" I asked. My voice sounded like I'd just developed Tourette's. I was sure the fed must have noticed it.

He just shook his head. "I'm not allowed to tell you that. Only about the threats. We feel they are real and that you should take them very seriously."

I didn't need him to tell me that last part; my nervous system told me I was taking the threats very seriously. My heart, breathing, and mind all raced like an out-of-control freight train.

"Have you told Sham...Michael and Dianne yet?"

"We just found out. You're the first one we've told."

"What's behind all this?" Even though I already knew some of what was going on, I was anxious to pick his brain.

He lifted his beer, took another small sip, and set it back down. "I can tell you some of what we know, Dan. Not all of it. A government investigation is involved."

I wanted to get up, get another beer, a pill. I struggled to stay seated, to not move, and waited for him to continue.

"We've been investigating drug smuggling along the New Hampshire seacoast for a while now. One organization in particular. They're real scumbags, vicious. More so than your average smuggling gang. We think they've been involved in killings. That's why I'd take this threat very seriously if I were you."

I flashed on the bales of pot that had washed up on shore. Still, I had to make sure. "What kind of smuggling?" I asked.

"Marijuana. Large loads. But they rarely make a trip without bringing along a significant amount of cocaine, too. We've only been able to move up the ladder so far...then that's it." He held his hands up like *he* was getting arrested for a change. "We've had more than one confidential informant turn up dead during this investigation. I can tell you that." He hesitated, then continued. "That's what I'd like to talk to you about."

"Dead informants?" I asked. Now my voice sounded like I was impersonating Mike Tyson.

Whitney seemed not to notice. He smiled. "No," he said, shaking his head. "I want your help."

"I thought you wanted to talk about the threats," I interrupted.

"I did," he said. "And we will some more. Along with precautions that can be taken. Things like that. But I also wanted to ask you what you might know about this organization?"

I knew next to nothing about any current drug smuggling organizations. At least I didn't think I did. Certainly less than the DEA, so I didn't feel like I was lying when I answered. "I don't know anything about any organizations. Maybe the Chamber of Commerce, that's about it."

Agent Whitney chuckled. "Very funny, Dan. But you must know something." He looked at me with a conspiratorial expression. "I have contacts on the Hampton police force. They've told me what's been going on with you. What you've been involved in. I think, whether you know it or not, you've stumbled across the people we've been trying to identify for quite a while now."

I wasn't sure who the hell he meant. Artie Neal, Marcy Wade, Morris Kruel, George Ransom, Rudy? How many of them could be involved in this? And a contract hit? "What do you want from me?" I asked.

He shifted in the rocker. "First off, I'd like to know everyone you've approached concerning this..." he hesitated, looked down at the notebook still in his hand, "Evelyn Kruel homicide." He leaned back and stared hard at me.

I didn't feel like I was doing anything wrong in telling him what I knew about a woman's murder. What I knew was just a bunch of speculation anyway. So I told him. Everything I knew. He bent over his little notebook, jotted it all down.

"Tell me everything you said to them and what they replied," he commanded.

I told him all that too. As best as I could recall.

When I was done, he sat back and stared at me.

My nerves were like sparking wires and I couldn't stand it another minute. "Another beer?"

He shook his head. "Get one if you want."

I did. But first I headed for the bedroom, popped a Xanax under my tongue, tasted it as it dissolved. I needed that pill, badly. And not just because of the news that there might be a hit out on me. Or the fact that there was a federal drug agent perched ominously in my front porch rocking chair. Sure all that was enough to make any man nervous, but I'd also recently had more trouble than a drunken tourist after dark in Tijuana. I'd held all that upset in, let it build. Not good. Anxiety can be like a glass of water—the glass can only be filled so much before it overflows. That's when a full-blown panic attack can occur. Right now, my glass of anxiety was spilling freely over the top.

I grabbed a beer, returned to my chair on the porch. I didn't bother with the glass. I hoisted the bottle to my lips and drained half in one swig. That seemed to be becoming a habit lately.

Whitney was scanning his notes; I didn't interrupt him. We were both quiet for a bit.

He finally looked up and put the notebook in the outside pocket of his coat. "All right," he said. "I'm going to make you a proposition. We give you something, you give us something. We can offer you and your two friends protection from these threats I've told you about."

"I like that," I said. "But what's the other part of the proposition?"

"The other part," he said, cocking his head, looking at me from an angle, "is the drug smuggling investigation I told you about. We'd like your assistance."

"That part I don't like so much," I said. My voice seemed steadier—Xanax under the tongue works quickly.

"You working with us is a lot better than what might happen to you and your friends if you don't agree to help," he said. "You, and your friends, will be protected at all times."

I didn't want to assist anybody on any drug investigation. Didn't believe in it. Still, I had Dianne and Shamrock to think about. "What exactly do you want me to do?"

"All right," he said, rubbing his hands on his thighs. "I can't tell you everything about the investigation but this I can tell you—the group I'm talking about got a big shipment of weed and coke a while back. Because of some problems, maybe heat or something or other, they've been unable to sell the stuff yet. Maybe your enquiries had something to do with it. Maybe you spooked them. Anyway, we believe the stash is hidden somewhere on the seacoast. They've been too paranoid to move it. That much we know for sure—the delivery came in and some of their regular distributors are still dry. So the shipment has got to be stored somewhere around here. We want to find out exactly where it is."

"How the hell can I do that?"

"We've got some ideas."

"That's it? You want me to find out where a load of pot and coke is located? Even when the federal government can't find it?"

He grimaced. "That's not all. We'd like to wire you up and get something incriminating on someone."

The idea shocked and repelled me. But I had to ask, "Who?"

"I can tell you that when you agree."

Find out for the cops where a shipment of drugs was stored? *And* wear a wire to record someone admitting to drug crimes? There was only one word to describe that job description—RAT. I didn't even know if these "people" were the same ones threatening Shamrock, Dianne, and me. Who knew if these threats Whitney spoke about were even real? Everyone knew some federal agents were as trustworthy as a street vendor in New York.

I shook my head.

He looked at me like I'd just lost thirty IQ points. "What do you mean?"

"I'm not interested. That's what I mean."

He pulled himself up in the rocker, leaned toward me. He was big and I could smell the beer on his breath. "These fucking people are trying to kill you and your friends, Marlowe. Don't be stupid."

He wasn't intimidating me. The pill had kicked in and I felt reasonably calm.

"I'll take my chances."

"What about your friends? What about them? Don't you care about them?"

"I'll warn them."

He looked at me, his head cocked. "I get it. You think you're too good to work with me. You don't know me. You don't trust me. I bet if it was Steve Moore sitting here, you'd be fine with it. Am I right? What if I got him to tell you I was okay? Would that make a difference?"

I didn't answer him. How well did this man actually know Steve? More importantly—how well did Steve know him?

"We could get you out of the other problem you got, too. You know the one where you could end up in Concord State Prison wearing a dress and lipstick for the Evelyn Kruel homicide."

He looked at me, waiting for a reaction. When he didn't get one, he stood up and stared down at me. "You're being stupid." He pulled a card out of his pants ass pocket. Flipped it baseball-card style onto my lap. "When you smarten up, give me a call." He turned and stomped down the stairs. I watched as he walked out on to the street and headed for his car. I heard the car door slam, the car start and pull away. I listened until the sound disappeared somewhere on its way to Ocean Boulevard.

I sat there for a long moment. I had a lot to think about. I had to tell Shamrock and Dianne about the threats. I glanced through the window at the anchor clock on the wall. The Tide would be in full swing; Dianne wouldn't have time to talk now. Neither would Shamrock if he was there. Either there or at the Shillelagh, too far in his cups by now to appreciate the importance of what I had to tell him. I decided to wait until first thing tomorrow morning to tell them both.

Chapter 31

THE PHONE WOKE me from a half-sleep. I eyed the illu-minated clock on the table beside my bed—3:05 a.m. My first thought was—the kids. Something happened to one of my kids. I threw the sheet off and flicked the wall switch on as I stumbled through the doorway into the living room. The bed-room light was strong enough I could see where I was going without killing myself.

I answered the phone on what I thought was the third or fourth ring. "Hello?" My throat felt like a chunk of cement was lodged in it.

"Dan?" It was Dianne and she was speaking very softly. "Can you come up here? Please?"

"What's wrong?" The chunk of cement broke into pieces.

"Just come, Dan."

"Are you all right?"

She didn't answer; I heard her sob instead.

"Where are you?"

"At the condo."

"I'm on my way."

Before I could hang up she said, "Come by yourself, Dan."

I don't know who she thought I'd bring. "All right."

I hung up the phone, ran back into the bedroom, and changed clothes faster than a runway model. I didn't have time for niceties like hair combing, so I threw a Red Sox cap on instead. I did have time for one thing though—my revolver. I didn't like the sound of Dianne's last words, "Come by yourself, Dan." Maybe someone was with her. If someone was, he wouldn't be one of the good guys. I spun the chamber, made sure the revolver was loaded. I stuck the gun in the back of my waistband, pulled my shirttail down over it, and raced out of the cottage, headed for my car.

Dianne lived on the second floor of an oceanfront condominium complex on Ocean Boulevard, almost halfway between the Ashworth Hotel and Boar's Head. The strip was deserted— even the twenty-something drinking crowd that closes the bars was long gone. I reached Dianne's place in minutes.

I parked in the tiny municipal lot across from her building, sliding into the closest spot open even though it had a reserved sign on it.

Hurrying across the street, I heard my name. I looked up and saw Dianne on her balcony. She looked down at me. "I'll buzz you in."

I didn't say anything, just raced for the door. The buzzer was already sounding when I came through the outer door. I went through the second door and took the steps two at a time. I came around the top railing, took a few steps toward Dianne's door. I stopped, felt for the gun in my back; it was still there. The door opened. It was dark inside and I didn't see anyone.

I took a deep breath and stepped inside. "Dianne?" There was only a small nightlight on in the kitchen. It wasn't enough to illuminate the whole living area. My eyes would have to adjust.

The door behind me began to close, startling me. My hand went instinctively for the gun, though I didn't pull it out. It was Dianne. She was wearing jeans and a plain blouse—her work clothes. Her back was to me and she was using both hands to gently close the door. When she had, she snapped the deadbolt into place.

"Are you all right?" I asked.

In the dim light I could see her shoulders rising and falling.

"Dianne!" I stepped up to her, grabbed her upper arms. "What's wrong?" I tried to keep the wave of anxiety rising in me from turning into a tsunami. Her shoulders heaved under my hands.

I turned her around toward me. She kept her head down, her long hair covering her face. I gently pushed her back a pace, trying to get a glimpse of her face. Bile in my throat.

I flicked on a light switch. The lights over the dining table popped on, lighting the whole area. "Look at me."

She did, but her face came up as slow as a rising sun. I took my hands and tried to brush her hair aside. She winced and pushed my hands away. She gingerly used both of her hands to push the long black hair back away from her face. I almost wished she hadn't.

It wasn't the tears that streaked her face that shocked me. Her right eye was closed shut. There were red welts on both sides of her face. I could make out the shape of fingers on her soft skin. I pulled her a bit closer and wrapped my arm around her shoulder. "Come on, sit down." I steered her toward a beige couch, forced her to sit. "Do you want a drink?" I didn't wait for an answer. I was already moving into the kitchen nook. Dianne didn't drink much but there was always a six pack of Heineken for me and Bud Light for her in the fridge. I didn't bother with them. I opened a cabinet door, pulled out a bottle of Absolute Vodka and a large can of cranberry juice. I used an opener to pop two holes in the can. I made the extra strong drink quickly, dropped in ice cubes, and brought the drink to Dianne.

I sat beside her on the couch. She used two hands to bring the drink to her lips, hands shaking. She took a small sip. Her lips pursed and she shook her head like she'd just swallowed a peeled lemon. "Are you trying to get me in the bedroom, Dan?" she said. She forced a little smile, but grimaced with pain. I forced a little smile back.

"Can you..." she began and motioned with the drink. I took it from her hands and set it on the glass-covered coffee table in front of us.

"What happened?" I already had a good idea and the guilt was building in me like a rising tide.

"After work..." That's as far as she got before she started to cry. She gazed at me with her good eye, a look on her face I'd never seen on her before. She looked like a scared little girl. And that sure wasn't Dianne. I pulled her close, let her cry it out.

Finally, she moved away, nodding. She made some unladylike snorts and started talking again. This time she kept it together.

"After work I parked in my spot like I always do. When I got to the front door, they came in right behind me. They must've been hiding somewhere but I didn't see them. They jerked some type of hood over my head." She stopped, looked down at the floor. "They must've taken it with them. Anyway, they marched me right up here, made me let them in."

"Two of them?"

"Let me tell you." She was angry that I'd interrupted her; that was a good sign. "Yes, there were two. They did *this* to me." She pointed at her face. "And this," she quickly added.

She released the top two buttons on her blouse, pulled the material down. There was an ugly mark on her breast the size of a man's fist. It was already turning a disturbing reddish-purple color.

I looked at it like it was the first bruise I'd ever seen. "I'm taking you to the hospital."

"No. I'm all right now." She closed the blouse, buttoned it up. "Dan, they said to tell you if you don't stop your questions on the beach and forget about everything you know, they'll be back to do this again." She started to cry again, lighter this time. Between soft sobs, she added, "They said next time it will be worse."

"Dianne, I'm so sorry."

She reached out, touched my arm. "It's not your fault, Dan." She smiled, showing her white teeth. Thank God they were all there. "They threatened to kill you and Shamrock." Her voice shook.

So they were covering all their bases, figuring that if I didn't care enough about Dianne to back off after the threat of her getting a worse beating, then maybe a death threat for Shamrock or myself might do the trick.

"I'll get some ice for your eye."

"No! I don't want anything to even touch it."

"You should have someone look at it."

She shook her head furiously, grimacing. Then she reached over, picked the glass off the table, raised it to her lips and drank. Her hands were still shaking, but not as much.

"Could you tell who they were?" I asked gently.

She shook her head, took another sip of the drink, then set it back down on the table. "I told you—they put something over my head. They shoved me in the closet and ripped it off before they left. I was scared, Dan. I stayed in there till I couldn't anymore. When I came out, they were gone."

"What about their voices?" I asked.

"Only one talked," she answered.

"How do you know there were two then?"

She looked at me like she were explaining something to a child. "Because the one who hit me and did all the talking, asked the other one questions."

"How did he answer if you only heard one voice?"

She started to whimper. "How the hell do I know?" She got herself under control. "The other guy must have moved his head, I guess."

"What else did they say to you?"

"I don't know. They asked what you'd told the police. If you'd told anyone besides me and Shamrock about all this. Stuff like that."

"What did you tell them?"

"Nothing at first. I didn't know what to tell them." She sobbed again.

I wrapped my arm around her, pulled her close, kissed her hair.

"That's when he hit me in the eye. Here too." She pointed at her breast. "And he slapped me hard when I didn't answer quickly enough. So I said you hadn't told the police or anyone else anything. I thought that was the best thing to say." She pushed me away from her. Her one good eye studied my face. "Was it?" she asked.

"Sure, it was fine, honey." I didn't know if she'd done the right thing or not, but it probably didn't make any difference. "What did he sound like?"

"Like someone punched him in the throat." If that didn't tell me who he was, her next statement did. "He stank of cigars, too."

Rudy, the dirty rat who'd almost burned me like a Salem witch. There was no doubt about it. Dianne's description was more accurate than fingerprints. Now I had another reason to get even with that animal. I kept the white anger boiling up inside of me in check. I would see that scumbag again if it was the last thing I ever did.

"And the other one didn't say anything?"

"*That's* what I said, Dan," she answered. I could see her thinking for a moment. "He didn't want me to hear his voice, did he?"

"Apparently not."

I thought about every shady character I'd met since I'd almost tripped over Evelyn Kruel's body on the beach. I went through them one by one. Who would want to hide their voice from Dianne? Morris Kruel? Dianne had heard his voice in the past, but not that much. He could have disguised a short response easily. I didn't know if Dianne had ever spoken to Marcy Wade or not, but if she had, it probably hadn't been a long enough conversation that Dianne would remember her voice. Besides, I didn't think Marcy had the stomach for something like this. Then there was George Ransom. I was sure that Dianne hadn't had much, if any, contact with him. And Eddie Hoar and Derwood Doller? Sure they were a couple of low-lifes, but even they weren't this low—it just wasn't their style.

That left one person. I wasn't a professional detective, but I wasn't a complete blockhead either. And I didn't need a PI license to figure out who the silent person had to be—Artie Neal. He had a voice so distinctive and so well known to half the population of New England that even if he tried to disguise it, his voice would still be as recognizable as Michael Jackson's.

"It was Artie Neal," I said aloud to myself.

Dianne's voice shook me out of my thoughts. "Of course. Anyone would know his voice. That dirty bastard. I'd like to kill him."

I looked at her, nodded, and smiled. I had me a smart woman. A tough one too. "That makes two of us," I said.

Dianne lifted the glass again, took a very small sip this time. Her hands were steady. When she set the glass down, she asked, "What should we do now?"

"I don't know," I answered truthfully. I ran my hand slowly above her eye, taking care not to touch the injured area and touching her hair instead. "Right now I'm taking you to the hospital."

She protested again—she didn't want to go. Of course I made her. On the drive, we didn't talk. I was lost in my thoughts; she must have been, too. I didn't need to concentrate too much on the driving. I'd been to Exeter Hospital so often lately that they might as well have put me on the Board of Directors. I was hoping that this would be my last trip for a long time.

Chapter 32

LATER THAT MORNING, I drove Dianne back home. She was in no shape to work and needed sleep. I talked her into closing the Tide for the day. She put up a weak protest but relented. I didn't offer to open up for her. I couldn't. There were things I had to do.

The hospital had tended to Dianne's eye, taken x-rays of her chest, and sent her home with a prescription for pain pills. If this kept up, we'd all be able to open our own pharmacies before long. Thankfully, there was no permanent damage to her eye or anything else for that matter. That didn't help me with my guilt, though. What happened to her was my fault; I knew it. We'd filed a police report at the hospital but there wasn't anything solid we could say, just supposition. I didn't think it would go anywhere.

I didn't try to get Dianne to stay with me; that could have been more dangerous. I did try to talk her into a couple of other places where she might safely stay but she refused. I did get her to agree to allow Ruthie, a Tide waitress who was also a friend of Dianne's, to come and stay with her. I called Ruthie, told her what had happened. I also called Shamrock and gave him a heads-up.

Ruthie came right over and she had her friend with her. Her friend was a .25 automatic. This was the Live Free or Die state; lots of people had guns.

After Ruthie and I had Dianne settled, I went back to my cottage. I wolfed down some food, took a quick shower. When I was done I got out the business card the fed had given me, called, and made arrangements to meet him at the White Cap that afternoon.

When I arrived, Agent Whitney was already sitting at a table. It was the same table Steve Moore and I had used the last time we had visited the Cap together. He was dressed similar to the way he'd been dressed the previous day. He had his leather coat on even though it was warm outside, probably to conceal his gun. I sat; he nodded and waved the waitress over.

Unfortunately, it was the same waitress who had waited on Steve and me. She didn't look too happy to see me.

"What do you want, Dan?" Whitney asked, pointing his finger at me.

I noticed he had what looked like a coke with nothing in it except a fat straw. "Heineken," I said to the young waitress. I wasn't in the mood for anything weaker. In fact, I probably could have used something stronger.

She scooted away to get my beer; I watched her as she left.

"You got back to me fast, Dan," Whitney said. "You change your mind already?" He was talking to me in a tone that suggested we'd been friends since grammar school.

I turned back to him. "Something came up last night." I told him the whole story. I was worried sick about Dianne. I couldn't let anything else happen to her or Shamrock either. Except for my kids, they were pretty much my whole life now. I had to protect them and that meant I had to bury my belief about not working with a narc. At least for now.

Whitney had his big arms on the table, the leather coat pulled tight as he listened. He stared at me, rarely blinked, and didn't interrupt. When I was done, he nodded as if I'd confirmed all his suspicions.

"So I guess I was on the money, huh? Just happened a little sooner than we thought." Then he added quickly, "I was going to get in touch with her today. Your other buddy, too. Kelly."

"You didn't have to wait," I said, sharper than I intended.

"Don't hang that on me, Marlowe."

So now it was Marlowe.

"You could've told her right away too. Didn't you say you were snoozing when your girl was beaten? And besides, you got her into this, didn't you, Danny?"

This guy changed my name more than AAA changed tires, but he was right on both counts. "Forget the Danny," I said lamely. "I don't like it."

Whitney smirked. "How is the broad anyway?"

"The *broad* is fine," I answered. All of a sudden, I liked this guy less if that was possible. For a minute I started having second thoughts about helping him. In the end, I didn't think I had a choice.

That's when the waitress showed up with my Heineken, a frosted glass, and another coke for the narc. I drank.

She flashed her order book and pretty smile. The smile was forced though; she must have been able to read our minds. "What can I get you, gentlemen?"

Before I could answer, Whitney piped up. "This is it. We're not hungry."

The pretty smile went away. She looked at me, and with a thinly disguised tinge of sarcasm, said, "No large french fries today?"

I know I blushed. This wasn't going to help my standing in the Cap any, but I had foolishly already eaten again. Still, french fries were better than nothing. "Sure, okay." She didn't bother putting it in her book, just nodded and walked briskly away.

"I'm not paying for that, you know," Whitney said.

I studied his face to see if he was kidding. It was funny how just yesterday he'd sounded like he'd treat me to a prime rib along with a lobster pie to go if I'd asked. Now that he figured I was running scared, he was probably going to stick me with the tab for his cokes, too.

"I'm not surprised," I said. I glanced around at the other occupied tables near us. There was no one I recognized. The table directly across from us caught my eye. An older couple, just short of elderly, looked like they were almost through with their meals. I hadn't heard them speak to each other since I'd sat down. They each acted as if they were alone at the table. How could a relationship get to that point? If I hadn't gotten divorced, would Sandy and I have eventually gotten that way? Would Dianne and I ever get to that stage?

"Forget the old farts, Marlowe," Whitney said, breaking into my thoughts. "You want to help us, right?"

"I don't want to. But I will." There was no other way to protect Dianne and Shamrock now. Neal—or whoever the hell was behind all this—had proven they were willing to go all the way. I had to swallow my principles for now, and work with someone I had always told myself I never would.

"Good," Whitney said, a pompous grin on his face. "You're making the right choice. They'd think nothing of killing you and your associates." He looked for my reaction. I tried to keep my face blank; I don't know if I succeeded. Finally, he said, "Can you add anything to what you told me the other day? Go through everything as a matter of fact. Refresh my memory.

I started to rehash what we had already talked about—Artie Neal, Marcy Wade, Morris Kruel, George Ransom, Jamaica, and the rest of it. I also ran back through what I knew about the events at Dianne's condo the previous night.

Before I finished, the waitress returned with a heaping plate of french fries. She set them down on the table between us, looked at me frostily, and left.

I continued my story. When I was done, he studied me for a moment. "So you think it was Artie Neal and this Rudy goon who worked over your girl?"

I nodded. "He didn't speak. It had to be someone with a voice Dianne knew."

"She knows other voices," he said.

"Of course she knows other voices, but no one who couldn't disguise at least a yes or no. *Except* Artie Neal. His voice is unmistakable."

Whitney waited a minute, took another sip of coke, then smiled smugly. "I think you're right. It just confirms what we suspected but weren't positive about—Artie Neal is the top man in this operation."

"You knew about Neal?"

"He was at the top of our list. But we weren't sure. Now we are."

"Why would Neal be involved in something like that?" I asked. "He must have more money than God."

Whitney snorted. "He makes at least a million a year. But remember his wife and kids get a lot of that. Plus that house up on the rocks cost plenty. He's also got a mini-mansion down in Massachusetts. A place in Florida too. And a guy like Neal? They never have enough money. Plus the fact that he probably thinks that he can get away with anything. He's got an ego so big he needs a wheelbarrow to lug it around in."

He was right about that last part. And the rest of what he said made sense too. Besides, a man who would spew the kind of bigoted venom out into the public airwaves like Neal did every day certainly wouldn't have any moral qualms about importing weed and coke. Probably didn't have any qualms against murder, either.

I looked at the plate of fries. Neither of us had touched them. They were probably cold by now. I looked warily up at Whitney. "What do you want me to do?"

He didn't hesitate a beat. "I want you to approach Artie Neal about a payoff."

"A payoff?" I had no idea where he was going with this.

Whitney reached over, grabbed a ketchup bottle, and slathered some on the cold fries. He picked up a fork, speared a couple, and ate while he talked. "That's right. A payoff in pot."

"What the hell are you talking about?"

He stopped chewing, pointed the sharp end of the fork at my face. "I'm talking about you telling Neal you want fifty pounds of pot to keep quiet about everything you know. Believe me, he wouldn't be going to all this trouble to knock you out of the picture if he didn't think you knew a lot. A lot that could hurt him."

I made a face that probably looked like a banker looking at a deadbeat's loan application. "He's not going to go for that."

"Why not?" Whitney said. "He knows your reputation." He hesitated, smiled. "Divorced, lost your restaurant, hurting for money. Not to mention your old drug baggage. Christ, he'll probably be amazed you took so long."

I wasn't surprised that Whitney knew about my past. For people in Whitney's line of work, information—dirty information—was their stock in trade. I shook my head. "Fifty pounds? That's a lot."

"Not to Neal. It's just a tiny fraction of what his organization has stored somewhere on the seacoast and I want to find out where it is." He resumed shoveling in the fries. He certainly was doing a good job for someone who hadn't been hungry just a short time ago.

"He's not dumb," I said. "Even if by some miracle he agreed to my proposition, he's not going to take me to his stash place."

"You're right, he's not. But you're going to light a fire under him by telling him you need the pot pronto or you're talking. Get him to go get it himself."

"And you people are going to follow him?" I asked. Whitney nodded as he chewed. "How do you know he won't call someone and just have the stuff delivered?"

"Two reasons. Number one—smugglers like Neal like to use the phone about as much as an asthmatic likes to have their face rubbed in kitty litter. Second—he knows we're trying to find the stash. He's probably told the rest of his people to stay away from it. He's got a big ego, like I told you. He'll figure he's the only one who can go there without being followed."

"He'll spot you."

Whitney grinned. "I don't think so. We're good at this. Besides, all the traffic around here makes it easy. He'll either think everyone's following him or no one. My bet is Neal thinks he's so sly, he'll go with the no one."

"What's to stop Neal from just killing me on the spot? Apparently he's not above murder."

"He isn't. But one of the first things you're going to tell him is that there's a letter explaining his whole setup that'll end up with the law if anything happens to you."

I shook my head doubtfully. "I've seen that one in the movies more than once."

Whitney smiled slyly and cocked his head. "Yes, you have. And that's because it works. Neal may not think you're the shiniest shell on the beach but he probably doesn't think you're the dullest either. Believe me, he won't take the chance."

I didn't like Whitney's comments about my intelligence, but seeing what I was getting myself into, I wondered for a moment if he was right. "You make it sound like it'll be easy," I said, even though I was none too sure of it.

"It will be." He arched his eyebrows. "Maybe I'll even have you come along when we tail him."

"Me? Why?"

"We can't be a hundred percent sure there won't be others at the stash site. If there are, maybe you can tell us who's who."

That sounded odd and I didn't like it, but I let it pass for now. There was one thing I didn't want to let pass though. "I'd like to let a Hampton cop in on this."

He stopped, a forkful of fries two inches from his mouth. "Who?"

"Steve Moore. You know him."

He set the fork, fries and all, on the plate.

"He knows a bit about this," I continued. "You can trust him. He's a good man."

Whitney folded his hands under his chin. "I'm sure he is, Dan," he said. "But this is big. We're not letting any local yokels know about this beforehand. I'm sure your Moore's okay, but he might mention it to someone who isn't. That's the way it's got to be. Agency policy. Agreed?"

I shrugged. I wasn't happy about it but from what I'd heard about the DEA, his statement rang true. "All right."

He nodded. "Okay. Then this is what we're going to do."

He laid the plan out, continuing to work on the fries. By now they were probably as cold as a skinny dipper in January. He finished the fries the same time he wrapped up his plan.

"You're okay with this, Dan?"

I wasn't but I nodded.

"Good. I want you to move on this quick. Call me the minute you've got anything definite set up with Neal." Whitney jumped up and walked away without saying goodbye.

I had an ominous feeling as I watched him go. For once, I hoped it was just the start of an anxiety attack.

Chapter 33

I DIDN'T DO much the rest of the day except go over ideas on how to approach Artie Neal so the pot shakedown would seem plausible. I wasn't sure there was a perfect solution to that problem and finally decided I'd be better off just playing the game with no frills and keeping my fingers crossed. If I got too elaborate with the spiel, I had a feeling I would trip myself up. I remembered the old saying, "Keep it simple, stupid." That seemed to apply in this case. Like most people in his line of work, Neal was more than likely a good judge of people—who was a danger to him and who was not. He had to be; otherwise, he wouldn't last long. My best bet would probably be to come on like some civilian trying to make some easy money and not be too sophisticated on how I was going to do it. That way I could hopefully fly under the man's warning radar.

I was still hashing the whole mess over when I finally fell into a troubled sleep.

When I got to the High Tide for lunch shift the next morning, Dianne was in the kitchen, standing at the speed table working very slowly with a large knife on assorted vegetables. She looked at me with her one good eye as I walked in. Her other eye had a dressing covering it. It didn't make her look any less attractive.

Guillermo was adjusting knobs on an oven and didn't look up. I wondered what Dianne had told him about her eye.

I stopped when I reached her and rested my hand on her arm—the one holding the knife. I wasn't worried that she might use it on me, although she would have been justified. It was just the closest arm.

"How do you feel?" I asked.

"I'm all right," she answered.

"Are you in any pain?"

"A little."

"Don't the pills help?"

She crinkled her nose. "I don't like those things. They make me feel funny. I took some Tylenol."

I wanted to take her in my arms right then and there, hold her. If Guillermo hadn't been in the room, I probably would have. But I'd put in her in an uncomfortable enough situation as it was.

"Is Shamrock here?" I asked.

She tilted her head in the direction of the bar. "Out front."

"Can I talk to you both for few minutes?" I had to tell them both about the fed and what we were planning with Artie Neal. I didn't like telling them, but they were in this, and any little bit of information I kept from them could be the one thing they might need to know to keep themselves safe.

"Sure." She placed the knife down on the table and wiped her palms on the front of the spotted white apron.

Just then I saw Guillermo step into the walk-in with a tray of something, the heavy door closed behind him. I put my arms around Dianne's waist and pulled her close, staring into her good eye. God, she felt good. "I'm so sorry," I said. I don't cry, but this time I almost did.

"It wasn't your fault, Dan."

"I knew something like this could've happened. If I'd warned you sooner…"

I could see the puzzlement in her eye. "I don't know what you're talking about."

"That's part of why I want to talk to you guys." I leaned closer, gently kissed the bandage on her eye. I moved my lips to hers and had just touched them when the walk-in door opened and Guillermo backed out of the big refrigerated box with a tray of perishables. By the time he turned and faced us, I was walking toward the bar.

"Don't ask me, Danny," Shamrock called as I shoved through the swinging doors. He was perched on his usual morning bar stool. "I'm not in a good mood today."

I walked over, slapped him lightly on the back, hung my arm around his shoulder. "Lost again, huh?"

He shook my arm off his shoulder. "It ain't just that. I'm very upset about what happened to Dianne. I could kick somebody's ass."

I put both hands on the bar and leaned against it with a sigh. "Tell me about it. She tell you the whole story?"

"I think so." Then he raised his voice. "What the hell's going on, Danny? We can't let *anyone* get away with hurting Dianne."

Just then Dianne came through the swinging doors.

"I want to talk to you about that," I said. "Some other things too." I pointed at a rear booth. "Come on over to my office," I said, trying to inject some levity. It didn't work, for Shamrock or for me.

The two of us trudged over to the same booth we always seemed to use for our little conferences. We got to the table first, slid in across from each other. Dianne had stopped to grab a cup of coffee on the way. When she reached the table, she scooted in beside Shamrock. For an instant I wondered why she sat there, then winced when I realized she wanted to be able to see my face clearly with her limited vision.

I brought them up to speed on everything I knew. Told them about the fed and what he had proposed. How I'd refused to help at first. I related the new threats Agent Whitney had mentioned. How my decision to not immediately tell Dianne and Shamrock about those threats made me responsible for what had happened to Dianne. Then I told them that I'd changed my mind and decided to help Whitney. When I was done, I looked at them both, wondering how they'd react. I kept my eyes mostly on Shamrock. I didn't like looking at Dianne. I felt bad enough.

Dianne spoke first. "Dan, you did exactly the same thing I would've done." She had a little smile on her face, though I thought it was a bit forced. "We didn't have time to talk to you Saturday night even if you did call. Did we, Shamrock?"

Shamrock hesitated, then jerked. I could tell Dianne had bumped his leg. He picked up on the cue. "Sweet Jaysus, Danny. We were as busy as a priest hearing confessions the day after St. Patrick's Day."

They were worried about me, trying to make me feel better, and it worked. For a moment at least, until I looked at Dianne's face again. Still, it felt good to know that two people cared more for my feelings than for their own safety. I was sure of one damn thing—I had two very good friends. I couldn't let anything else happen to either of them. No matter what happened to me.

We were silent for a short minute. I studied my hands on the table.

Then Dianne spoke up. "Dan, I don't like the sound of this. If you and this Whitney are right and it's Artie Neal who's behind all this, how do you know he won't just kill you when you approach him?"

"She's right, Danny. I better go with you. He won't make a move on you with Michael Kelly there." He tapped a beat-up thumb against his chest.

Now it was my turn to smile, though I kept it a little one. I didn't want to insult Shamrock. Still, the smile felt good. "Thanks, Shamrock but that's not a good idea. It's going to be tough enough to get Neal to swallow this. He won't want a witness."

They both stared at me, skeptical looks on their faces.

"And Whitney thinks this will work?" Dianne asked. She had more doubt on her face than a first-time skydiver.

I shrugged. "That's what he says. Says he's done a lot of these type of stings in the past. Says a guy like Neal would prefer to buy somebody off for cheap money and use killing only as a last resort."

"But, Danny Boy, won't Artie think it's just a setup?" Shamrock's red eyebrows pulled together into one bushy brow. "I'd be thinking you were going to have the police waiting for me when I returned with the contraband."

I shrugged again. "Whitney seems to think that Neal won't plan on returning to his house with it. Instead, he'll want to leave the fifty pounds somewhere else. God knows where. I guess someplace that can't be traced to him. Maybe a storage room or something. He says Neal'll figure on letting me know where the pot is so I can pick it up myself. That way when I get it, Neal won't even be there. He won't be caught holding anything. But Whitney's not going to let it get that far. They're going to grab Neal when he gets to the stash site."

"Hmm." Dianne cocked her head and looked at me sideways with her good eye. "So they'll arrest Artie Neal where he stores all the marijuana?"

I nodded. "That's the hope, I guess."

"Wait," Shamrock said. "Why won't he kill you when you first approach him? You'd be by yourself in his house, for God's sake. He could dump you on the beach like Evelyn Kruel."

"If he tries anything, I'm going to tell him I've left a note behind with the entire story, including that I visited him that day. I get out alive—note gets destroyed. I disappear—note goes to the cops."

Dianne shook her head doubtfully. "I've seen that one in more than one old movie."

I threw up my hands. "I said that too. But Whitney says that's because it works. Neal can't take the chance of killing me with the possibility I've left a document incriminating him behind."

"I don't know, Dan," Dianne said. I could see the worry in her eye.

"It'll be fine," I said, trying to reassure them both and maybe myself, too. "Whitney says I'll be under surveillance by other agents at all times. He says nothing can go wrong."

"You know the old saying," Shamrock piped in. "The one about famous last words."

Dianne lightly smacked Shamrock's shoulder. "We can't think that way." She turned back to me. "What can we do to help?"

I shook my head. "Nothing. Soon it'll all be over."

"Dan, we want to help," Dianne said. Out of the corner of my eye I could see Shamrock nodding.

"There's nothing you can do," I said. "It's a one-man job." I saw the doubt and concern on their faces. "Honestly. If there is anything you can do, I'll let you know. I promise."

Neither of them looked convinced but they both grumbled agreement. "When is this going to happen?" Dianne asked.

"Tomorrow, I think. That reminds me. Can I have the day off?"

Dianne pursed her lips. "And if I said no?" She didn't wait for an answer. "I'll get somebody. You just be safe, Dan Marlowe. And you better call us if there's anything we can do."

"That's right," Shamrock said. "And let us know the minute this is over. I'll be so nervous I'll probably break more dishes than a wife on the warpath until I hear you're okay."

We all chuckled, then got up from the booth and went back to our jobs. Today I'd be working on automatic pilot. I had a lot on my mind and there was no way pulling drafts and delivering baked haddocks was going to let me escape that. No way at all.

Chapter 34

MY SHIFT WAS over and I was more than a little nervous. I wasn't going to waste any time before visiting Artie Neal. The longer I put the job off, the more I would worry. Better to get it over with as soon as possible. And for more than one reason.

I knew Neal had an afternoon show at the Boston radio station that ended at five o'clock. I planned to wait till around eight and drive up, see if he was home by then. Before I left the Tide, I called Agent Whitney and let him know my intentions. I also told him I wouldn't wear a wire. I felt Neal was too smart for that. Whitney reluctantly agreed. He told me that I should meet him at a motel parking lot on the opposite side of Ocean Boulevard, about fifty yards from Neal's house, as soon as I'd finished talking to Neal. I said I would. *If* I got out of the place alive. Whitney chuckled; I didn't.

Back at the cottage, the hands on the anchor clock moved like they had rheumatoid arthritis. When the hands had finally dragged themselves to the seven forty-five position, I figured I'd waited long enough. I took one Xanax, placed it under my tongue. The pill dissolved, releasing its unique medicinal taste.

The effects were a lot quicker than swallowing the pill and quick is what I needed. I would have to be a rock with Neal. If his radar caught even a hint of any excess nervousness, he might balk. The deal was going to be a hard sell as it was, I had no doubt about that.

Outside it was raining, the wipers sloshing water back and forth. I drove for a short while before I eased my car to the side of Ocean Boulevard just feet from Artie Neal's driveway. I could make out his Caddy parked at the end of the drive, close to the house. I pulled my car in and parked beside Neal's. I took a couple of deep breaths and got out of the car, then went through the little gate and up to the door. I rang the bell without hesitating. I could hear the damn tune the chimes played again; I didn't like that song.

Within a minute Neal answered the door. He was dressed casually. "Marlowe!" he said, sounding as shocked as if the Beatles had been standing there.

"I'd like to talk to you," I said. I wasn't nervous now. Like I said—pills kick in quick under the tongue *if* they're the dissolvable type. The rain probably had something to do with it too. I was soaked and wanted to get out of the rain and inside so bad I probably wouldn't have cared if he'd had the Boston Strangler over for drinks.

"Are you crazy? Last time I let you in, you did this." He touched a discolored area on his cheek, grimaced.

I smiled. "I'm not here for that, Artie. I've got a proposition."

I could see his mind bouncing around like the balls in a pinball machine. After a bit, he said, "All right, Marlowe. I'm curious to see what silliness you have on your mind this time. But keep your hands to yourself. I'm warning you." He raised his voice on the last part; I guess he was trying to sound threatening. But he was no more intimidating than a Mexican Chihuahua.

He led me back through the hallway. I shook some of the water off as I walked. I was just about to sit in the fancy love seat I'd occupied on my last visit when Neal shrieked, "Hold it." He opened one of several foldout chairs leaning against a wall, brought it over to me, set it down.

"Do you know how much that's worth?" He aimed his chin at the love seat. "You're wet. You'd ruin it."

I sat in the chair he offered. It was more comfortable than the love seat anyway.

"Mind if I have a drink, Marlowe?" he asked. He walked to the bar and poured himself a hefty snifter of cognac without offering me one.

He returned and sat on the sofa opposite me, drink in hand. He took a sip of the amber liquid, watched me over the rim of the glass. After he swallowed, he brought the glass down and let out a contented smile. Probably trying to rub in the fact that he hadn't offered me a drink. "All right, Marlowe. Let's hear this...ahh, proposition of yours."

I was on now. I had to make it good; I'd get only one chance. "I know a lot of what's going on, Neal."

He looked at me like he was a tolerant school teacher and I was the class dumbbell. Like I said, he was a good actor. "What do you know, *Mr.* Marlowe?" he said, not trying to hide the sarcastic tone.

I leaned forward, put my arms on my legs. "I know about the smuggling ring you're involved in for a start."

"Smuggling?" he said as if he'd never heard the word before.

"That's right. Smuggling. Cocaine and marijuana."

He raised himself on the sofa in a good impersonation of an indignant man. "Are you out of your mind?"

"From Jamaica," I said quickly, hoping to hit him hard and fast with a lot of details all at once. Throw him off balance.

For some reason I felt that was a good idea. "Brought into Hampton Harbor by sailboat. Then your girlfriend Marcy Wade takes the money back down to the island."

"She's not my girlfriend," he said. Odd that that was the part he had a problem with.

"No, Evelyn Kruel was your girlfriend."

Neal's eyes narrowed.

"Until she stumbled across your little operation, Neal. Did she find out that you were using her property to keep in radio contact with the sailboats? Did she threaten to go to the police? Is that why you killed her?"

"You've got to be kidding."

"Was she angry that you got her brother Morris involved with your dope operation?" I hadn't been sure of that one, but when his brows jumped like I'd made a move to whack him again, I was certain that Morris was in the mix.

"You don't know what you're talking about, Marlowe," he said, but his demeanor told me that I'd hit a sensitive nerve.

"I don't?" I decided to play another bluff. "How about George Ransom?" I let the question hang there. If he denied it, I wasn't sure what I could say connecting him to Ransom. Luckily, I didn't have to worry about that. Except for a noticeable bob of his Adam's apple Neal didn't respond—that told me something. We just sat there, staring at one another. He nursed his drink, stalling for time. I could almost see the smoke rising from his overworked brain. I was determined not to speak first.

Finally, he said, "Not one thing you've said is true, *Mr.* Marlowe. But just out of curiosity tell me about this proposition you mentioned earlier."

This was it; I had to be good. "The police don't know anything," I said. "And I imagine you'd like to keep it that way."

Neal's hands flew out, palms up. He motioned for me to stand. I hesitated until I realized what he was up to. I was glad that I had deep-sixed the idea of me wearing a wire and that I'd left my gun in the car. I stood; Neal stood. He walked over and gave me a thorough frisk. Up, down, and around my body. It was a good sign. It meant he would at least consider the proposition. When he was satisfied I was clean, we sat back down.

"Okay?" I said.

"Talk, Marlowe." He looked at me icily, drained the last of the cognac, and set it noisily on the glass coffee table.

"All right," I said. I felt confident, calm. "I want fifty pounds."

"Pot?" Neal looked at me like he hadn't expected that.

"That's right."

"Why pot?" He looked at me suspiciously. "Why not money?"

I was ready for that. "Because I figure I can sell it off in small pieces and make a lot more than you'd ever be willing to pay me in cash." I thought the little ploy made sense and was hoping it would appeal to Neal's known tightness with a dollar. Whitney and I had discussed this part of the plan extensively. We were betting that not only would he buy the idea I was making the proposal for monetary reasons, but that he'd also be happier to pay me off more cheaply with pot rather than with his precious money.

It didn't take Neal long to decide. "How do I know you'd keep your mouth shut down the road, Marlowe?"

"Because I'm not greedy and I'm not crazy. This'll be enough for me. I'll be able to get my restaurant back. That's all I want." Like everyone else on Hampton Beach, I was sure Artie Neal knew that I used to own the High Tide and how

I'd lost it. "Besides, I've seen what you and your people are capable of. I don't want anything happening to me or my two friends."

He straightened at that last part, apparently quite proud of himself. "And it would, too, if you ever opened your mouth or tried another shakedown. You understand that, bartender?" He was trying to sound like Bogie. It didn't work and I almost laughed. I kept the smile from my face. I had succeeded and didn't want to blow the scam now.

"I won't ever bother you again, Artie. You got my word."

He sat there, mulling my proposition over. I held my breath. After a couple of minutes he slapped his knees. "You be at your house tomorrow. All day."

I nodded.

"Give me your phone number. I'll call you there."

"All right," I said. "And Artie? Don't try anything heavy. I've left a letter—with all the details about your operation and my visit here today—that'll go to the police if anything happens to me."

Neal spoke quickly. "There'll be no need for that. You'll get what you want."

"Okay." It looked like Neal had bought it lock, stock, and barrel just like the fed had said he would. Neal had me pegged for a greedy, ex-junkie, divorced bartender desperate to get his restaurant back. For once my negative reputation had helped me in a positive way. Well, hopefully it had. I should know within twenty-four hours.

I reached over, took a pen from the coffee table, wrote my phone number on the back of an *Architectural Digest*. Then I stood. "I'll find my way out, Artie."

He stood too. "Remember, Marlowe, about keeping your trap shut down the line." He actually had a snarl on his face as he said it. Again I fought to keep a smile off my face. I walked out of the great room, along the hallway, and out the front door into the pouring rain.

Chapter 35

I DIDN'T GO FAR. I drove a short distance to the motel across from Neal's home and pulled my car into the lot. The headlights on a car blinked off and on. It was parked in a row of other cars close to the street. I pulled up beside it. The car was a gray compact Honda. I could see Agent Whitney behind the wheel. He waved for me to join him.

I don't know why but I took the .38 from the glove box, shoved it in my rear waistband. I put on the windbreaker I brought with me to cover the gun. I got out of my car and hopped in beside Whitney. I slammed the door after me. "Where's your other car?" I looked around, noticing the lack of a two-way radio.

"This is a surveillance car," he said irritably. "You didn't think we were going to bird-dog him in that government boat, did you?" He didn't wait for my answer. "What the hell happened? Did he buy it?"

I told him everything that was said during the encounter. Told him I thought Neal had swallowed it, but I wasn't one hundred percent sure. Neal was a slippery character, after all. Maybe he just wanted me to think he had taken the bait.

Whitney's face was illuminated by the light from a street lamp. It made his grin look evil. "You got him, Marlowe. He's a greedy little prick and he thinks you're the same. I knew he'd jump at the chance to buy you off for a measly fifty pounds of pot."

I looked through the rain-streaked windshield in the direction of Neal's house. Whitney had the car situated so we had a perfect view of Neal's driveway. If he started to leave, we'd see him. The wipers moved rhythmically back and forth, marking the time.

"I still don't see how you can be sure he won't send someone else," I said.

Whitney shook his head. "No chance. These dirtbags are all the same and I've taken down plenty of them. He was paranoid before you came; now he'll be worse. That's good for us because he won't let anyone else go to the stash place. He'd be afraid they'd be followed. Not him though. He thinks he's smart. Thinks he'd notice a tail. He's going to learn he isn't as smart as he thinks."

"I might as well get going." I reached for the door handle. "You don't need me anymore. I'll let you know when he calls."

Whitney spoke in a condescending tone. "I told you. It's not going to get that far."

I let go of the handle, looked at Whitney. "You still think that?"

"I do. He's not planning to call you until he's got the product out of the stash house and safely tucked away somewhere else. *Then* he'll call you and tell you where you can pick it up. He's not going to get out of the stash house, though. That's where he'll be arrested."

"You hope." I looked out the passenger window at the rain. "How long will we have to wait here?" I asked.

"It could be all night. Although with guys like Neal..." He put a hand on my shoulder. "Get down. He's moving."

I lowered myself so I was peeking over the dashboard. Sure enough, I could see Neal's car backing out onto Ocean Boulevard. It began moving north, heading past us. Just as it went by us another car at the other end of the lot, a car I hadn't noticed before, turned on its lights and pulled out in the direction Neal was going. It was a little Ford Escort. There was one car between them. Whitney and I popped up. He put the car in drive and we whipped out of the lot onto Ocean Boulevard.

"You think he's going for it now?" I asked.

"Yes." Whitney had both hands tight on the steering wheel in the ten-and-two position.

"He didn't waste any time." I could feel my heartbeat increasing—the pills could only do so much.

"He figures the faster he moves, the less time anyone will have to set something up."

"Oookay," I said.

Even with the rain and the wipers, I could still make out Neal's car with its unique taillights, three cars ahead of us. Those taillights made keeping Neal's car in sight much easier. After a while Neal took a left hand turn. There was still one car between our car and his. That car looked like the one that had pulled out of the motel lot before us.

I pointed at the Escort. "A friend of yours?"

"This is a two-car job," Whitney answered. "I could've used more, but..." he hesitated, "but we're shorthanded."

"Maybe they've got an old farm up here in Rye or North Hampton," I offered.

"Maybe," was all he said.

Neal didn't go to an old farm. He got to Route 1 and headed south. The other cop car pulled into a lot and we passed it. I turned, looked back, and saw the Escort pull out behind us.

Whitney saw me looking. "We'll be hopscotching back and forth all the way," he said. "So hopefully this dick head won't make us."

"He's smart," I warned.

"You'd be surprised. Sometimes the smarter they seem, the easier they are to follow. His type's so paranoid, sometimes they think everyone behind them is law enforcement. And there's usually nobody there. When they get sick of being paranoid, they go to the opposite extreme and think everybody's Mr. Rogers. That's when we usually *are* there." He shrugged. "That's just the way the bad guys think. Stupid shits."

"I hope you're right this time."

We kept our position in the caravan until we reached downtown Hampton. When Neal pulled over to the curb, I wasn't surprised to see the Kruel building across the street. Whitney went past him, took a right into a commercial cul-de-sac, and pulled into a parking spot facing away from Neal's car. Whitney looked into the rearview mirror, adjusted it. I looked over my shoulder just in time to see the Escort go by on Route 1.

"Careful," Whitney growled. "Don't turn around."

I turned back enough so I was facing Whitney but could still see Neal's car out of the corner of my eye. His wipers were going and his headlights were still on. A woman in a raincoat ducked out of the Kruel building and raised an umbrella over her head, then hurried across the street, folded the umbrella, and hopped in the front passenger seat with Neal. I didn't see her face but I had no doubt who it was. Marcy Wade.

"He sure took the long way around," I said. "There's shorter ways here from his house."

"Counter surveillance," Whitney said. "Do you know who that woman is?"

"It's got to be Marcy Wade," I answered. Then I added, "I guess you called it wrong this time, Bob. Either he's going over the fifty-pound deal with her for some reason, or he's getting a little something."

"Not this guy. Not now. He's going to use her as a beard. Smart too. Looks a lot less suspicious with a man and woman walking into a stash place than a single guy. But it won't help him this time."

"So you think he's still going for the pot?"

"He is. These guys all work the same way even though they think they're so fuckin' smart and original. And maybe they are where ordinary citizens are concerned, but when it comes to professionals," he raised his head, "it's a different story."

Neal pulled his car out into light traffic, headed south on Route 1, and disappeared around a store at the head of the cul-de-sac. Whitney jammed the Honda into reverse, changed direction, and pulled onto the roadway after Neal. Ahead, I could see the Escort on the road with one car between us. Beyond that, I could see Neal's taillights.

The parade turned onto Winnacunnet Road. We continued trading places with the Escort all the way to the beach, across the Hampton Bridge, and into Seabrook where Neal's car pulled into a small strip mall. Both our car and the other surveillance car continued on. Whitney and I pulled into the lot of a small clam shack. We could see Neal's car. It was facing away from the stores and was pointed toward 1A.

"What's he doing?" I asked.

"More counter surveillance," Whitney answered. "We're close now."

"You don't think he's seen either car?"

"Nope. He wouldn't be doing this if he had. He'd be heading home." The agent sounded awful sure of himself.

After about five minutes, Neal's car pulled back out onto 1A and headed south. Whitney let him have a good lead, then followed. I didn't see the Escort, but assumed it was around somewhere. We didn't have far to go before Neal's right turn signal went on and I knew instantly where he was going. He pulled into the parking lot in front of 1A Fireworks. As we drove past, I saw his car disappear around the red, white, and blue cinderblock building. The store was closed. Soft light came from the interior through the large plate glass windows. Probably security lights.

Whitney pulled our car into a convenience store down the road.

"What now?" I asked. My heart was going at a good clip; the pill was almost useless.

"We give them a few minutes. Make sure they're inside."

"Where are the other agents?"

"They're here."

I couldn't see anybody or anything that looked even remotely cop connected. Maybe that was the way tails were supposed to be. I didn't have much time to dwell on it though. A few minutes after we'd stopped, Whitney slapped the steering wheel. "Here we go." He hopped out of the car.

I was surprised but followed. We walked briskly along the shoulder of 1A. Oncoming car lights blinded me.

"Have you got a gun?" Whitney glanced at me.

My hand went to the small of my back. I'd almost forgotten the .38 was there, hidden by my windbreaker. "Yeah."

"Keep it there."

When we reached 1A Fireworks we eased up along the side of the building. Whitney had his back to the wall and slid quietly along it to the front of the building and around the corner. I followed behind him and when I reached the corner,

I peered around it. Whitney was peeking through the closest window. He cupped his eyes against the glass. Before I could blink he turned, brushed past me, and headed for the rear of the store. I trailed behind.

"What'd you see?" I asked.

He didn't answer. At the back of the building, he peeked around the corner like a kid playing hide and seek. I didn't feel like I was playing a kid's game. Just the opposite—and this grownup game might have a very bad outcome.

I stood there looking at Whitney's back, wondering what he saw and where all this was going to take me. I could hear cars flying by on 1A. Wouldn't be good if one of those cars reported two suspicious people prowling around a closed business. I knew the Seabrook police had a reputation for taking care of business first and asking questions second. I wasn't confident they'd pull up with only flashlights in their hands.

Finally, Whitney looked back at me. On his face was an expression I didn't like. I'd seen that look before, back in the day. On the faces of people who were full of either greed or drugs. Sometimes both. I tried to convince myself that I was imagining things. More likely the good guys got as screwy as the bad guys when it came to the final act. That had to be it.

I don't know how long it takes a thought to race through your mind; I didn't look at my watch. But as soon as I had displaced the foreboding notion, Whitney whispered, "There's a storage building out back." He was breathing like a swimmer caught in a riptide. "It's got to be there. We're going in. You keep your gun where it is."

I looked around, expecting to see unmarked cars bouncing into the parking lot. Nothing. Whitney pulled a 9mm from a holster on his hip, held the gun at his side. I swallowed hard. Whitney moved around the rear corner of the building with me right behind him. It only took us seconds to cross the grassy area separating the main building from a large windowless concrete structure. Neal's car was backed up to a large double door in the center of the one-story building. We shimmied along the front of the building, our backs to it, until we reached those doors. They were closed.

Whitney looked sideways at me. "All set?" he whispered. I held my breath; it only seemed to make my heart beat more rapidly. He reached over with his free hand and turned the knob. Locked. He turned back to me and grimaced. "We wait."

I guess he figured the door was too strong to break down. I knew he wanted to catch them off guard, so I was fine with that. Even a novice like me realized that this was the part where if there were going to be any gunfire, this would be when it would happen. So anything that put that action on the back burner was okay with me.

We both stood there, backs to the wall, our breathing the only noise except for traffic on 1A. I scanned the area, looking for the rest of Whitney's team. Not only couldn't I see anyone, I didn't even see the Escort that had helped us tail Neal here in the first place. The road was blocked by the main building, so I couldn't see much anyway. For all I knew that's where the cavalry was now—in the lot in front of the store, just waiting to come roaring around the corner as soon as the door Whitney and I were standing beside opened. That's what I thought. And of course, that's what I hoped.

Chapter 36

WE STOOD THERE for what seemed like an eternity. Bob Whitney, DEA agent, and Dan Marlowe, bartender. It was an unlikely pair; I was aware of the irony. The rain had slowed to a light mist, but it was one of those drizzles that gets you thoroughly soaked. To take my mind off it, I rehashed the events of the past few days, wondering how the hell I'd gotten into all this and how the hell it was going to end up. I don't know how long I was mulling over these troublesome thoughts before they suddenly dropped into the trash bin section of my mind at the sound of the doorknob turning. Whitney brought the gun up in his right hand, raised it over his head.

I could see the top of the door move as it slowly opened with a squeal. My legs had been stiff from standing there waiting, barely moving. Now they felt as loose as a sailor's after a three-day bender. I held my breath, watched as the door opened wider. No light came out of the building.

Whitney's shouts of, "Federal agents. Search warrant. Search warrant," made me jump like I'd just been jolted with electricity. He pulled the door all the way open and bulled his way into the building. I couldn't see who or what was there, but I followed close behind him, expecting to be torn apart by gunshots at any second.

I bumped into Whitney who stepped aside. The interior was in semi-darkness but I could make out Artie Neal sprawled on the floor in front of us. Apparently Whitney had bowled him over as he entered. There were two large cardboard boxes on the floor beside Neal. And behind him, visibly shaking, stood Marcy Wade. She had her hands over her head.

"Please, please, don't shoot," she said, sounding almost hysterical.

"Close the door," Whitney said to me.

I turned and pulled the door closed.

"Lock it."

I didn't think; I just slid the deadbolt home.

"Now find a light."

I found a switch on the wall, clicked it on. A series of overhead florescent lights flickered on. The inside of the building became fully illuminated.

We were in a large room that seemed to take up the entire structure except for two doors adjacent to each other on a sidewall. One I assumed to be the bathroom; the other was probably an office. Lined up against the far wall straight ahead were neatly stacked boxes that resembled the two that Neal was now sitting beside. The boxes were piled three high, about five across. At this angle I couldn't tell how far back the stacks ran.

I walked up and stood beside Whitney. "Open one of those boxes," he said to me, nodding at the boxes on the floor beside Neal who had yet to speak. I knew what was in them; we all did. The odor of marijuana was overpowering. I started to move toward the boxes.

"You'll need something to open them," Whitney added. I stopped, looked around, saw a long wooden bench down near the stacked boxes. I walked over to the bench. In addition to a large flat beam scale, there was also a fifty-pound capacity dial scale, a notebook that looked like it was being used as a ledger, and a hunting knife. I took the knife and returned to the boxes.

Whitney had been right—I needed the knife to get through the strapping tape that secured the boxes. I opened one, reached inside, and removed a plastic-wrapped object that was about the size of a hardback book. I held it up for Whitney to see. He smiled, nodded.

I didn't need him to tell me what it was—a small, two pounds probably, very tightly pressed brick of Jamaican marijuana, the opposite of the looser press, ten- to fifty-pound bales of Mexican pot usually distributed on the seacoast. I'd heard this Jamaican pot was good stuff, only knocked down a few notches in desirability because the tight press made wholesale and retail weights look tiny compared to comparable weight in Mexican weed. The box was full of similar bricks.

"That's what it's all about, baby," Whitney said. Then added, "Put it back."

I dropped the brick back into the box.

Neal was still sitting on the floor, his hands palms down on both sides of him. "You don't look so smart now, asshole," Whitney said to him, a smirk on his face. He still had the gun pointed at Neal.

Neal had looked like he was in a state of shock when we'd first piled in. Now it seemed he was gaining some control over himself. "You've got the wrong idea, officer," he said, looking back and forth between Whitney and me. I don't think he liked me too much at this point—the great Artie Neal suckered by a lowly bartender. "I'm doing research for my radio show."

The man was quick; I had to give him that.

"A caller tipped me off about this little stash and I wanted to make sure it was on the level before I bothered the police."

Whitney snickered. "I've heard a lot better than that, Neal. But at least you tried. I guess you can only work with what you've got."

I heard Marcy whimper. Whitney did too. "You can put your hands down, Miss," he said. She lowered her arms and I could actually see her body shaking.

I was about to ask Whitney about his backup when I heard something pull up out front. It sounded like a truck. I could hear the vehicle maneuvering about. Whitney stiffened, looked in the direction of the noise. Finally, a vehicle door opened and closed. A moment later there was a series of knocks on the door.

"Open it," Whitney said to me.

I must have been stupid or naive or both. Or maybe it was my anxiety, now in overdrive, that was interfering with my awareness. *Something* was off kilter, I just didn't know what.

I slid the deadbolt free and pushed the door open, expecting to be greeted by men wearing bulletproof vests and jackets marked with various combinations of three letters. Instead, Rudy Valentine—the man I was sure had beaten Dianne—stepped through the door. He smiled when he saw the look of shock on my face. Yes, I was shocked. But I was more angry. My mind clicked louder than the tumblers on a second-rate safe and I reached for the small of my back. A light, blunt pressure in the center of my back stopped my hand.

"Too late for that, Marlowe," Whitney said. I felt his hand go under the back of my coat and pull the .38 from my waistband. Rudy closed and locked the door behind him. He walked around me, bumping into me on purpose as he did. His cheap cigar odor smelled even more repulsive when compared to the sweet smell of marijuana.

"You can turn around now," Whitney said. I did. "Get over there beside him." He waved the gun at Neal. "You too, Miss."

Marcy and I moved to stand on either side of Neal who was still sitting on the floor. Whitney handed my gun to Rudy and they held their guns on the three of us.

"Oh, don't look so surprised, Neal," Whitney said. "Old Rudy's been with me for quite a while now, haven't you, Rudy?"

Rudy nodded and grinned in a way that reminded me of Jack Nicholson in *The Shining*. "Yeah. And I dumped the car and got the truck."

"Good," Whitney said.

"Who are you?" Neal barked, looking at Whitney.

"I *thought* he was DEA," I said.

Whitney glared at us. "I *was* DEA. For a lot of years. Until they railroaded me out. Over a...a misunderstanding. Stole my fuckin' pension too." He waved the gun at the boxes behind us. "Now I got my pension back."

I should have kept my mouth shut, but it didn't matter now. There was no way this guy was going to let us leave here alive. Besides, I was pissed that he'd conned me so easily. "A misunderstanding?" I said sarcastically. "What'd you do? Shake down too many dealers, Whitney? Or did you shoot the wrong person ten times? Maybe you and your rats got caught helping yourselves to what you were supposed to be turning in? Probably all of the above, huh?"

I could see Whitney bristle. I'd hit a nerve; maybe more than one.

Neal glared at Rudy. "You dirty rotten little..."

Whitney cut him off. "Shut the fuck up." He pointed the gun at Neal and Neal shut up. "You should have watched your people a little closer, Artie. Been less greedy, too. Should have paid Rudy more for his collection services. He might have stayed loyal to you. And you should've paid him in cash for his work, not coke. That's your downfall—trying to save a few bucks by paying people like Rudy here, and even Marlowe, in product." He gazed in my direction for a moment, then back at Neal. "You see Rudy's been a snitch..." he glanced at Rudy. "Sorry—a confidential informant—for me before. The agency knew there was a big smuggling group up around Hampton somewhere. Couldn't get a line on it but we did get a line on somebody selling a key of coke down in Lawrence. And who'd it turn out to be but my old CI. Right, Rudy?"

Rudy scowled. "Stop wasting time. Let's do what we got to do and get out of here."

Whitney ignored him and kept his gaze fixed on Neal. "For some reason my friend here didn't like the idea of fifteen years mandatory. He liked working with me again better. And when I got dumped, Rudy decided to come with me." He looked at Rudy. "I told you it would pay off." Then he turned back to Neal. "So you see, Artie, if you hadn't been so tight trying to save money and paid Rudy here in cash instead of coke, you wouldn't be in this situation. But you did and you are. My good luck and your bad."

Rudy scowled again. "Wrap it up, will ya?"

"All right. I'll wrap it up," Whitney said. "The only smart thing you did," he said to Neal, "was not letting Rudy here know where the stash place was. Nice idea, too—a fireworks warehouse. Nobody'd think anything of trucks pulling up and unloading boxes. Not bad, Neal."

"Come on," Rudy said. "Hurry the fuck up." For an enforcer he seemed very anxious; I wondered if he had an anxiety disorder. "Let's do this and get outta here."

"All right, all right, hold your horses," Whitney said. "That's the trouble with all you drug people...no patience." He moved closer to Neal. "Where's the coke?"

Neal looked like he'd just been asked a tough chemistry question.

"I know it's here," Whitney said. "We're taking the pot and I want the coke, too. Now where is it?"

Neal played dumb again.

Whitney took three quick steps forward; he was very fast for a big guy. The 9 mm in his hand lashed out in a back-handed motion and made a sickening noise when it thudded against Neal's mouth. Marcy screamed and the sound went right through me. Neil gasped, spitting out blood and teeth. Tears flooded from his eyes. I thought he was going to pass out, but he didn't. In what seemed like seconds, his shirt was drenched in blood. He covered his face with his hands but they couldn't stop the red rivers pouring between his fingers.

Whitney didn't give Neal any time to recover. He raised his gun, preparing for another strike. "I'm gonna beat your fuckin' skull in unless you talk now."

That was it for Neal. I couldn't blame him. As it was he'd probably need years of dental work. Even with that he'd probably never sound the same on the radio again.

He held up his hands in front of him; they dripped blood. He was sobbing, whimpering. He reminded me of a little girl. I couldn't understand half of what he was saying with all the blood and chips of enamel that sprayed from his mouth as he tried to talk. The man was pissing his pants; I could see the stain spreading.

Whitney reached over and yanked Neal to a standing position by one arm, then held him away from him. "Don't get any of that blood on me, asshole. Now where is it?" Neal turned toward the two doors on the side wall. Whitney gave him a hard shove on the shoulder and he stumbled in that direction, moving like he had the DT's. Marcy and I just stood there. I was watching them go; she wasn't. I looked at her, wondered if she was in shock. She probably was and was lucky because of it. The punk, Rudy, still had a gun on us—*my* gun—and I didn't have enough room to make a move on him, unless I wanted to be dead. I wasn't that desperate...yet.

When Whitney and Neal reached the two doors, Neal opened the closest one. Whitney was right behind him. Neal suddenly collapsed and there was a roar from the office. Whitney stumbled backwards and crashed to the floor. There was no doubt he wasn't getting up.

Rudy spun in the direction of the blast. I didn't have time to figure out what had just happened. I charged Rudy. He saw me coming, but it was too late. He couldn't get the gun on me quick enough. I grabbed his gun wrist with both hands and bowled him over, both of us thudding to the floor. I was on top, hanging on to that wrist with every ounce of strength I had. He bounced around under me like a bucking bronco.

He struggled with the gun, trying to twist the barrel so it pointed at my head. An explosion went off so close it made my eardrum feel like Ringo Starr was beating on it.

That noise put the fear of God in me. I'd never believed in those superhuman strength stories—until then. I gave his wrist one last push with everything I had and his arm went straight. My hands held his gun hand down on the floor above his head. When I was sure I could hold his gun down with just one hand, I let go with my right and punched as hard and as fast and as often as I could at his nose. I didn't hit him like I was punching a bag. I used my fist like I was banging a stubborn nail into wood. After a half dozen of those blows, I heard the gun clatter across the floor. I continued to batter at that nose like there was a million dollar payday if I did it right. The man who had beaten Dianne and almost burned me alive was on the ground under me. I was looking at Rudy, but I was *really* seeing Dianne and her bad eye.

I don't know how many times I hit him. I could vaguely hear someone yelling for me to stop. I didn't. Not until a sharp blow caught me in the shoulder and knocked me off Rudy's motionless body. I turned and looked up.

George Ransom was standing there looking down at me. He held a pump shotgun in his hands. Probably what he clubbed me with. He motioned for me to get up. I slowly struggled to my feet, breathing heavily. Behind Ransom stood Artie Neal. The skin on his face not covered in blood was picket-fence white. Marcy was still glued to the spot I'd last seen her in, definitely in shock.

I looked down at Rudy. He was making a horrible noise I guess you could call breathing. I tried to locate his nose; I couldn't. No one would ever be able to get a good night's sleep sharing his bed that was for sure. I looked at my right fist. It was a mess. I'd probably need to borrow some pain pills from Dianne or Shamrock if I ever got out of this. I looked at the body of Bob Whitney. Then back at Neal and George Ransom and the shotgun pointed squarely at my stomach.

After all that action the only thing I'd accomplished was to hand over my life from one group of bad actors to another. I froze. There *was* one thing I'd accomplished—I felt no anxiety. Not a smidgen. Nothing. I couldn't remember the last time I'd been without *any* anxiety. I thought about the fact that I was probably going to die—still no anxiety. First Whitney. Now Ransom. It really didn't matter who got the role of my executioner. Dead was dead. Any way it came.

Chapter 37

"MARLOWE, you dirty cocksucker," Artie Neal sputtered, drops of blood sprinkling from his mouth. "This is all your doing. You set me up." He pointed at Rudy Valentine. "Your cop friend would never have found this place with just that piece of shit. I never trusted him, but I needed him. To take care of people like you, as a matter of fact."

"He wasn't my friend," I said, wrinkling my nose. The odor of gunpowder mixed with the stench of blood, urine, and pot.

"What the hell are we going to do with them?" Ransom said, looking from me to Rudy on the floor and back again.

"There's only one thing we can do," Neal answered, sounding like he was trying to talk and gargle at the same time. "There's a goddamn dead DEA agent on the floor, for Chrissake."

"He ain't no DEA. I was listening. I heard him say they threw him out."

"Doesn't matter. He *was* a fed. Believe me they'll pull out all the stops to get who killed him. And they'll never let it die. I had one of them on my show once and that's what they believe. They'd probably never even give us a chance to surrender." Neal wiped at his face with a handkerchief. The cloth came away blood stained. I didn't think it was the blood he was worried about though; he was sweating like an overweight tourist in July.

"How's the insulation in this place?" Neal asked.

"If you're wondering if someone could hear the shot," Ransom said, "the answer's probably no. There's nobody around now and this building's tight. I've tested new brands of blockbusters in here before and nobody said shit."

It didn't look good for me, to say the least. I had to try something. In desperation, I latched onto the oldest of bluffs. It was straight out of half the cheap detective paperbacks I'd ever read.

"You won't get away with it, Neal. I've already told the police everything about you. And remember the letter I left for the cops in case anything happened to me."

"Artie, let's go. I don't feel well." It was Marcy. I'd almost forgotten about her. She didn't look well and it was a pitiful sight. She was a washed-out woman and about as attractive now as one of the cardboard boxes behind her.

"We'll go," Neal snapped. "When we're done." He turned and glared at Marcy. "You aren't going to fall apart on me, are you? I wouldn't like that."

She wasn't as out of it as she looked. "No, no, Artie. I'm fine. I'd just like to leave as soon as we can."

"Yeah, all right," Neal said. His tone told me it might go either way for Marcy Wade. The shiver I saw run through her body told me she knew it, too.

Neal turned back to me. He tossed the handkerchief he'd been using on his face on the floor. The bleeding hadn't stopped, but it had slowed considerably. What was left of his front teeth made him look like a carved jack-o'-lantern.

"As far as what you said, Marlowe, who are they going to believe? A very popular radio talk show host or an ex-junkie they already suspect of murdering Evelyn Kruel?" He looked at me smugly, or at least as smugly as you can look with a mouthful of nubs. "And I don't believe there was any note. Whitney wouldn't want legit cops finding out about this. He wouldn't have let you tell anyone for the same reason. The man played you like a violin. You're stupider than even I thought. And just in case you did tell somebody you were seeing me tonight, well."

He held up one hand and put on what he probably thought was an innocent face. "Mr. Marlowe never made it to my home, officer." He looked over at the fed and then at Rudy. "I guess you three must have had some sort of partners-in-crime disagreement. You sure had the history for it. And unfortunately, you all ended up shooting each other. Speaking of that..."

Neal took a few steps, picked up my .38. "Put the shotgun down, George. We don't want to ruin the scenario."

Ransom lowered the shotgun and pulled an automatic from his belt.

I was done; I knew it. There was no way out of this now. Still, I wanted to know something. "Why did you kill Evelyn Kruel, Neal? I thought she was your girl."

"I didn't kill her," he said, then pointed a foot at Rudy. "That piece of shit did. I told you I had to have him around to do some things that were a little below my station."

"Why?" I asked.

"You had the right idea, Marlowe. She found out too much. Just like you for that matter. She got suspicious. Had a big Jew nose. She went over to the house, the one that she owned. The one that Morris, her brother, had lined up for us. He knew the score; I paid him well. We've used different properties he managed for his sister for various things along the way. Never had a problem until she went to the house when nobody was there, got in somehow, saw the radio equipment and some papers, added that up with a couple other things she'd picked up on. You can imagine what happened next."

I wasn't anxious for this conversation to stop. I knew what would happen next if it did. So I didn't let more than five seconds of silence hover in the air. "So she didn't like you using her property to keep in touch with the sailboats coming up from Jamaica?"

Neal snorted. "Where her property was concerned she was a smart bitch. She knew zero about dope but she did know about forfeiture laws. She knew the cops could seize any of the places we'd used for our operation. And she had no idea how many we'd used. She probably thought we'd used them all at one time or another."

He let out an evil little laugh, then stopped. He moved his jaw around like he was in pain. By the looks of his mouth and the way he spoke, he must have been hurting pretty good. Sometimes I had to struggle to understand him.

After a minute he stopped the facial isometrics. "The slut knew she couldn't claim ignorance, not once she realized her property manager, who happened to be her brother, was in with us. They'd never have believed that she wasn't involved, too. She figured the feds would latch onto half the shit she owned on the seacoast. To say she hit the roof is an understatement."

He shrugged, pursed his lips. "So she had to go and Rudy here did his job. Not the way I ordered, though. She wasn't supposed to be found, but it's too late for that now."

"What about the bales on the beach," I asked.

"Those fuckin' kids," Neal said. "They thought they saw a Coast Guard boat and panicked. They threw over some of the load before they realized it was a false alarm. And it was the good stuff too. Big bales, nice loose press. I could've got big money for them."

"More than these tight..." I began before Neal interrupted.

"Enough." Neal turned, walked back to Whitney, leaned down and picked up the 9 mm. He returned with the gun, pointed it at me. My gun was still in his other hand down by his side.

"You'll never get away with this, Neal." I looked at Ransom, then back at Neal. "They'll find the bodies and George'll crumble faster than a chocolate chip cookie." It was worth a shot to try and sow distrust between them. It didn't work.

"Come on, Marlowe," Neal said like he was talking to a child. "You don't think we're going to leave your carcasses here to rot, do you? We'll let this act play out on some nice little stage somewhere else. You'll be found with an untraceable shotgun in your hand and the fed's bullets in you. His gun will be beside him. With the reputation you got—and with him being ex-DEA—they'll bury the thing as fast as they can."

What about him?" I asked, pointing at Rudy on the floor. His breathing was louder than a drunken bed partner at three in the morning.

"I guess he got caught in the crossfire between the two of you. Of course, he'll have to get it in the face to cover up the damage you did to him. Nice job, by the way. They'll chock it up to three sleazebags trying to rip each other off. Like I said, your deaths'll be buried faster than rotting fish." He smirked again. "And just on the outside chance you did say something, we'll have our merchandise moved to a more discreet location before the sun comes up. And the mess cleaned up not much later than that."

The bastard seemed to have all the angles covered. I hated going out like this; I hated going out in any way. But going out at the hands of human waste like Artie Neal was a very poor way to leave this earth. I turned to Marcy, hoping that she might put in a word for me, not that it would have done any good, but I was beyond desperate now. She looked back at me like I wasn't there. Her eyes were glazed and her body shook. I wasn't going to get any help from her. She wouldn't even be able to help herself for a long time to come. I wondered if Neal would risk letting her live or if she'd be found along with the rest of us—wherever the hell that was going to be.

Neal stalked over to Ransom. "Here," he tried to hand him Whitney's gun, "take care of him with this."

Ransom looked at Neal like he was selling ice cream during a blizzard. "You do it. I did the fed. And saved your life, by the way. I want to make sure you ain't got nothing over me."

Ransom wasn't as stupid as I'd thought. He didn't trust Neal. He also must've realized that if they ever got caught, putting the finger on a fed's killer, even though he was an ex-fed, might be enough to allow Neal to cut a deal on a smuggling rap. By making Neal a murderer as well, the cops might not be inclined to plea bargain.

I could tell that Ransom wasn't bluffing. He wasn't going to pull the trigger. Neal must have known it, too.

"All right. I'll do it," he said in a reluctant voice. His arm straightened out, the gun pointing directly at my chest, and I could see in his eyes that he was going to pull the trigger.

I didn't say my prayers; I never believed in that. I did say a lot of other stuff though. I was running the reel of one fucked-up life through my head and waiting to get knocked on my ass by a 9mm slug when a loud explosion made every nerve in my body jerk. It wasn't the roar of a gun though. The sound came from the front of the building. It was the doors. They'd flown inward, coming off their hinges.

Neal and Ransom turned toward the doors just as I did. Men in tactical dress—faces covered with black masks and holding automatic weapons—stormed in. For the second time that night I heard shouts of "Search warrant. Search warrant."

My hands shot into the air. The situation looked very dicey—I could see myself being gunned down by nervous cops. I'd heard of that happening. Neal and Ransom dropped their weapons faster than a hot pan on a stove. Their hands flew above their heads. Marcy let out an ear-piercing scream. Apparently, she'd been shaken out of her stupor.

"Don't move, don't move," the intruders yelled. There were three of them and they held their automatic rifles like they meant business. It was a very frightening scene. I felt a little better when Steve Moore, gun drawn, stepped through the doorway. Behind him came other plainclothes cops, all with their guns drawn. And behind them trudged two young nervous-looking Seabrook police officers.

Steve came up to me, holstered his gun. "Are you all right."

I nodded and lowered my arms.

"Is that Whitney?" he asked, looking over at the man on the floor. I nodded again.

Neal and Ransom were shoved roughly to the floor, guns to their heads, arms cuffed behind their backs. Marcy was spared the indignity of being made to kneel, but was cuffed, too. The little progress I thought she'd made as far as her mental health went was gone. She had reverted to her previous state of shock, shaking like a junkie during a drought.

An older man in civilian clothes walked up to us. The man seemed to be in charge and Steve made an introduction. There was a lot of activity and noise so I didn't catch his name. I did hear something about a Northern Mass-Southern New Hampshire Drug Task Force.

The man put his hands on his hips, stared at the stacked boxes against the back wall. "How much pot we got here?" He looked at me. "You know?"

I'd done a little estimating in between bouts of terror. "More than a thousand pounds, I'd guess."

The task force boss let out a little whistle. This was probably the biggest bust they'd ever made on the seacoast. Seizures this size were usually corralled by federal agencies.

Suddenly there were shouts and hollers from the office. The top man jogged in that direction. Other cops—mostly uniformed locals, but a few plainclothes—streamed in the front door, adding to the confusion.

Neal and Ransom were dragged off the ground and marched toward the smashed entrance. When Neal passed by, he looked at me and snarled. "You dirty junkie, Marlowe."

I think he meant to be derogatory, but his words came out sounding like a perverted lisp. I'd been called worse.

"At least I'll be showing up for work tomorrow, Neal," I said, a big grin on my face. "I think I'm going to apply for your job, too. You won't need it anymore. And besides, my voice is in much better shape than yours."

He bared his remaining teeth and tried to speak, but only ended up spitting blood on one of the cops escorting him. The cop cursed and shoved Neal forward. Neal stumbled the rest of the way through the door. Ransom and a couple of other cops followed.

"How'd you find me, Steve?" I asked. The task force men had a few of the boxes open and were going through them. They whooped and high-fived each other.

"Dianne. She called me, told me you were mixed up with Bob Whitney and that she was worried. I made a quick call to a buddy on the task force. He knew Whitney and told me he'd gone bad and been busted out of the DEA."

Just then a couple of EMTs came through the door, examined the semiconscious Rudy, loaded him on a gurney, and headed for the door.

"Rudy?" Steve asked, watching the gurney roll by.

"Rudy," I spit out.

"You?"

I smiled. "Yeah."

"Anyway," Steve continued, "The DEA didn't want Whitney prosecuted. Didn't want the bad press, so they just busted him out. They might have trouble keeping this quiet though."

"You followed us here?" I asked. I felt a little lightheaded and the floor felt soft. Probably a delayed reaction to all that had just gone down. I needed a pill—so much for being rid of the anxiety. At least I'd had a taste of what normal felt like. Now all I had to do was make it last.

"Didn't have to." Steve rubbed his chin. "I went to see Morris Kruel, put the squeeze on him about murder. He folded like a card table. Told us about this place. His sister was landlord here, too. Looks like we got here just in time."

We both turned and watched as a female Seabrook cop came through the door and took charge of Marcy Wade. When she was paraded by us, I said some inane thing, but I might as well have been talking to Whitney lying on the floor—she wasn't with us anymore. I felt kind of sorry for her. Some people really do get in over their heads and Marcy was definitely one of them. She would never have gotten involved in something like this except for being in the wrong place at the wrong time. Working for Evelyn Kruel, meeting a slime bucket like Artie Neal, and then being seduced into doing things that she otherwise would never have even thought of. That kind of person you had to feel sorry for. At least I did.

There was a shout from the office door and we turned to look. The task force boss came out of the office. He and a uniformed cop were each lugging a dark blue duffel bag. Top cop had a big smile on his face. He walked up to us, set the duffel down on the floor. He unzipped the bag and pulled out a plastic-wrapped package about the size of the pot bricks but a lot thicker. There was lettering on the package. I didn't need anyone to tell me what it was. I don't think anyone else did either.

A few of the other task force men gathered around, big grins on their faces. One of them said, "Now *that's* a lot of coke."

"How much?" Steve asked.

The boss tossed the brick back into the duffel, grabbed the strap with one hand, and lifted it off the ground. His arm shook with the strain. "More than a gram. That's for sure." A hearty laugh went up from the men around him.

Steve laughed too; I didn't. Like I said it was all starting to catch up with me and laughing was the last thing on my mind. The lightheadedness had been replaced by a sense of doom. I knew from experience that it was just a symptom, that nothing terrible was going to happen now, but that didn't make the feeling seem any less real. My heart pounded and insisted on skipping some beats. I tried to get my mind off the anxiety by taking a couple of steps but the floor turned to quicksand beneath my feet.

"Are you okay, Dan?" Steve asked. I assured him I was and hoped he didn't hear the cracks in my voice that sounded as loud as a bullwhip to me.

There was no doubt he had picked up on my condition, though. "Come on, I'll give you a ride."

Before we left, he spoke to the top cop, asked permission to take me home or to the hospital. Said something about me being interviewed later. The man hesitated, studied my face, then nodded grudgingly. Steve and I walked through the shattered doors out into the night. The air was cool and I felt a tiny bit better if only because the walls of the world out here gave me a little more breathing room than the walls inside the building.

I climbed into Steve's car and asked him to take me home. My voice didn't sound any steadier. I had assumed his mention of the hospital had just been a ploy to get me out of there, so when he said, "Are you sure?" I was surprised.

"Yes," I answered.

On the short ride, we were both silent. He turned right after the Hampton Bridge, took a couple more turns, and pulled into my driveway.

I opened the door, started to get out.

"Do you need any help?" Steve asked.

"No thanks," I said. *Not unless you want to put the pill in my mouth and hold the beer to my lips.*

I had a Xanax under my tongue and a bottle of Heineken in my hand before Steve's car was out of earshot. I put a cold compress on my right fist, and like a gift from God, remembered some old pain pills I had squirreled away. In less than an hour, I was half a man again.

Epilogue

THE FOUR OF US—Steve Moore, Shamrock, Dianne, and I—had been sitting at a corner table in The Crooked Shillelagh for almost an hour now. We'd done some drinking and not much talking while the Irish band played. They finished a rousing rendition of *Seven Drunken Nights*, hopped off the small stage, and took a break, leaving the room quiet enough to talk. We wouldn't get another chance until after their next set.

Shamrock was first to speak, of course. He was wearing his restaurant whites. "I wonder what's going to happen to George Ransom's fireworks store now?" He lifted the glass of Guinness to his mouth, took a quick large swig. "I always wondered about that business. There's probably a lot of money in firecrackers."

Steve was sitting beside Shamrock and shot him a look. "I don't think you want *that* business, Shamrock. There's already a federal forfeiture lien on the place."

Shamrock let out an audible sigh. "Great. I finally get some...I mean...I never have any luck."

I picked up on his meaning, though I don't think anyone else did. I flashed back on those bales of pot on the beach and the dark figure wearing white pants I'd seen that night scurrying across Ocean Boulevard with something in his arms and smiled.

"I don't think you'd want to get involved anyway, Shamrock." Dianne sat beside me, directly across from Shamrock. She was wearing a maroon blouse made of another soft material I couldn't identify. If she wore makeup, it was very light as usual. Her black hair was down. She no longer wore the dressing on her eye. The eye was still discolored just a bit. I liked to look at her when she talked; I think Steve and Shamrock did, too.

"Why?" Shamrock asked, a twinkle in his blue eyes. "You don't want to lose me?"

We all laughed.

"Well, that goes without saying, Michael," Dianne said. "Besides that, I heard there's a good chance they may outlaw fireworks again or at least some of them. You don't want to get stuck holding the bag."

"No, I certainly don't." Shamrock took another quick sip of his Guinness. "I'll keep my eyes open for another opportunity, though."

Dianne and I smiled. Shamrock loved to talk about business opportunities when he was in his cups. Maybe more so now, I realized.

"So will Ransom get the death penalty for killing Whitney?" I asked. In front of me on the table sat a glass and a bottle of Heineken. The beer here was always very cold—I liked that. My hand still had a bandage because of the beating I'd given Rudy Valentine; I liked that too.

Steve raised his eyebrows. "It's possible. If he'd killed him a bit further down the road, he would've been in Massachusetts—no death penalty. Here we got one. But they never use it."

"Isn't there a federal charge for killing a DEA agent?" I asked.

Steve put the bottle of Bud he'd been drinking down on the table. "Yup, but it doesn't cover Ransom. Whitney'd already been fired."

"Here you are, gents...and lady." It was the waitress and if she didn't sound and look like she'd just been teleported here from Dublin, my name wasn't Dan Marlowe. She set fresh drinks in front of all of us.

I hadn't heard anyone order. "You must have read our minds."

"Not really," she said, laughing. She looked at Shamrock; he beamed. I guess there was a special communication between countrymen.

"Whistle if you need me, lads." She spun and disappeared into the dense crowd near the bar.

"What will happen to Marcy Wade?" Dianne asked. She sipped at her drink—Absolute and cranberry juice. This was a celebration, after all. I envied the lime almost bumping her nose.

"Jesus, that woman's in pitiful shape," Steve answered. He shook his head. "She had some kind of breakdown. Usually these things are staged bullshit, meant to get a judge's sympathy. But I saw her at the station and again at the arraignment. She's not acting; she's a freakin' basket case."

"I feel kind of bad for her," I said. And I meant it. I'd known people like her in the past, people who'd gotten sucked into something they wouldn't have normally. Not bad people; good people as a matter of fact. People who hadn't realized they were getting into something more serious than they'd thought.

Shamrock waved his hand through the air, smoke from the cigarette between his fingers trailing after it. "Ahh, maybe they'll just put her in the booby hatch for a while."

"You might be right," Steve said. "She needs the vacation, that's for sure.

I turned, looked over my shoulder. The place was jammed. I wanted to make a trip to the head, but by the time I got through the throng, the band would be back, and that would be the end of our conversation. There were still some things I wanted to know. I decided to wait.

"What about Morris Kruel?" I asked.

"He flipped faster than an Olympic gymnast." Steve was smiling as he spoke. "He was in charge of getting property—the communications house up on North Beach, boat slip, stash houses, even Ransom's fireworks shop. Evelyn was the landlord of most of it. So he'll do some time, but it's Neal the feds want."

"I thought it was state charges?" I interrupted.

"Nooo. Like I said, the feds want Neal. Big boy, big name, lots of press. They like that." Steve played with the label on his bottle of Bud. "Besides, even Neal won't be able to beat the federal charges. State? You never know. Feds give more time, too. The state's aware of that so they usually go along with it. And the feds have precedence, anyhow—if they want it."

"What do you think he'll get?" I asked.

"Well," Steve said. "Considering someone like him is probably blubbering like a baby right about now and giving up everybody who ever farted the wrong way in his presence, he...."

I interrupted again; Steve didn't seem to mind. "Who can he squeal on? I thought Neal was the one the government wants so bad. The top man."

"Oh, they do and he is," Steve answered, nodding. "But he'll give up his Jamaican connection right off the bat for starters. That might not mean much though. The feds might already know who the connection is. Besides, they may not be able to do much down there. Then he'll probably rat on everyone in the distribution chain below him that he knows about, up and down the whole damn seacoast and who knows where else. You can be sure of that." Steve put his hands palms up. "So *maybe* he'll be able to bargain down to twenty years. At best. That means he'll do around eighteen and a half, federal time. And *that's* if they can't fit him for ordering a murder or two. With Rudy Valentine alive—*if* they can hang Evelyn Kruel's murder on him—then Neal's going to have a big problem. Guys like Rudy are about as standup as a punch drunk boxer."

"So even if they don't get him for murder," Dianne said, "he'll still spend a lot of time in prison?"

"Decades," Steve said.

"Good," Dianne said. "He deserves it. He's a very bad man."

"And don't forget," Steve added, "the government's already seizing anything they can find that he owns too. His house on Plaice Cove'll be going up for auction if anybody's interested."

"That's not Plaice Cove, Steve," I said, trying to sound knowledgeable. "It's really North Beach."

"I know that, Dan. It's just called that."

Apparently, I'd been the only one asleep when this information was made common knowledge on the beach.

"Will I have to testify about that horrible man hitting me?" Dianne asked. I couldn't tell by her tone if she was apprehensive or looking forward to it.

"I doubt it," Steve said. "Like I said, they're trying to fit Valentine with Evelyn's murder. I doubt they'll even have to bother with what he did to you."

"Good," she said firmly. "On the murder charges, I mean. I wouldn't have minded testifying against him. Asshole."

"Hey, wait a minute," Shamrock said. He was bringing his beer glass down from his lips. He had a beer mustache and his eyes were just a touch glazed. "We forgot all about Eddie Hoar and Derwood Doller. What about *them*?"

"Jesus, I forgot about them," I said.

Dianne laughed. "Well, don't forget they're still banned at the Tide."

Steve put on a mock serious face. "How can you forget your two drinking buddies, Dan?" A round of laughter circled the table.

I held my glass up in a toast to the two nimrods, Eddie and Derwood. "To the two most bumbling hustlers on Hampton Beach," I said jokingly.

Everyone raised their drink, laughed.

"Will they be arrested, Steve?" Dianne asked.

Steve shook his head. "I doubt it. I don't know what the hell they'd be charged with. The pot they stole from the boat got ripped off from them. I don't think there's anybody who could testify they ever even had possession of it. Anyhow, those two are minnows in all this. I don't think any prosecutor'd even want to bother with them." He hesitated, then added, "And if the prosecutor's office decided to do anything, they'd probably just want them to confirm where they got the pot from."

"Would they talk?" Shamrock said. But then catching himself before anyone could answer, "Oops, stupid me. They'd talk like a comedian on speed."

"Hey, that's a good one," I said. "A comedian on speed. I have to remember that in case I ever want to write a book about this someday."

"The feds don't really need anyone else though," Steve said. "They got the sailboat crew, the off-loaders, and a lot of the distributors. You can bet most of them have made deals, too."

Across the crowded room and out the window, I could see the lights of cars drifting up Ocean Boulevard. Red brake lights twinkled on and off. The traffic was heavy, bumper-to-bumper. We didn't have to worry about that though. None of us had to drive, except Steve. His car was around the corner, on Ashworth somewhere, in the driveway of someone he knew.

"So," Dianne began, cocking her pretty head, "does all this mean I won't have to worry anymore why the customer at the bar is using the restroom every fifteen minutes?"

The three of us stared at her. "What?" she said. But I'm fairly sure she knew. I think she was playing with us.

Steve, I guess, wasn't so sure. "I don't think your bathroom traffic will be any less, Dianne. There's probably other big coke dealers on the seacoast. And even if there aren't, someone will move in right away to take over. Too much money to be made not to."

Dianne straightened in her seat. "I was only kidding, Steve. I catch anyone making frequent bathroom trips in the Tide, they're shown the door."

"I know that, Dianne," Steve said. "Everyone does."

"Forget the coke, that's bad stuff," Shamrock piped in, apparently forgetting who he was with. "Now the herb. There's nothing wrong..." Then he must've remembered who he was sitting with. "Oops." He looked at Steve sheepishly.

Steve chuckled, flicked his hand in the air. "You're busted, Shamrock." Dianne and I laughed. A tint of red oozed onto Shamrock's face.

"Only kidding," Steve said. "I hope I got more important things to do in this life than chase people smoking pot."

The color receded from Shamrock's face and he joined the laughter. Then he raised himself in his seat, and looked around for the barmaid. When he caught her eye, he signaled for another round. Steve shot his arm up and waved his hand in her direction, shaking his head at the same time.

"I have to get going," he said to the three of us. He pointed with his thumb toward the front window. "Traffic...and besides, looks who's coming. We're done with talking for a while."

We looked. It was the band, pushing their way through the crowd toward the tiny stage. A couple of the members were nursing Guinness. The female member had what looked like a Black and Tan.

Steve pushed his chair back, stood and shook hands with me, then Shamrock. He came around the table, leaned over Dianne, and gave her a kiss on the cheek. "I'll talk to you all soon. Let you know what's going on. Take it easy."

We all said goodbye and watched as he elbowed his way through the crowded room and went out the door onto Ocean Boulevard.

"He's a real nice guy," Dianne said.

"Yes, he is," I said.

"Thank God for that," Shamrock said. "I forgot he was a cop when I started talking about weed."

"He doesn't care about that," I said.

"Speaking of *that* though, Shamrock," Dianne began in an angry tone. "I could have sworn I smelled some illegal substance when I came into work the other morning."

Shamrock blushed again. "That's impossible, Dianne. Like you said, I should only indulge outside. It must have blown in with me when I came back in through the door."

"I hope so," she said as if she were a mother scolding her child.

"Look, the band's ready to play," Shamrock said quickly, changing the subject.

He was right. The red-haired girl with the fiddle was tuning up and the other musicians were downing their beers and getting their instruments ready. The crowd was quieting down, at least as much as a mob in an Irish bar on a summer weekend night in Hampton Beach was capable of doing. Just then the fiddler kicked up her leg, slammed her foot down on the stage, and started moving the bow across the strings so fast I expected the fiddle to burst into flames. The other musicians joined in. It was a song I'd heard before, *many* times. It was one about Irish rebellion. I never knew the name of the tune. I don't think it mattered. I looked at Shamrock. There was a faraway look in his eyes. I wondered for a minute what it was like to be so far away from your home country. I guess, like a lot of Americans, I would never know.

The waitress delivered new drinks. She said something. I couldn't hear a word, so I just nodded. When she was gone, I moved my chair closer to Dianne's; my hip touched hers. I felt her hand move to my thigh. I glanced at Shamrock. He was watching the band, beaming now, his head moving around with the beat of the music. I wondered if this was really the music you'd hear in a bar in Ireland or if this was just the Americanized version. Maybe something like St. Patrick's Day, which in the old country supposedly wasn't a drunk fest like it was in the states. No matter, I figured. Shamrock—born on the Island—and I—two and three generations away—were both enjoying it. So the music had to mean something good to both of us.

I lasted for two songs before I leaned close to Dianne. I could smell lavender. "Do you want to leave?" I asked.

She looked at Shamrock. "We can't leave Shamrock alone," she said in my ear.

Shamrock turned in our direction. Apparently we hadn't been as quiet as we'd thought.

"Don't you two worry about Michael Kelly. I won't be lonely. If there's a fly walking on the wall in here, I know its name."

He pursed his lips, nodded heavily. "Besides, there's a lassie over by the bar who looks a wee bit lonely. I think I'll go over, cheer her up." Shamrock stood, reached for his wallet.

I waved him off. "No, Shamrock, I got it."

"Thank you, Danny, my friend."

"No. Thank *you*, Shamrock." I gave him a wink. He smiled.

"See you tomorrow, Dianne," he said.

"Good night, Shamrock."

We watched him fight his way through the crowd and up to the bar. I think he was already talking to the woman before he even reached her. I looked at Dianne; we both laughed.

The bar maid was passing by and I grabbed the check from her. Left money for the drinks and a good tip for her.

Outside, you couldn't have asked for a nicer night. I pulled Dianne close to me, kissed her the way I'd wanted to all night. She felt so good. I heard the good-natured catcalls of some twenty-somethings heading for the front door of the Shillelagh.

Dianne pulled away first. I never would have. I'd have been happy to stay that way forever. At that moment I wouldn't have cared if I was kissing her standing on the Seashell Stage on a sunny afternoon during Seafood Festival. I was that crazy about her.

She held my arms, leaned back, and looked into my face. "Shouldn't we take this inside?" she said, smiling. It was a wonderful smile. The type of smile that gave me hope that everything was going to end up all right.

"Your place or mine?" I said.

"Well, at my place we can sit out on the balcony, have a drink, and watch the ocean."

I thought about that for all of two seconds. "But my place is a *lot* closer."

We looked at each other, burst out laughing. I put my arm around her shoulders, pulled her close. We scooted between parked and moving cars and crossed Ocean Boulevard.

Somehow, even after all I'd been through the past few weeks—no, the past few years, I guess—I felt good. Awful good, as a matter of fact. I didn't know how much of that feeling was because of Dianne and how much of it was time passing and me just getting better. I did know that she was a big part of the equation and she was more than I deserved.

Just as we reached the walkway that led to the cottage we stopped. She snuggled close to me and we looked up at the sky above the dunes. The moon was a huge orange ball. It hung there, just being. The sound of the surf and the smell of salt in the air rolled over the dunes. We stared at the moon for a bit, until I felt a gentle nudge from Dianne.

I kissed her head, took one last look at that beautiful sight in the sky, and then walked with her down the walkway, up the stairs, and into my cottage where we said goodnight to Hampton Beach.

About the Author

JED POWER is a Hampton Beach, NH-based writer and author of numerous published short stories. *The Boss of Hampton Beach* was his first novel in the Dan Marlowe crime series followed by *Hampton Beach Homicide*. Both books are available in paper and as ebooks.

Find out more at www.darkjettypublishing.com

Made in the USA
Middletown, DE
14 August 2015